A LICENCE TO MURDER

A BELFAST MURDER SQUAD MYSTERY

DEREK FEE

MIST MEDIA

For Aine, Bobbie and Sean

Copyright © 2018by **Derek Fee**

All rights reserved. No part of this publication may be reproduced, distributed or transmitted in any form or by any means, without prior written permission.

Publisher's Note: This is a work of fiction. Names, characters, places, and incidents are a product of the author's imagination. Locales and public names are sometimes used for atmospheric purposes. Any resemblance to actual people, living or dead, or to businesses, companies, events, institutions, or locales is completely coincidental.

Book Layout © 2017 BookDesignTemplates.com

❀ Created with Vellum

BOOK 1

Belfast, 2017

1

Rasa Spalvis folded her arms and hugged herself as she walked slowly along Linenhall Street in central Belfast. Mid-October wasn't as cold in Ireland as in her native Lithuania, but winter had come early. Her tank top and mini-skirt exposed far too much flesh to guard against the bitter north wind that blew from the direction of City Hall down the exposed street. She watched each car that passed, hoping it contained a punter who would beckon her inside and out of the cold wind. It didn't matter that she would be expected to perform sexual acts with them. That was why she was in Belfast. She was one of four girls being moved around the United Kingdom by the Lithuanian mafia in a parody of a tour. She had already turned tricks in London, Southampton, Bristol, Newcastle and Glasgow. And every day there was the ceremonial handing over of the money to the man who owned her.

A large BMW came slowly down the street and she put on her most professional smile. At twenty-three she was in her prime. She had a taut body and her tank top displayed the narrowness of her waist and the swell of her breasts. Her hair was naturally blonde and she had high Slavic cheekbones. She watched the face of the man in the car as he looked her up and down. This was the part of the ritual she disliked most. It reminded her of films she had seen about the slave markets in Africa with the traders examining the teeth of the females on sale. She could almost see the little cogs in his mind asking himself the question, Will I, won't I? Then the car sped up and he drove on towards City Hall. The smile faded from her face. 'Šunsnukis,' she shouted after the car. What the hell was he looking for? Who did he expect to see on the street? Julia Roberts. She spat on the ground. A Mercedes was coming towards her slowly. Her smile automatically returned and she thrust her chest forward so that her breasts strained against her top. Instinctively she could feel the driver was interested. She allowed her mini-skirt to ride a little higher and show off her milky-white thighs. The man looked older than her father. Generally, she didn't like servicing older men. When she was younger, she would sometimes refuse an older client but she couldn't afford to be so choosy these days. Valdas hurt the girls who failed to bring in the requisite amount of money. She walked slowly towards the passenger side window, which was opening. She looked at the man behind the wheel. She had been a prostitute for seven years and she had serviced every type of man. She fancied that she was now as good a judge of men as you could get. Her first reaction was to let this one pass, but it was cold and Valdas had already taught her a lesson with his fists. She leaned on the open window. 'Are you looking for a party?' Her English was heavily accented and that seemed to please the client.

'I haven't seen you here before,' he said.

'I'm new to Belfast.'

'I think I would like to party with you. Get in.'

This was the moment of truth. Was she going to fight against the little alarm bell ringing in her head? Her experience told her that this man had a streak of cruelty in him. Perhaps it was his thin lips or the smile that wasn't quite right.

She had been beaten up more times than she could remember. The last time had led to a week's stay in hospital. She opened the door. 'Twenty pound for a blow job and one hundred for penetration.'

The old man removed a roll of notes from his pocket, counted out six twenty-pound notes and laid them on the passenger seat. He looked up and saw the greed in her eyes. 'And there may be more.'

She was both excited and repulsed by the thought of extra money. She thought she had satisfied every sexual perversion, but she also knew men had an infinite capacity for thinking up ways to hurt women. She hated men. She hated Valdas and sometimes dreamt of killing him. But that was in the future. She scooped up the money. Maybe everything would be all right. She sat into the car and they moved off.

THE MAN WHEEZED and looked down at the girl. The Mercedes was parked in a secluded area off the main path at the western end of Whiterock Road. His hands were still round the girl's neck and his penis was still inside her. He looked down at her eyes. They were staring straight back at him, unblinking. She had probably just passed out. He slapped her face. 'Wake up, you dozy bitch,' he shouted. He hadn't squeezed that hard. Had he? His penis lost its strength and slipped out of her. Although he found it distasteful, he put his lips over hers and attempted the kiss of life. Then he remembered the course he had done on CPR and started to rhythmically press her chest. After ten minutes he stopped and got out of the rear of the car. There was nobody around. He walked to the edge of the copse and took in a deep breath. A ferry was making its way down Belfast Lough towards the port. He removed a mobile phone from his pocket and dialled a number. 'I need your help,' he said when the phone was answered.

2

Detective Superintendent Ian Wilson looked at the mountain of paper on his desk. He missed the days when his former sergeant, Moira McElvaney, would sneak into his office and arrange the mass of paper into some order that he could tackle. His team members were occupied with completing the necessary documents for the Public Prosecution Service on the murder of Tom Kielty and the attempted murder of Jock McDevitt. All except Detective Constable Peter Davidson, who had requested to work full time on Wilson's theory that former politician Jackie Carlisle had been murdered. It was rare to see Davidson, who was an old-timer with no promotion prospects, being so fired up about what was after all a punt in the dark. He picked up a file from his desk and opened it. The coroner had concluded that the man found in the boot of the burned-out BMW had been murdered. If he were a betting man, he would have put a month's salary on the body being that of Mad Mickey Duff, an ex-employee of new gang-boss Davie Best. He would add another month's salary to an accumulator that said Best may not have fired the car but was certainly behind the murder. He flipped through the pages in the file. The crime scene photos would certainly shock a jury if one ever got to see them. Who was he kidding? The newspapers and the evening news showed worse from Mosul, Raqqa, Manchester and London. It seemed that violent death was all the rage.

A ping from his computer indicated the arrival of a new email. It was from the chief constable and had been sent to every PSNI employee. He reluctantly clicked on the enclosure and a letter from the CC appeared on the screen. Apparently, it gave the CC great pleasure to announce that Deputy Chief Constable Royson Jennings would be retaking his post after a highly successful period assisting Cumbria Police in restructuring their operations. Wilson had heard the rumours that his nemesis was returning but had hoped they were false. The timing couldn't have been worse. He had a string of unsolved murders sitting on his table. Jennings could use each of them as a stick to beat him. It was almost half a year since Sammy Rice had been murdered. Wilson had solved the crime, in that he knew the names of the killer and of the men who had hidden the body, but he had not a shred of evidence to back it up. Unless Sammy's body rose from its hiding place, along with the weapon used to kill him, the case would remain open on his desk. He switched off his computer. The email from the CC would spawn a flood of sycophantic responses of the 'great to hear of the return of the DCC' variety. Every crawler from sergeant to assistant chief constable would want to ensure the DCC knew that they were over the moon at the thought of his return. Jennings would not expect to see Wilson's name among the brownnosers. Wilson didn't fancy facing a refreshed Jennings. It prompted him to remember the phrase in Joni Mitchell's 'Big Yellow Taxi'. He didn't know what he had got until it was gone. He should have had a greater appreciation of the Jennings-less era than he'd had. Now that it was over, he knew he was going to miss it.

A look at his watch told him it was almost four o'clock in the afternoon, which meant that it was almost eight o'clock in the morning in Los Angeles. Stephanie Reid would probably be just getting out of bed or perhaps she would be enjoying a breakfast on the deck of her mother's house in Venice Beach. It was too early to Skype her and give her his bad news. He missed her. The yearning had started as he watched her heading for the departure gate at Belfast International. She hadn't looked back and he was grateful for that. They had both used the word 'love' in their final exchanges and they had been in contact every day since she left. It was becoming apparent that she would be away for longer than either had anticipated.

His phone beeped and he looked at the message. Jock McDevitt, crime correspondent for the *Belfast Chronicle*, messaged at least twice a day. Following the launch of his book, McDevitt was the flavour of the month, and not only in literary circles. His ready wit had made him a success in his television interviews. Aside from Northern Ireland Screen extending money for development of a film version of his book, Ulster Television was now courting him to front a new crime programme. Wilson assumed that his new-best-friend would soon leave him behind, but McDevitt continued to astonish him with his loyalty. That was the reason he would be accepting his invitation for an after-work drink in the Crown.

3

DCC Roy Jennings pushed open the door of his office at PSNI HQ in Castlereagh. It was exactly as he had left it. He walked round looking at the photos on the wall. He was well aware of those who had worked hard to get him back in the second highest post in the PSNI and he knew why they wanted him there. Nobody did something for nothing. He had long ago sacrificed his integrity on the altar of his ambition. He moved behind his desk and examined his realm. It would have hurt the chief constable to accept him back. Norman Baird had the reputation of being an honest man. But the real powers in the province didn't want an honest man at the head of the police force, they wanted loyalty and not just loyalty to the political system but loyalty to them. Jennings had displayed his loyalty many times before and would obviously be required to do so again. He sat in his chair. All those who had put him in this chair would be paid back. And those who had been responsible for his exile would also be paid back.

There was a knock and Assistant Chief Constable Clive Nicholson stepped through the open doorway. 'I heard you were in the building, welcome back.' Nicholson walked to the desk and the men exchanged a Masonic handshake.

'I've missed it,' Jennings said. 'But thanks to you and several others I've been kept abreast of events.'

'You should be chief constable now.' Nicholson sat before the desk.

Jennings gave a wry smile. He would have been if he hadn't been exiled when the old chief constable died. He had been next in line but they had used his rehabilitation against him. Now he had to kowtow to Baird.

'You would have been if it wasn't for that bastard skewering you,' Nicholson said.

'And how is my old friend, Detective Superintendent Wilson?'

'Thriving it appears. At least you managed to get rid of Spence.'

'I don't count that as an accomplishment. Spence was already halfway out the door. I assume Wilson has been behaving himself.'

'I have a man inside – Wilson's new sergeant, name of Browne. A bloody shirtlifter. You want to see the stuff I have on him. But somehow I don't trust him.'

'Will he provide the goods when the time comes?'

Nicholson's silence was answer enough.

'What about this Davis woman? Can we manoeuvre her on board?'

'She's ambitious. You know the type, sacrificed her family for the job and now she wants what she thinks she's earned. Baird has made it clear that he wants women in the higher echelons and she fits the bill.'

Jennings brought his hands together in a praying motion. 'You didn't answer my question.'

'She's a woman and Wilson has an effect on the damn creatures.'

'So we can't depend on her?'

'I don't think so.'

'But she hasn't had to deal with me yet. Perhaps she'll have an occasion to regret her decision to concentrate on a career in the PSNI.'

Nicholson smiled. The old Jennings was back. He'd wondered whether his former chief would have been changed by his period of correction. It appeared not to be the case.

'Bring me all the files Wilson has been working on. I want to be completely up to date. I'm willing to bet that he's engaged in some form of mischief – a leopard doesn't change his spots.'

4

There were many days when Sandra Ferguson wished that she had selected another breed of dog. That didn't mean she didn't love her two Jack Russells. It just meant they had the ability to drive her to distraction. Like at that very moment for example. They were on their usual walk on the edge of Redburn Country Park when the two little tykes broke away and disappeared into the undergrowth. Ferguson had spent ten minutes calling out for them without success. She was tempted to march back to her car and leave them to fend for themselves. She looked at her watch. It was eight thirty. She was supposed to start work at Holywood Golf Club at nine and the secretary of the club was a stickler for punctuality. She needed to find those bloody dogs and get them home. She ploughed into the undergrowth and thought she heard them crying somewhere straight ahead. She marched on, calling their names as she went. She found them sitting beside a mound of earth into which they had been digging. 'Bad dogs,' she said, waving their leads at them. Neither dog moved and as she bent to put their leads on she saw that they had exposed something that looked like mottled flesh. She picked up a branch and started to poke the soil that the dogs had disturbed. Clumps of earth fell away to reveal more skin and possibly a ribcage. The mound of earth was no more than two feet long so it wasn't possible that it concealed a body. She continued to move soil away and eventually exposed what looked like a breast. She dropped the stick and whirled round in time to send a stream of vomit onto the ground behind her. She quickly connected the leads to the dogs and ran out of the bushes. As soon as she reached the open fields, she removed the mobile phone from her pocket. Her hands were shaking as she placed a call she never expected to have to make.

5

Detective Sergeant Rory Browne drove the police car across the grass towards the two police Land Rovers that were parked at the edge of the area of bush in Redburn Country Park. He and his boss, Detective Superintendent Ian Wilson, hadn't spoken a word since they had been scrambled by the news that a half-interred body had been discovered. Wilson had initially been excited to hear of the find, hoping Sammy Rice had defied the odds and risen Lazarus-like from the grave. He had immediately rushed from the station, but then news had come over the radio that the body appeared to be that of a young woman.

Wilson and Browne got out of the car and accepted two plastic jumpsuits from a uniformed policeman. While Wilson was putting on his suit, he saw a young woman sitting in the rear of one of the Land Rovers. She appeared to have two small black and white terriers on her lap. 'Is that the girl who found the body?' he asked the uniformed officer.

'Yes, sir, Sandra Ferguson, she followed her dogs into the undergrowth.'

'We'll talk to her later,' Wilson said, taking the clipboard containing the sign-in sheet and passing it to Browne. 'Any sign of Forensics?'

'Not yet, sir,' the constable said.

'What about the pathologist?'

'On the way.'

Wilson pulled the top of the suit over his head and bent under the crime scene tape that was being held up by the uniformed officer. The two detectives walked into the bush taking care not to disturb the site. They finally reached the area where the ground had been churned up. Wilson noticed the branch Ferguson had used to disinter the corpse. Except it wasn't a corpse. It was a torso. From what he could see there was no head, arms or legs. As soon as Forensics finished with the site, he would order up the cadaver dogs. The missing body parts might be buried somewhere in the vicinity. He bent down and looked at the torso. The news on the radio was accurate. One breast had been exposed and it certainly belonged to a woman and probably a young woman. He didn't want to move any of the soil surrounding the torso. Despite the covering of earth there was another smell intermingled with the sweet smell of decaying flesh. Wilson tried to identify it. It could be ammonia, but he would leave that determination to the forensic technicians.

'What do you think, Boss?' Browne asked.

Wilson stood up. 'Early days, Rory. Without the head and the hands, identification is going to be difficult, if not impossible.' He thought about the body they had recovered from the burned-out car. Something clicked in his brain and he found himself staring ahead but not really seeing anything. It was odd having too unidentified bodies in a row.

'What's the matter, Boss?' Browne asked.

Suddenly Wilson was back among the bushes. 'As an educated man you know what déjà vu is. Well, I have the strangest feeling that I've been in this scene before. Not necessarily at this location, but the feeling is very strong.' He knew it was something to do with the smell, but he couldn't put his finger on what. Maybe it would come to him later.

Browne leaned over Wilson's shoulder and examined the torso. 'You've probably attended more than a hundred crime scenes like this. Those images are imprinted on your brain and it only needs a trigger to bring them back.'

Wilson wasn't so sure. This feeling was particularly strong. 'Let's have a word with Ms Ferguson.'

They tried to retrace their original steps into the undergrowth in order to cause minimum disruption to the site. As they emerged from the bushes, they saw the forensic van arriving. Wilson started to peel off his suit. 'Check in with the chief of the team. Then join me in the Land Rover,' he said.

SANDRA FERGUSON WAS CUDDLING one of her dogs on her lap while the other lay at her feet. Both dogs started howling as soon as Wilson opened the passenger door of the Land Rover and climbed in. He waited patiently for the noise to abate before turning and looking directly at the young woman. 'I'm Detective Superintendent Wilson and I understand you're the person who found the torso.'

'Yes.'

Wilson could see that Ferguson was in shock. He thought she would normally be pale anyway, but her face was currently ghostly pale. He reckoned that she was somewhere in her mid-twenties. She was an attractive young woman with black curly hair and clear blue eyes. He could see the marks of the tears where her mascara had run. The day she found the woman's torso would be in her memory until the day she died. 'Do you live locally?'

She held the dog on her lap close. 'Firmount Crescent, not far from the care home.'

'Would you prefer to talk to me there?' Wilson turned as Browne opened the driver's door and sat into the Land Rover.

'No, here's fine. I don't know what I can tell you though.'

'Just explain how you found the torso and what you did when you saw it.'

'The dogs got away from me and wouldn't come back. They're little brats when they get off the lead. I could hear them scuffling in the bushes and called them out. But, of course, they ignored me, so I went in after them. I could see that they were digging in the ground and at first I thought it might be a dead animal. Then I saw the skin. I picked up a branch and started to root around where the dogs were burrowing. Once I knew for sure it was a body, I put the dogs on their leads and I called 999. I'm afraid I also vomited.'

'Don't worry about that. Do you walk the dogs here every day?'

'Most mornings.'

'And you've never seen anything strange going on?'

'I often see a few joggers, but nobody burying a body.'

'Do you work locally?'

She looked quickly at her watch. 'Oh Jesus, I forgot all about work. I'll be fired.'

'No you won't,' Wilson said. 'And you won't be going to work today. Give Detective Sergeant Browne the phone number of your workplace and he'll make all the arrangements with them. You've received a very big shock, which probably hasn't fully hit yet. Sergeant Browne will arrange for a car to take you and your dogs home. When you get there, make yourself a nice cup of tea.' He didn't tell her that she would probably spend the rest of the day wrapped up in bed crying.

6

Dr Andrew Muriuki pulled his car up as close to the crime scene tape as he could. He climbed out and removed his sky-blue plastic jumpsuit from the boot. He had recently qualified as a pathologist and had expressed serious reservations about taking the locum position covering Professor Reid's leave of absence. Although Belfast was no longer the murder capital of the United Kingdom, a quick examination of the files indicated that he might have to deal with a least one murder during his sojourn in Belfast. Now his knowledge was about to be put to the test and he was worried that it might be found wanting. He saw that the forensic van had already arrived and assumed that the several figures in white plastic jumpsuits moving around in the undergrowth were forensic officers. He had just completed dressing himself to look like an overgrown condom when he was approached by a very tall, well-built man wearing a suit and moving with an air of authority. He removed his bag from the boot and stood by his car.

Wilson extended his hand as he approached the new arrival. 'Detective Superintendent Ian Wilson, and who might you be?'

Muriuki shook the extended hand. 'Dr Andrew Muriuki, I'm replacing Professor Reid during her leave of absence.' Reid had left him very detailed notes on the procedures at the Royal Victoria and the open files that would require his attention. However, it was her assistant during their tea breaks who had filled him in on the cast of characters he would meet in the hospital and the local police force. Heavily featured in their discussions was the man standing in front of him. He had been told that the policeman who was also Reid's lover was an imposing individual, but he was not prepared for the angle he had to crane his neck at in order to look into Wilson's eyes. Muriuki had been taken from his mother before he was five months old, principally because she had twice tried to kill him by throwing him into the village's long-drop latrine. As a result of being underfed as a child, his growth had been stunted and he was happy that he had reached a height of five feet five inches.

Wilson looked down on the pathologist. Two red-rimmed dark eyes looked back at him from behind glasses that resembled bottle tops. He looked for all the world like a young student or an aspiring actor auditioning for the role of an African Harry Potter. He'd heard that Reid's locum was a Kenyan but that was about it. The words 'leave of absence' brought home to him the indefinite nature of Reid's stay in Los Angeles.

'I understand that we're dealing with a torso of a woman,' Muriuki said, levelling his gaze at the area where the forensic team was at work.

Wilson followed the pathologist's stare 'The head, arms and legs are missing. As soon as you and Forensics are through, I intend to organise a detailed search of the park for the missing body parts, including the use of the cadaver dogs.'

'Then I'd best get to work,' Muriuki ducked under the tape and strode towards the crime scene.

Wilson was two yards behind him. He wanted to see how Reid's temporary replacement handled himself.

The forensic team had already exposed the full torso and one of them was taking photographs of the scene. Wilson noted that the head had been removed from the shoulders and the arms from the shoulder sockets while the thighs had been severed at the hips. What remained was the chest, the pubic area and the rear.

Muriuki could see that the dissection of the body had been done in the most rudimentary fashion. The operation had certainly not been carried out by a medical practitioner. He would leave it to the forensic technicians to establish the implement that had been employed. He knew that the police would be interested in the cause and the time of death. The decay process was under way, but he wouldn't be able to give an estimate of the time of death until he had a chance to test the growth of maggots in the lab. There was very little he could do here. He stood up and turned to face Wilson's chest.

'Anything?' Wilson asked.

Muriuki walked towards the cars. 'The murder didn't take place here and neither did the amputations. The earth is clear of blood. Other than the dismemberment, there is no sign of violence on the torso. I would assume that the head, arms and legs were removed so as to disguise the way in which this poor woman died. I'll need to run some tests on the rate of maggot growth back at the lab before I can give even an estimated time of death. I'll carry out a full post-mortem on the torso and let you have the results as soon as they're available.'

Wilson was impressed. He doubted that Reid would have been able to go any further. It looked like they would have to locate the head and the limbs if they wanted to find out how the woman died, and who she was.

As they exited from the bushes, they saw that an ambulance had pulled up alongside the Land Rovers and two paramedics were standing outside the crime scene tape. The chief of the forensic team approached them carrying a body bag. 'Are you finished?' he addressed the question to Wilson, who in turn looked at Muriuki.

The pathologist was already heading towards his car. 'I'm finished. Tell them to deposit the torso at the Royal Victoria mortuary.'

Very businesslike and very professional, Wilson thought as he watched the small man slip gracefully out of his jumpsuit. Reid would be missed, but her replacement didn't appear to be the worst pathologist he'd worked with.

7

Wilson peeled off his jumpsuit and placed it in a plastic bag. He was standing at the top of the escarpment looking across the park to the Holywood Golf Club in the distance. He was no land surveyor, but he estimated that there were more than two hundred acres of wood and bush directly in front of him. If there was a better place close to Belfast to hide a body, he didn't know it. Except, he wasn't dealing with a body. All he had was a torso. There were no wounds on the torso itself so the cause of death would remain undetermined, unless by some miracle the cadaver dogs find something or another couple of stray Jack Russells decided to help out. Searching Redburn Country Park was going to take time and be resource intensive. This was the part of policing that the politicians didn't think about when they played the numbers game. It's easy to cut the number of police officers and trumpet the positive impact that could immediately be seen on the bottom line. But solving crimes requires resources, which means boots on the ground. This evening, or tomorrow, some half-assed journalist like his friend McDevitt would start writing about the threat to young women from the man, or men, responsible for carving up whoever the torso belonged to. Twenty years ago there would have been dozens of detectives on a case like this. Today it will be him and his small squad of journeymen aided and abetted by a few dozen uniforms spending their days tramping round a two-hundred-acre park looking for a patch of disturbed ground. Good luck with that.

'Tea,' the chief of the forensics team thrust a cup in Wilson's direction.

'Thanks.' Wilson took the cup. 'Sandy, isn't it?'

'Aye, I hope you like sugar. We find it helps.' He took a slug from his own cup.

Wilson tasted his tea, five spoons of sugar for sure, possibly more.

'She's all packed up and away,' Sandy said. 'We've taken some soil samples but there's not much else. The ground has been pretty well churned up. I don't blame the wee girl or her dogs. It just is what it is. If there's any evidence about, we'll find it. Mind you, I wouldn't like the job of searching this park. I live in Dundonald and we used to come here with the kids. There are plenty of nooks and crannies.'

'I was thinking the same thing. The uniforms won't thank me.' Wilson finished his tea. He could still feel the sweetness in his mouth. He passed the cup back to Sandy.

'Do you think the other bits are buried close by?' Sandy asked.

Wilson looked across the green fields and woods that covered the park. 'Could be, but if we do find the rest of her I'm going to buy a lottery ticket.'

Browne joined them. 'Ferguson is away home. We'll call on her tomorrow for an official statement. I've contacted her employer and explained the situation. Is it time for the cadaver dogs?'

Wilson looked at Sandy, who nodded. 'Make the arrangements. We're also going to have to close the park while the uniforms carry out a detailed search. I'll give the chief super a call and see what can be arranged within the limits of the budget.'

'You'll have the photographs before close of play today,' Sandy said. 'And the forensic report as soon as possible. Best of luck with this one, you're going to need it.' He turned and started walking back to the van.

'Any thoughts, Boss?' Browne asked.

'We need to find the head and the limbs. Otherwise we're up shit creek without a paddle. Check the CCTV situation in the area. My guess is that there isn't too much. There'll be some at the golf club no doubt, but it'll be bugger-all use. Harry will have to manage the search of the park. There are three issues that I'd like to clear up quickly. Where exactly was she murdered? How did she die? And last but by no means least, who the hell was she? Someone has gone to great lengths to deny that information to us. Why? What is so important about this murder that we have to be left completely in the dark? On the face of it, I can't see any of these questions being answered without the expenditure of an enormous amount of shoe leather.'

8

Detective Constable Peter Davidson was living the dream. On most nights he exchanged his dingy bedsit in central Belfast for Irene Carlisle's four-bedroomed home in Hillsborough. He regularly clapped himself on the back for having the courage to follow up on the widow Carlisle's subtle encouragement. Their arrangement was entirely suited to two mature individuals. He had learned that Irene's life had not been the bed of roses most people might have expected. Her husband was a career politician and as time progressed his interest in politics had increased and his interest in his wife had diminished. She was ready for some male and attention and Davidson's life had been devoid of female companionship for some time, so their arrangement had been mutually agreeable. He was keeping quiet about his understanding with Irene. He was supposed to be investigating the possibility that her husband's suicide had in fact been murder. His boss, Ian Wilson, wouldn't be at all happy about his extracurricular activities. He was five weeks into the investigation and he was getting nowhere. That wasn't exactly true. He had learned that the hospice dealing with Jackie Carlisle had received a call on the morning of his death cancelling an appointment that involved him receiving a morphine injection. He knew for certain that neither Carlisle nor his widow had placed that call, but he was still having trouble getting the hospice to agree to their telecom provider releasing the data on the calls for the day in question. The pace of the investigation didn't bother him and since it was an off-the-books exercise, Wilson was allowing him a free hand. So far there were only two leads to follow up, the phone call and the source of the morphine. The tox report from the autopsy had established that the shot of morphine Carlisle had received had been almost one hundred per cent pure and that the quantity injected was sufficient to kill a dray horse. There were few enough places in Belfast where product of that nature could be obtained. One of those sources being new ganglord Davie Best. A dead politician and the possible involvement of a gang-boss didn't auger well for the health of the person investigating the connection. It was a case of treading very carefully and not awakening the monster.

Davidson had got into the habit of dropping by the widow Carlisle for an early morning coffee. In order to cover for this activity he was also canvassing the neighbours concerning the day of Carlisle's death. He had just enjoyed a cup of coffee and a cuddle with Irene and as he was leaving he noticed a car in the driveway of one of her neighbours who had been away on holiday when he did his house-to-house. It was a fine autumn day with relatively few clouds breaking up the blue of the sky. Davidson was in a positive mood when he marched up the tarmacked drive and knocked at the door of the imposing residence.

The man who answered the door was slightly older than Davidson and was wearing a check shirt with a cravat. Davidson suppressed a smile. Who the hell in this day and age wore a cravat? He produced his warrant card. 'Detective Constable Davidson.'

The look on the man's face showed that he had had very

limited contact with the police. 'Has something happened? It's not my son is it?' The accent was south of England.

'No, sir, nothing like that. You are no doubt aware that one of your neighbours, Jackie Carlisle, was found dead recently.'

'Yes, we all knew Jackie, life and soul of any party. Great fount of inside stories and all-round nice chap. What's the problem?'

'No problem, sir, we're just looking into suspicious movements on the day Mr Carlisle died. His life had been threatened and while we agree with the coroner's verdict of suicide, we're anxious to follow up on any threats he might have received just before his death. You didn't happen to see anything suspicious on the day he died?' Davidson knew his story was full of holes. The problem with lying is not that one gets caught in it but that one has to keep thinking up new lies to validate the original one.

The man thought for a moment. 'No, I didn't see anything unusual. I think I was gardening that day. The roses needed pruning, the damn things always seem to need pruning. I remember seeing Irene leaving and a short time after that a chap got out of a car and went up the drive. Jackie must have been expecting him because the door opened and he was admitted immediately.'

'Is there anything you can tell me about the man?' Davidson withdrew his day-book from his pocket.

'He was a big fellow, six feet plus. He was wearing some kind of white jacket. I think there was another chap in the car he got out of.'

'You mean a white sports coat?'

'No, damn it, if I meant a white sports coat I would have said so. It was the kind of jacket that a chef or a doctor might wear. I went inside just after that so I didn't see him leave. Is that suspicious enough for you?'

Or a male nurse, Davidson thought. And yes, it was bloody well very suspicious. 'And Mr Carlisle let him in immediately?'

'That's what I said. Are we finished?'

'More roses to prune, sir?' Davidson put away his day-book. And when he looked up the door had been shut in his face. He smiled before turning and walking back down the drive. Most people would have let Carlisle's death go and been satisfied to bid him good riddance but not Detective Superintendent Ian Wilson. No, his boss had an antenna that could pick up the weakest signal of a crime. He was the kind of man who worried a small inconsistency into a major line of enquiry. The cancelled phone call. The large overdose of pure product. And now the two men, one possibly wearing a nurse's uniform. He was enjoying his little gallop with Irene Carlisle and he hoped that this new piece of information wouldn't put an end to it. Whatever way you spun it, the prime suspect in a murder enquiry into the death of Jackie Carlisle was his merry widow.

9

Chief Superintendent Yvonne Davis held her head in her hands. The man sitting across from her had just blown her budget to smithereens. Redburn Country Park was two hundred and fifty acres of woodland, bush and scrub. Searching it for the body parts of the obviously murdered woman would cost a fortune in overtime and pull officers off the roster. 'We'll have to search the whole park,' she said, more or less to herself but loud enough for Wilson to hear.

'I would assume so.' He remembered a time when the chief super spent most of his or her time chivvying the troops along and mentoring the ones who were going to make a career. He doubted that Davis, with all the administrative tasks she had to perform and meetings she attended, had the time to even think about chivvying her troops along. In fact, he doubted if she would even recognise some of the troops who laboured in the bowels of the station. It was the age of the management cop. In the new order, you don't get to the top because of your grasp of the fundamentals of crime detection and prevention. Now, the road to the top is paved with memos, management courses and brownnosing. Wilson had never seen a crime that had been solved with a memo on organisation structure or the takeaways from a management course. He found himself constantly pitying Davis because from what he had heard she had been a pretty good cop.

'The park has been closed off?' she asked.

'The road in has been blocked. Just as I left, two TV camera crews arrived. We're going to be on the news tonight so we better get the ball rolling.'

'How did they find out so quickly?'

'In the old days they would probably have some intern monitoring the police radio, but today I'd put my money on the ambulance crew. A woman's naked torso is a tasty morsel for our friends in the Fourth Estate.' He would also bet that Jock McDevitt and his friends would be salivating at the thought of a string of front-page by-lines.

'Does it ever stop? We seem to stutter from one crisis to another. And they are all centred round you.' She pushed aside a lock of hair that had fallen over her right eye.

Wilson put his hands up. 'I promise I didn't kill the woman and cut her body up.'

'Very funny, but you're not the one who's going to be hauled over the coals when the bean counters see that discrepancy between my funding provisions and the actual expenditure.'

'Force majeure. We can't avoid looking for the other body parts since I'm fairly sure that they are relevant to our investigation. I'll be a damn sight more bothered if we don't find them. Anyway, a case like this will draw a lot of public attention, which means a lot of television appearances. And you've got a new hairstyle to show off.' He smiled as he delivered the last sentence.

Davis put on a harsh face but was aware that she was blushing. 'I think you're the most aggravating man I've ever met. No, I take that back. You're a royal pain in the arse, but my ex was a roaring bastard.'

'You're going to have to moderate your language for your

television appearances. How many bodies can you liberate for the search?'

She looked down at the chart on her desk. 'I can spare four and HQ have managed to find another five.'

'Yes, and I bet they're the brightest and the best.' He knew that his search crew would consist of officers who were otherwise under-occupied and most certainly under-motivated. He assumed that was the current euphemism for malingerers. Harry Graham might have his work cut out for him.

She looked at her watch. 'I have a meeting at HQ in half an hour and I still have to read the report that we're supposed to be discussing. What do I say if someone asks about Redburn Park?'

Wilson stood up. 'You tell them that we have happened across the torso of a young woman who appears to have been the victim of a murder and that we are investigating according to established procedures. I'm putting Harry Graham in charge of the search at Redburn.'

'Any estimate on the time it's going to take?'

Wilson smiled. He knew what she wanted him to say, but searching two hundred and fifty acres of woods and heavy bush was a mammoth task. 'We'll do our best.'

10

Wilson found Siobhan O'Neill sitting alone in the squad room. He sometimes wondered what policing in the future might look like. During his old friend Spence's reign as head of the Murder Squad all seven desks had been occupied. Today, Rory Browne was following up on the forensic report from Redburn Country Park, Harry Graham was organising the cadaver dogs and the search and Peter Davidson was chasing a shadow that Wilson had conjured up. Should he pull Davidson off the Jackie Carlisle investigation? It was almost six months since Carlisle died and the majority of the evidence connected with that death seemed to be interred with the body. They were pissing against the wind, but he felt that there was enough there to keep investigating, even at Peter's slow pace. He walked to the front of the room and examined the whiteboards. The central board was covered with black-and-white photos of the burned-out car in Helen's Bay and the charred body that had been removed from the boot. There was precious little else. They knew where the car had been stolen from but had no idea who had stolen it. There was CCTV footage of the car moving east through central Belfast before heading for Helen's Bay. Nobody had come to claim the body and nobody had seen Mickey Duff since the conflagration. The conclusion was obvious, but there wasn't a shred of proof. The good news was that there was no pressure from HQ to clear the case. Who the hell cared about the death of a small boy, his junkie prostitute mother and her drug-pusher boyfriend anyway? By rights he should ask O'Neill to take a photo of the board and pack it away, but he wasn't going to do that yet. Life in the Murder Squad wasn't only about catching the culprit and a few rounds of drinks in the Crown afterwards. Cases weren't always cleared and sometimes the wheels of justice moved exceedingly slowly. His truncated squad should know that they laboured against the odds and he hoped that fired them up. He thought about the battered body of Josh McAuley on the steel tray in the mortuary. If the charred body was Mickey Duff, and if Duff had killed the boy, then he supposed that justice had been served.

He pulled up a chair and sat beside O'Neill. When she had joined the squad she had been forty pounds overweight. She was systematically shedding the pounds and looking the better for it. Her thinner face sparked a memory, but, as several times before, he couldn't put his finger on it. 'We need to set up a new board, but I don't want to take the Josh McAuley board down.' He might have added 'yet', but he resisted the temptation. He thought back to the remark made by Willie Rice before he went to meet his Maker. In the old ganglord's jaundiced eyes the new mobsters were more vicious than their predecessors. Wilson chose not to agree. Rice and men like him had been cold-hearted killers. There was a streak of mercilessness in everything that had happened in the province for more than thirty years. The current generation of criminals had been mentored well.

'Why is it always a woman's torso?' O'Neill asked. 'I'm sick of it, all this violence being perpetrated against women. And leaving her naked only increases the indignity. She had a father and probably a brother and a husband. And they may well have been good to her. But somebody murdered her and carved her up. And it was almost certainly a man.'

Wilson could see the film of tears in her eyes. He knew she was almost certainly right. Violence against women was probably as old as the Garden of Eden. Except it wasn't reported in the Bible just as it wasn't in the newspapers until recently. He had no doubt that when they unmasked the killer it would turn out to be a man. 'We'll get him.' It was the mantra of every squad leader in every police force in the world. And few of them really believed it. The number of unsolved murders gave the lie to it. 'And the sooner we get cracking on putting the evidence together the more chance we have of bringing the bastard to book. Forensics is sending the photos taken at the burial site over before close of business. I want them on a board with a couple of shots of Redburn Country Park showing the location of the torso. Also, I want a schematic of the roads leading to the park and the location of any traffic CCTV cameras.' He saw that her eyes had cleared. 'It's not our job to change the world or any of the sleazeballs in it, but it is our job to put this woman's killer behind bars.'

Wilson walked to his office in the corner of the squad room. By the time he sat at his desk, O'Neill was already busying herself setting up the new board. He hoped he hadn't just handed her a line of crap. He looked at his watch. Four thirty in the afternoon in Belfast was eight thirty in the morning in LA. Reid would probably still be rubbing the sleep from her eyes, but he was in need of seeing and talking to her. He opened up Skype and it showed that she was online. He pressed the green phone.

The call was answered after two rings.

'That was quick,' he said. 'You a little psychic today?'

The screen suddenly changed and he could see her framed against a blue sky. Eight thirty in the morning and already her world was flooded in sunshine. He wondered what the temperature outside might be. The picture on the screen and the radiance of her smile seemed to make his office less dour. California suited her. Her light blue cotton shirt set off her tan perfectly. Her blonde hair was tied back and she had an unmistakably healthy look. She was sitting at a small breakfast table set on the deck in the garden of her mother's house in Venice Beach. He wanted to climb through the screen and sit beside her. His summer had seen the usual mix of rain and cloud interspersed with ever shorter periods of sunshine. Global warming had bypassed Northern Ireland.

She held up a coffee cup and a glass of orange juice. 'Breakfast California-style. You're calling early today. What's the reason?'

He smiled. 'Maybe I just wanted to talk to you.' Something had happened in their relationship since they had stood on the pavement outside the Redeemer Central Church on Donegall Street. The evening before she'd left she had used the word they had both been avoiding. But now the genie was out of the bottle and nothing was ever going to be the same again.

'I miss you too.'

'Yeah, but it doesn't look like you're missing rainy old Belfast.'

'This place would be perfect if you were here. Now, tell me what's happened?'

'The naked torso of a young woman was found this morning in a shallow grave in Redburn Country Park.'

'Only the torso?' She returned the coffee and the glass of juice to the table.

He could see the interest in her eyes. 'We've closed the park off and we're instigating a search for the arms, legs and the head.'

'Only the torso,' she repeated as though to herself. 'Any apparent wounds?'

'No.'

'Have you met my replacement?'

'Dr Muriuki. Yes, he seems to be professional. Not up to your standard of course. How's your mother?'

She looked round and her voice dropped. 'Not great, the disease is progressing. I'm on hand when the pain becomes severe, but she needs more morphine to control it.'

'No breakthrough from your brother or father?'

She lowered her voice further to just above a whisper. 'Peter is a totally lost cause. Dad has been on Skype, but he has no intention of coming over.'

'How long does she have?'

'She's already passed the time they'd given her. She's hanging in there hoping for some kind of rapprochement with Peter. But she's beginning to see that that's not going to happen.'

'I wish I was there with you.'

'I know, but the naked torso of a woman found in Redburn Country Park this morning.'

'Is it okay if I call you again tonight?'

'It's better than okay. I won't sleep if you don't.'

He blew her a kiss and she blew one back. Then the screen returned to the Skype home page. His office became gloomy again. She was right. All he had to do was turn up at Belfast International and put his credit card on the desk. The next day he would be sitting beside her in the sunshine. But she was also right about the reason he wouldn't do that. Someone had murdered and dismembered the body of a young woman. He wanted to know why and then he wanted to know who. Finding the answer to those two questions was the devil that drove him.

11

Siobhan O'Neill looked at the photos that had arrived from Forensics. They made her feel ill. This wasn't one of those occasions where the killer had medical training and had neatly severed the limbs and head. This was a case where the limbs and head had been roughly hacked from the body. She had to review all hundred plus photos before selecting the five that she would print and attach to the whiteboard. She had already obtained a photo of Redburn Country Park and its environs and had dropped a pin on the GPS coordinates established by Forensics. She had put in a request to Traffic for the location of the CCTV cameras that might be active in the area. She printed the photos she thought best represented the situation at the burial site and was in the process of attaching them to the board when she glanced into her boss's office. Wilson was leaning back in his chair with his hands behind his head. Sometimes when he looked at her she thought he was on the point of remembering where he had met her first. But the look of recognition in his eyes always vanished as quickly as it appeared. She wondered what he would think if he knew he was responsible in large measure for her joining the PSNI. Her friends thought she was crazy to waste her computer skills checking up on villains. Sometimes she was forced to agree with them. Computers had been her life since she had been presented with a second-hand laptop by her older sister. Within a year she had mastered coding and was writing her own programmes. After college, she had joined a tech start-up, one year later the company was sold and her one per cent of the shares dropped fifty thousand pounds into her hands. By one of those ironies of fate that seem to direct our lives, the day she was offered a position with the new company in New York was the same day her mother was diagnosed with Alzheimer's. The dream of living and working in the Big Apple was born and died in an instant. She could have found another tech start-up but putting in the all-nighters was now out of the question. The priority in her life became the woman who had brought her into the world. Her mother had already promenaded down their street in her underwear so a twenty-four-hour watch had to be established. She had never appreciated the capacity of their friends and neighbours to rally round in times of crisis before. The next crossroads in her life arrived soon after when she saw Ian Wilson on television. Memories flooded back and the next day she applied to become a police officer. She already had her little nest egg and she would be able to repay the kindness of the people of her native city. She finished affixing the photos and the map to the board. She had written 'Jane Doe' at the top of the whiteboard. She tried to think of something more original but nothing came to mind. Wilson was still leaning back in his chair as she returned to her desk.

DC Harry Graham was standing on a knoll surveying the expanse of Redburn Country Park below him. Off to his left, where the road into the park ended, two television vans were parked and a small group of journalists had assembled. They had already shot footage of the cadaver dogs being unloaded and being set to work. That footage would be splashed across TV screens tuned to the evening news with the scant details that the police already knew. Graham looked at the ten officers already deployed in searching a wooded area to his right. He hadn't noticed many bright sparks among them and although the light might last until seven o'clock, the gloomy conditions would probably force them to suspend operations at six. They would resume early the next morning. When he'd heard that he was being put in charge of the search of the park he'd been none too happy. But when he arrived and saw that almost half the two hundred and fifty acres of park was open parkland, he felt considerably better. Still, it would take the guts of three days to cover the entire park. And three days in a murder investigation was a hell of a long time.

12

The three men sat in a stark room in a military installation near Carryduff. DCC Royson Jennings sat on one side of the wooden table. He was in full dress uniform and was somewhat perplexed at being called to this very hush-hush meeting within days of arriving back in Belfast. He had been easing himself back into the saddle. He'd missed the last elevation to the main job but Chief Constable Norman Baird wouldn't last forever. Powerful people still depended on him, so it was a question of being patient. He'd met the men on the other side of the table before. They had been doing business together for the past fifteen years. The fact that neither one was wearing his uniform rang an alarm bell for Jennings.

Sitting directly across from him was a man he had known as Major Milan. A member of Military Intelligence, he handled British agents embedded in Republican organisations. Jennings wasn't so naïve as to believe either that the man was a major or that his real name was Milan. Although he had seen him in uniform once, Milan was generally dressed in mufti. He was tall and thin. The moustache he had worn when they had first met had disappeared and his once brown hair had become salt and pepper. Seated beside Milan was Chief Superintendent

Robert Rodgers, a senior officer in the PSNI Special Branch and responsible for the infiltration of subversive groups. Jennings had the impression that the location for the meeting had been carefully chosen. There was no coffee and biscuits and after a perfunctory handshake the three men had taken their seats. The three men sat silently looking at one another. Jennings gave a half-smile at the sight of the two other men sitting side by side. Although ostensibly on the same side, PSNI Special Branch and Military Intelligence were bitter rivals in the collection and cultivation of undercover agents. Often an agent working for one of the organisations had murdered an agent of the other. Coordination of state activities in Northern Ireland had never been a high priority.

'It's been a while,' Milan said finally.

Jennings and Rodgers nodded. Fifteen years to be precise, Jennings thought. He remembered the scene with the witches in *Macbeth*, 'when shall we three meet again'. Except they weren't witches. They were something considerably worse.

'We have a problem,' Milan said.

Jennings took off his cap and placed it on the table in front of him. 'Again.'

Milan's man's face contorted as though he had sucked a lemon. '*Pecavit*,' he said.

Jennings' school Latin was sufficient to know this meant someone had sinned and he also knew it wasn't him this time. He had already done penance for his sin. A bad feeling began to work its way up from his stomach and he thought he could taste bile. He looked at Milan but didn't speak. Jennings had no idea what Milan's background was, but he knew the type: classics scholar at Oxford or Cambridge, commission in the army, nice secure job in an office block on the Embankment, wife in the professions or possibly working for a charity, two point four children attending the 'right' school.

'Our friend has made another error of judgement,' Milan said. 'We have already assisted with the clean-up, but we must decide on our future approach. The intelligence Icepick provides is of the highest order and is considered vitally important by our political masters. That must be taken into consideration, whatever we decide.'

Jennings stared at the two men sitting across from him. They were the remnants of the great intelligence war against the IRA. He had no idea why an agent was called Icepick, but whoever had come up with that cover name was a hundred times move inventive than the idiot who had come up with Steaknife. 'Redburn,' he said, almost to himself.

The men on the other side of the table nodded.

Jennings looked down at the table then raised his eyes to stare straight ahead. The men on the other side of the table dropped their eyes. Their previous dealings together haunted Jennings' dreams. If their joint past was ever exposed, it wouldn't only bring him down and finish his career, they would all go to jail. Well, he and Rodgers would go to jail and their English friend would probably end up pruning roses outside a country cottage somewhere in deepest Sussex. 'You are surely not asking for protection for the bastard?'

'We are talking about the most productive asset we have ever developed in the province,' Milan said.

Jennings gave one of his trademark cynical smiles. 'We are talking about a man who has now murdered two women, if not more. Am I to understand that some of your thugs were responsible for dismembering the body?'

Neither of the men on the other side of the table spoke.

'What do you have in mind?' Jennings asked.

Milan took out his pen and made a note in a leather-bound book. 'The asset must be protected at all costs. He has risen to a position of such prominence that we cannot afford to throw him to the wolves.'

'Perhaps we can arrange a little accident,' Rodgers spoke for the first time.

Typical Special Branch, Jennings thought, always us a

sledgehammer to crack a hazelnut. 'I'm assuming that there's a reason why that suggestion is out of the question.'

Milan put the cap back on his pen. 'Our friend has purchased himself some insurance. If anything happens to him, he has lodged a detailed account of our previous assistance to him with his solicitor and other unnamed persons.'

'But he doesn't know our names,' Rodgers said.

'Don't be an idiot,' Jennings said sharply. 'Once they know that his crime was covered up by the PSNI, Special Branch and Military Intelligence they'll find us. If the powers that be don't throw us under a bus first.'

Rodgers turned to the Milan. 'I don't like it. He's your asset. You promised us that it was a one-off the last time. He got carried away, et cetera, et cetera. Now we're in the position of having to protect the bastard again, while he sits close to the top of the totem pole presenting himself as Mister Clean.'

Milan closed his notebook. 'It is precisely because he is so close to the top of the totem pole, as you put it, that our political masters feel we should protect him. What's the life of one prostitute in the great scheme of things?'

'To hell with the great scheme of things,' Jennings said. 'Don't think that I don't realise where this is going. The last time *I* was the one who did ninety per cent of the dirty work.' Milan opened his mouth to speak, but Jennings held up his hand. 'I know, I know, you came through with a couple of quick promotions. But I was the one who was out there.'

'What about Gilligan?' Milan asked.

Jennings smiled. It was Chief Superintendent Matt Gilligan who had convinced him to play ball with Military Intelligence and Special Branch in 2002. And although his role had catapulted him up the PSNI ladder, he hadn't stopped looking over his shoulder since. 'Gilligan did bugger-all. Anyway, he has nothing to fear now that he's dead.' Sometimes he wondered whether the title Military Intelligence was a misnomer. 'Who exactly was the woman?'

'Some Eastern European tart he picked up,' Milan said.

'Won't she be missed?' Jennings asked.

Rodgers smiled, exposing two rows of stained teeth. 'Yes, I can just see her pimp turning up at Musgrave Street station complaining that one of his tarts is missing.' Within the force, Rodgers was known as 'Black Bob' because of his work running black operations that the PSNI would disavow if discovered. He was not a man to be trifled with.

'Why didn't they just dump the body?' Jennings asked.

'One of our maxims is never plan in haste,' Milan said. 'It generally ends in a cock-up. Some idiot thought that he was being clever. The girl was covered in DNA from the asset. The first priority was to get every ounce of DNA off her and these things are not time independent.'

'Tell it to the inquiry,' Jennings said. He wasn't in a position to throw stones about cock-ups. His legal brain was looking for a way out. The last time he was closer to the investigation and could interfere at will. This time it wouldn't be so simple. And the case had landed in Wilson's lap. But so had the one in 2002 and he hadn't managed to solve it then. 'Detective Superintendent Wilson is SIO on the case. He's possibly the most experienced murder detective in the United Kingdom. Pulling the wool over his eyes is going to be no easy matter.'

'You did it before,' Milan said.

Jennings smiled at the memory despite the fact that the event haunted him. 'I can't promise anything. We're at a very early stage. Wilson doesn't even have a name or the woman's profession.'

'He won't find the limbs or the head,' Milan said, 'and the clothes have been burned.'

'Then we shall live in hope that there are no more screw-ups.' Jennings stood up.

Milan's eyes followed him. 'We've done our part to protect

the asset. Now it's up to you. In the meantime we're trying to locate the incriminating documents he claims to have secreted.'

'There are no guarantees on this one.' Jennings looked from one to the other of the men facing him. 'Bit of luck that I'm back in the saddle, eh!' As he left the room, he wondered whether that was the case.

He had been running through possibilities since he'd heard that the mess in Redburn Country Park had been handled by Military Intelligence.

13

It was almost seven o'clock and Wilson was still at his desk. The squad room was empty and dark. The search at Redburn Country Park had been suspended and would resume in the morning. The autopsy, such as it was, would also take place the following morning and Wilson had passed the pleasant task of attending to DS Browne. He now had two choices. He could pick up a takeaway and head straight back to his apartment in Queen's Quay, plonk himself down in front of the television and try to stay awake until it was time to place his second call of the day to Reid. Or he could stop off at the Crown for a pint or two before picking up the takeaway. It had been a crap day, enlivened only by his call to Reid. But it was the butchered woman who was on his mind. It took a certain callousness to take a chainsaw to someone. At some point in the investigation there would be the inevitable profile of the murderer. Perhaps that would lead them somewhere, but he was a proponent of the school that says shoe leather beats psychobabble every day of the week. The initial profile would have him chasing fifty per cent of the male population of Belfast. It was evidence and running down leads that solved crimes. He was about to leave when his phone rang.

'Your boss is on television,' Jock McDevitt said. 'The new hairstyle suits her. I hadn't thought of it before, but maybe you should introduce us.'

'I actually like her, so there's no chance of that.'

'Fancy a pint? Life must be dull now that the good professor is off sunning herself in California. Or have you already found a replacement?'

'Don't talk shite.' He didn't like to think that the suggestion would have been true in the past. 'But I was contemplating a pint before going home.'

THEY ARRIVED at the Crown almost together and Wilson was in luck that his habitual snug wasn't occupied. He noticed that McDevitt was still gentle with his right shoulder. Bullet damage takes a while to repair.

'My twist,' McDevitt said as he handed the barman a ten-pound note.

Wilson picked up his pint of Guinness. 'What are we celebrating?'

McDevitt took a draught of his drink. 'My agent and I met with a couple of Hollywood-types this afternoon. We're crawling at a snail's pace towards a deal for a film of the Cummerford book.'

'Belfast will soon be too small for you,' Wilson said.

McDevitt's face was glowing with excitement. 'Unlikely! My agent says that initial sales are not encouraging. Not enough sex apparently. You fell down on the job there. If there had been a bit of grappling between you and Cummerford it wouldn't have hurt sales. Anyway, Hollywood was always pie in the sky. Now what about the woman's naked torso in Redburn Country Park? If there isn't a sex angle to that, I'm a monkey's uncle. My nose for a story is smelling something sensational.'

It was only day one, but Wilson was sure that McDevitt was right. Although it might turn out to be the result of a family argument. Husband kills wife was far too regular an occurrence to fan the interest of the populace. 'You might be right there,' he said. 'Unfortunately, that nose of yours is not an exact science.'

'I see it's going to be one of those "blood from a stone" sessions.' He pressed the bell for service. 'Ready for another pint or would you prefer a whiskey?'

Wilson was only halfway through his first drink and he had no desire to spend the entire evening in a pub. 'Don't waste your money. There's nothing to tell. Everything that we know for the moment was in the statement put out to the press. The list of things that we don't know is as long as your arm. Someone has made a damn good effort to give us precious little to work with. If she's a housewife, someone will report her as missing. If she hasn't turned up for work, her colleagues will eventually give us a ring. Right now we're looking at a blank page and we're going to need time to detect the dots never mind trying to connect them.'

McDevitt ordered another round of drinks. 'My heart bleeds for you. What about the guy who was incinerated at Helen's Bay? Any sexual overtones there?'

'HQ have put it down to a drug-related crime.' Wilson finished his first drink and pushed the glass away. 'Mind you, the conflagration would have destroyed every scrap of any narcotic that might have been present in the car. Pretty harsh treatment for the boy that was in the boot though, what do you think?'

McDevitt accepted two pints of Guinness from the barman and handed one to Wilson. 'I don't suppose that you've seen the pictures of the decapitated heads along the road in Mexico? Those drugs boys don't mess around. Too much money involved.' He raised his glass and drank. 'How's the other half getting on?'

Wilson sipped his drink and recalled Reid sitting at her

breakfast table. 'She's tanned and relaxed. The sun is shining and there's a swimming pool in the background.'

McDevitt smiled, the picture Wilson had painted was a million miles from Belfast. 'Are you sure she's coming back?'

Reid staying in America was an outcome that Wilson had considered but dismissed. Perhaps he had been hasty. If he was in her position, would he come back? He looked at his watch. It was lunchtime in LA. That was the way he looked at time since Reid had left. LA time was now his base. He could call her in an hour.

'How's her mother?' McDevitt continued.

Wilson shook his head. 'Matter of time.' He wondered how long.

McDevitt leaned forward. 'Okay, tell me, I know that you had the opportunity, why the hell didn't you bonk Cummerford?'

14

Peter Davidson and Harry Graham had been born three hundred yards and fifteen years apart. They both knew the Shankill like the back of their hands and had been to school with most of the 'characters' who inhabited the warren of Victorian streets. While they were welcome in most of the pubs in the area they had organised to meet in the more upmarket surroundings of the Union Street bar, where they had selected a corner table some distance away from the nearest patron.

'What's so bloody important that we have to meet outside work?' Graham said. 'I have three youngsters at home and their mother is giving me grief about not being around enough.' He enjoyed a drink after work but instinct told him this wasn't a social catch-up. Davidson had been acting peculiarly over the past few weeks and Graham was already wondering what he was up to. He liked working with his older colleague but never forgot Davidson's dodgy reputation.

Davidson looked furtively round before sipping his pint of Guinness and following it up with a whiskey chaser. 'I have a bad feeling about the Jackie Carlisle thing.' He told Graham about his latest interview with the neighbour. 'Two men in a car waiting outside the house until Irene, I mean Mrs Carlisle, left. Then one dressed like a nurse in a white jacket goes into the house while the second guy stays in the car. Then they drive off and Jackie Carlisle has given himself a massive injection of morphine. I don't like it.'

'You're screwing her aren't you?' Graham took a large draught of lager. 'You randy old bastard. I knew there was something weird about you over the past few weeks. And you've cleaned yourself up. You're at it with the widow Carlisle.'

'Okay, you're right, but that's not what's going to get me killed. Looking into whoever was responsible for offing her husband might just do it.'

'Pull the other one, Peter. You're keeping the investigation alive because it keeps you close to the widow. Don't tell me that you've fallen for her?'

'Good God, Harry, will you stop thinking with your wee man. This business is fucking serious. I managed to get the phone log from the hospice and the call cancelling Carlisle's appointment was made from a mobile that was active for only one day. That mobile made two calls. One to the hospice and the second to another mobile. I've asked the tech guys to give me the location of the second mobile. It looks like the boss was right. Someone killed Jackie Carlisle and that someone has got to be pretty powerful. There are too many examples around of former UVF commanders naming names. As soon as they're lifted they start spilling their guts. There are people in this city who don't want their misdeeds put into the public domain. Some of them are well capable of silencing anyone with a big mouth.'

Graham had never seen Davidson in such a funk. 'For God's sake man, we're PSNI.'

'Who the hell do you think I'm afraid of?' Davidson downed his Guinness and followed with his whiskey before raising his arm for the refill. 'The dalliance with Irene was fun until I found out about the men in the car and the mobile phones. Now I see the investigation in a very different light. If the people behind Carlisle's death see me nosing about in their business, they won't think twice about getting rid of me.'

'Have you told the boss yet?'

Davidson shook his head just as the barman arrived with two fresh beers and a double whiskey. Once they were alone again, he continued the conversation. 'I'm hoping he might drop the investigation, what with this woman's torso and the guy in the burned-out car.'

Graham sipped his lager. There would be hell to pay when he got home late for his dinner, but Peter was an old friend. He also realised that he was the only one who knew what Davidson knew and that Davidson would give up his name in a minute if he was tortured. 'Now I know.'

Davidson put down his glass. 'I didn't think of that. But nobody knows that you know.'

'What the hell did Carlisle know that got him killed? Sure the man was at death's door anyway.'

'It seems they wanted him through that door as quickly as possible.'

'You have to tell the boss.' Graham drank half of his lager in one gulp. Davidson had thrown a funk into him as well. He wanted to be home with his family. Investigating murder was one thing; getting mixed up with the power elite was another. He could understand his friend's predicament. 'You really have to tell the boss.'

15

Wilson sat cradling a cup of coffee and looking out the picture window of his apartment at the city of Belfast waking up. Somewhere out there someone was missing a wife, mother, sister, daughter or maybe just a friend. Sooner or later that person would make the connection between the missing person and the torso found in Redburn Country Park. In the meantime, his team would be struggling to identify who the torso belonged to. It was evident that the murderer had created this situation purposely. As long as the owner of the torso was unknown, they couldn't follow the normal investigative procedure of looking into the life of the deceased. There was no one to be interviewed and precious little evidence to collect. Clearly whoever had perpetrated the crime was no neophyte. He made a mental note to ask O'Neill to look for similar crimes on the mainland or even in Europe. Not only had the murderer killed before, he had examined how best to set an investigating conundrum for the police. Wilson preferred a flat race rather than having to go over hurdles, but it was what it was.

He had been awake since five and had already had his run and showered. It was night in LA and Reid would be asleep or perhaps she was having a late dinner in Musso and Frank before heading off to a club with a new acquaintance. He hoped not. Using the word 'love' had not only let the genie out of the bottle, it had also invited the green-eyed monster of jealousy into the room. The solution was easy. He could jump in a taxi and get the first available connecting flight. But they were adults and not love-struck teenagers. And yet it was a tempting solution. For almost a year he had been struggling with cases that lay unsolved on his desk. Maybe he needed a break in the sun, a month to recharge his batteries. Just like McDevitt's Hollywood dream, it was pie in the sky. He couldn't remember the last time he'd had the possibility of taking a month off.

Many of the officers he had attended police college with had already retired from the force. Some had left of their own accord whereas others had had their health decimated by the stress and the long hours. Where was he on the spectrum between enthusiastic raw recruit and worn-out potential retiree? He supposed it depended on the day. Taking UVF commander Walter Hanna off the streets had made him feel good. But it was one victory in a war of lost battles. The animal that had torched the car in Helen's Bay was still prowling the streets of the city he was paid to protect. He sat on his couch and watched the sunlight slowly spread from the east and the lights of the city gradually flicker and die. He remembered himself as a young detective. They had impressed the police mantra of means, motive and opportunity on his young mind. He wished it could be that simple.

16

It was eight thirty and the team was assembled at the whiteboards at the end of the squad room. Wilson looked at the faces of his four team members. They looked as tired as he felt.

'There's no way, Boss,' Harry Graham said after Wilson had outlined his plan to keep all the investigations going at some pace, even a snail's pace. 'We're talking about two heavy-duty investigations. The body in the burned-out car, even if that body is Mickey Duff, involves the Best gang and opening up that crew is going to involve thousands of hours of investigative time. Now we have the torso in the park and if no one comes forward to identify the torso's owner, we could be wasting thousands of hours there as well. Think about Redburn Country Park, Boss. Two hundred and fifty acres to be searched by ten uniforms and we have no idea whether any of the other body parts are even buried there. They could be scattered around every park in Belfast. Most of us are already running on empty. We've got to have more resources.' He looked over at Davidson. 'Can we really afford Peter's hobby?'

Davidson went to protest, but Wilson cut him off. 'I know where you're coming from, Harry. I can keep asking upstairs and the chief super can keep asking at HQ, but the bottom line is that we live in an era of austerity. It's all about cutbacks. Every force in the country is feeling the effects and the criminals are beginning to catch on.'

'And so are the bloody terrorists,' Browne interjected.

Wilson continued, 'We have no option but to move on with the resources that we have. Someone killed this poor woman and then desecrated her dead body. I want to find the person or persons who did that, and I know that you all do too. I also want to bellyache, but I know it's not going to get me anywhere.' He wanted to add that they could all retire like a lot of their colleagues but decided to keep things positive. 'So we'll search Redburn Country Park because that's the obvious thing to do and we'll pray for the phone call from a distressed parent or husband that'll tell us who the dead woman is. If that call doesn't come, it doesn't mean that we can drop the ball. We have to look at other possibilities. And I don't want the investigation that Peter is undertaking to be considered as a hobby. A lot of peculiar happenings surrounded Jackie Carlisle's death and I'm convinced that he was murdered.' He missed the look that passed between Graham and Davidson. 'So, the bottom line is that we keep the pressure on for Helen's Bay, the torso *and* Carlisle. For my part, I'll put the case for additional resources to the chief super again.'

17

The nine o'clock meeting in Chief Superintendent Yvonne Davis's office was limited to superintendents, chief inspectors and inspectors. This officers-only affair took a whole hour out of Wilson's week and he detested it. He had never studied meditation, but he had developed the ability to tune out some of the more inane remarks made by his colleagues. Davis had explained more than once that the purpose of the meeting was to exchange views on the operation of the station and to be informed of any new administrative developments. It had, however, developed into a pissing contest where various participants endeavoured to prove that they were the smartest man in the room.

Wilson endured today's meeting by letting his mind wander to how nice it would be to sunbathe beside Reid before lunch and a bottle of chilled Californian white. As the meeting wound down, he was in the process of pushing himself from his chair when a look from Davis made him stop and sit back into the seat.

Davis allowed the other participants to leave. 'You'll be delighted to hear that I got a call from HQ this morning.'

'Subject being new administrative rule on how to hang up one's coat properly?'

'Subject being high level of interest in the naked torso found in Redburn Country Park.' She poured herself a cup of tea from the pot in the centre of the table and selected a chocolate biscuit.

'Seventy calories,' Wilson said. 'Who exactly is interested?'

'DCC Jennings.'

Wilson's eyebrows rose. 'Must be the first time in his life that a naked female torso has interested him.'

Davis spluttered a shower of biscuit crumbs over the table. 'You are completely incorrigible. Does the fact that the DCC is interested in your case not fill you with a certain amount of dread?'

'It fills me with a certain amount of curiosity. We only discovered the torso yesterday. You went on television last evening. By the way, Jock McDevitt says you looked good. He asked me to make an introduction.'

She sipped her tea. 'I'll ignore that remark.'

'It's a bit soon to have HQ looking over our shoulders.'

'HQ seems to spend an inordinate amount of time wondering what you're up to.'

'You've noticed that as well. Now that Jennings is back I was expecting an increased level of scrutiny. It's been part of his doctrine never to forgive and never to forget. That's how he got to the great heights that he has. You'll need to develop the same skill.'

'So where are we?'

'Exactly where we were when you made your TV appearance. We have one body part, the search for the rest of the body should have already resumed. You will not be pleased to hear that the general opinion of the murder team is that the search will be costly but fruitless. So far we are unable to think of any method to extract a name for the torso. The pathologist will take a DNA sample and we'll run it through our databases when it eventually arrives. I wouldn't hold out much hope there either. Quite frankly, I'm pinning my hopes on someone responding to your TV appearance or reacting to the sensational piece that I'm assuming has appeared this morning in the *Chronicle* under the by-line of your admirer.'

'And if we don't find the name of the victim?'

'I don't want to speculate on that eventuality. The team are already pissed off because we can't put a name to the charred corpse in the freezer at the Royal Victoria. I don't suppose that someone at HQ is watching that case carefully?'

She finished her tea and pushed her cup away. 'Your squad is not exactly performing at the moment.'

'Then give me more resources.'

She smiled as though he had made a joke. 'Keep me informed.'

He pushed himself up from the table. 'Yes, ma'am.'

'By the way, Ian, how are you finding the staff meetings?'

'Most informative, ma'am.'

'Liar,' she said under her breath. She watched him as he left. He seemed tired. She'd heard that his pathologist friend was in America looking after her dying mother. He looked like a big bear that needed to be cuddled. 'Snap out of it,' she said to herself. The man was a walking landmine and she'd stood on one of those already.

18

DCC Jennings had been in his office since first light. Because of his meeting the previous evening, he had missed Davis's TV performance. As soon as he arrived at HQ he asked for a recording and a copy of the forensic photos from Redburn Country Park. He was somewhat aware that a seminal moment was arriving in his life. He'd waited fifteen years for his past to catch up with him. Depending on an idiot who had murdered his own people before letting his bloodlust loose on some poor prostitute was probably a definition of madness. When they've killed once, killing becomes easy.

As he watched the recording of Davis he thought he must have taken leave of his senses. He didn't equate Davis's performance with the timid chief inspector and superintendent he had met before she took over from Spence. She was growing into the job and she was representing the PSNI with poise. He wondered whether she was corruptible. He thought possibly not, but you never can tell. He wasn't the only person who had made a deal with the devil. He liked the English – they were a pragmatic people – but their intelligence service was a shambles. The antics of Burgess and Maclean should have dealt the old-boy network a fatal blow, but the Oxbridge set was so entrenched that the classics brigade remained in charge. Had he been involved in getting rid of the prostitute's body, they wouldn't be facing the problems they were at the moment. He wondered whether there was any way he could turn events to his advantage. Perhaps he could get Wilson to put his foot in the shit pile. That would be some sort of double whammy. There was a knock on his door, which then opened to reveal ACC Nicholson.

'Come in, Clive,' Jennings said, waving his hand. 'I was just thinking about you.'

Nicholson approached the desk. 'Word has it that you were in the office at the crack of dawn. You've obviously been champing at the bit.' He tossed a copy of the *Chronicle* onto the desk. 'McDevitt has gone over the top on the naked torso. The little bugger has excelled himself. You'd swear that Belfast was threatened by a horde of flesh-eating zombies.' Jennings was scowling and Nicholson saw that his attempt at humour had fallen a bit short.

Jennings looked at the front page. McDevitt was another name on his list. His articles after the Cummerford trial had been the last nail in his coffin. Now that McDevitt had the bit between his teeth they could expect a stream of salacious articles. It was going to be hard to make this case somehow slip between the cracks.

Nicholson noticed the frozen picture of Davis on the television screen. 'She did well yesterday, comes across well on the box.'

'Ambitious?' Jennings tossed the paper aside.

'Very.' Without being asked, Nicholson pulled up a chair and sat facing Jennings.

'Corruptible?'

'Doubtful.' Nicholson was wondering where this conversation was going. 'She already has the chief constable's ear and she's just serving her time until she joins us here in some senior capacity.'

Maybe she's after your job, Jennings thought. That wouldn't make Clive very happy. Nor him. Nicholson was one of his more important pieces on the PSNI chessboard.

Nicholson could see that his boss was mulling something over. 'I think that Wilson has already infected her.'

'But you have a man watching Wilson,' Jennings said. 'You told me that you'd recruited his sergeant.'

'Yes, Browne, the sodomite. I don't really trust him.'

'But you have something on him?'

'Photos, in flagrante delicto.'

Jennings joined his palms and steepled his hands in front of his face. Nicholson was old school. People were coming out all over Northern Ireland, some of them were officers in the PSNI. Some of the province's former leaders would be very displeased indeed with the new morality, but Jennings had never understood the obsession with sex. He harboured feelings for neither women nor men. He was totally self-sufficient. Given the direction of the current moral compass, he doubted the potency of Nicholson's photos. 'Anything else?'

Nicholson shook his head.

'What has he produced so far?'

'It's early days.'

Jennings would like to have cried in frustration. He was going to be alone. Nicholson and his acolyte Grigg would be helpful, but the full import of what he was charged with could never be explained to them. 'Thank you, Clive, I'm sure you have some important duties to attend to.'

Nicholson took the hint and rose from his seat. He saw that Jennings was disappointed with his efforts to infiltrate Wilson's squad. If that rebounded on him, the sodomite would feel the full weight of his wrath. The way he saw it, it would also be a judgement from God.

When Nicholson had left, Jennings picked up the *Chronicle*

again and read the lead article carefully. McDevitt had confined himself to repeating the facts as outlined in the PSNI statement. But McDevitt was Wilson's friend and sooner or later he would repeat some titbit that Wilson had imparted. But a leak wouldn't be enough. He needed time to think.

19

DS Rory Browne was gowned up and standing by the steel table in the autopsy room of the Royal Victoria. He was getting back on an even keel after his disastrous sexual adventure with 'Fab Vinny'. How had he managed to get involved with such a narcissistic sociopath? The previous evening was the first time since ending that toxic relationship that he had ventured out. He had entered Kremlin with some trepidation, his heart pounding at the possibility of his former lover being present inside the club and throwing a strop. Fortunately there was no sign of Vinny and he had spent a pleasant evening. There had been several possibilities for sex, but he had turned every invitation away. Deep down, despite equality laws and people's good intentions, he knew that there was an incompatibility between his sexual orientation and his career. It was unfair but true. He was relieved that he had come out to Wilson and admitted how he had been recruited by Nicholson to spy on him. At least he had a clear conscience in that direction.

The replacement pathologist was busy on his computer. Reid would have been on station at precisely the time arranged. The new man obviously wasn't a stickler for time.

The door from the mortuary opened and the pathologist's assistant wheeled in a steel trolley covered with a sheet. Browne nodded at him and watched as he transferred the torso from the trolley to the table in the centre of the room.

DR ANDREW MURIUKI looked up from his computer and saw that the torso was already on the table. He was gowned and ready for the first autopsy of the day. The police had sent along the young sergeant he had met at the burial site the previous day and he was pacing nervously in the autopsy room. He was struggling to remember all the names of the new people he had met. At least the sergeant had an easy one. Muriuki liked Belfast and he liked the Irish people. He had attended a Catholic school in Kakamega that had been managed by a group of Irish missionaries. He closed his computer and stood up.

'Good morning, Sergeant Browne isn't it?' Muriuki extended his hand as he joined Browne at the table.

Browne shook the extended hand. 'Detective Sergeant, Dr Muriuki.'

'Just so,' Muriuki extended his hands towards his assistant, who slipped on a pair of blue plastic gloves. 'I suppose we better get on with the business at hand.' He pulled down the microphone. 'On the table is the torso of a young woman.'

It wasn't Browne's first autopsy, but a murder victim whose head and limbs had been severed from her body was something one didn't come across every day. The piece of human body on the table looked like a prop from a Hammer horror movie. The edges where the head, arms and legs had been removed showed jagged flesh and bone. He watched the pathologist at work. If, by chance, they discover the identity of the dead woman, he could only imagine what the impact of seeing what the murderer had left behind would be on her loved ones. It would certainly be a closed casket funeral.

Muriuki stopped speaking and turned the microphone off. He motioned for his assistant to bring the tray bearing the tools of his trade closer. He donned the helmet and motioned Browne and his assistant away before making the traditional Y cut in the sternum. The two arms of the Y running from each shoulder joint to meet at mid-chest and the stem of the Y running down to the pubic area. Muriuki then cut along the boundary between the ribs and the cartilage connected to the breastbone. He turned on the microphone again before using a scalpel to examine each organ in the body. He then removed the organs, taking a sample from each. He examined the stomach contents and took samples of urine and blood as well as bile from the gallbladder.

Browne continued to watch as the organs were returned to the body and the inside was lined with cotton wool before the assistant applied the traditional 'baseball' stitch to close up the wounds. He was impressed with Reid's replacement. The professor herself couldn't have done a more professional job.

Muriuki went to a sink on the side of the room where he peeled off his gloves and gown before washing his hands.

Browne removed his gown and placed it on top of Muriuki's. 'Any conclusions?' he asked.

Muriuki looked at the young sergeant through thick-lensed glasses. 'I won't have a full report until we do lab tests on the organs and the samples we took. Of course, issues like cause of death and time of death are either impossible or only estimations. I took some samples of larvae and we'll see what the lab says about them. One thing you can tell your superior. I worked with prostitutes in Mombasa so I have a certain experience with STDs. I noticed some lesions in the pubic area, which I would identify with chlamydia and I'm sure she also had herpes. I'll need further tests to establish whether she has had anything more serious such as gonorrhoea.'

'Are you saying that this torso belonged to a prostitute?' Browne said.

'Any sexually active lady could have picked up these STDs. I am not in the business of impugning the reputation of a person I don't know, but you are free to draw your own conclusions.'

'That's what they pay us for,' Browne said.

'Also, the torso has been washed in what I have established was oxygenated bleach,' Muriuki said. 'I took a swab yesterday and it's been analysed.'

'Why would the murderer do that?'

'To get rid of any DNA that might have been on the body.'

Browne stuck out his hand. 'Thank you. How soon will we have the report?'

Muriuki took his hand. 'You will have it when I do.'

OUTSIDE, Browne and took out his mobile phone and called his boss.

'How did it go?' Wilson asked.

'A very professional job. Our victim may have been a prostitute.'

'How so?'

'Evidence of a cocktail of STDs. Our pathologist seems to be a bit of an expert on prostitutes, but he wouldn't commit himself.'

'It's a line of enquiry.'

'Also, someone washed the body in oxygenated bleach.'

'I know why they do that.' A faint little bell rang in Wilson's head. 'Get back here and we'll talk.'

WILSON WENT STRAIGHT to the whiteboard and underneath the photos of the victim's torso he wrote 'Prostitute?' and beside it 'Davie Best'. The first piece of a complex jigsaw was now in place. Somewhere, in some university or police college, an academic has classified the types of victim preferred by murderers. And right at the top of the list are prostitutes. Wilson had read somewhere that the most dangerous profession was jump jockey, but he thought that whoever had made that statement hadn't really considered prostitutes. If Muriuki was right, and Wilson without any direct evidence was inclined to believe that he was right, they were about to plunge into a very murky pool.

Meanwhile, the news from Redburn Country Park wasn't positive. The cadaver dogs roaming the wooded area since early morning had come up with nothing. The search was proceeding, but Wilson was convinced that the arms, legs and particularly the head were not going to be found. He took out his mobile and called Davidson's number.

'Boss,' Davidson answered.

Wilson noted that he was breathless. 'Where are you?'

Davidson pressed his finger to Irene Carlisle's lips to tell her to remain silent. 'Running down some of Carlisle's neighbours. The residents of Hillsborough appear to spend as much time holidaying as they do in their homes.'

'I need you at the station, something requiring your specific expertise has come up.'

'You're taking me off the Carlisle investigation?' Davidson was secretly elated, but his companion in the bed didn't look pleased. 'I'd prefer to continue as I am.'

'I don't have time for discussion. Get your arse over here as quickly as you can.' Wilson stood back and looked at the whiteboard. There was something nagging at him that he couldn't yet identify. Every now and then it appeared to be about to break into his consciousness before descending back into the recesses of his mind. He became aware that he had written Best's name without thinking. A recent memo that he'd read from one of his colleagues indicated that Best had now consolidated the prostitution racket in a large section of Belfast. He had a feeling he would soon be paying Best a visit.

20

Davidson had been wondering whether Wilson had cottoned on to his extracurricular activities. In general, the boss had seemed happy to see him looking into Carlisle's demise, hoping for a clue to emerge that might lead to a full-blown investigation. Wilson had no idea that he had already come across that clue and had imparted that information only to Harry Graham. As he entered the station, it occurred to him that Graham may have turned him in, and he felt apprehensive about Wilson's response. The boss was the epitome of the 'fist of steel inside a velvet glove'. He could be either your best friend or your worst enemy.

'Boss,' Davidson pushed in Wilson's office door and had to restrain himself from gushing out the story of the investigation into Carlisle's death and his relationship with his widow. The smile on Wilson's face stopped him in his tracks. 'What's up?'

'I need your expertise, take a seat.'

Davidson felt relief course through his body. 'Of course, Boss.'

'Word from the pathologist is that the victim in the torso case was probably a prostitute. He has to validate that opinion in the lab, but it's the only thing we have to go on for the moment. We need to identify this woman as soon as possible. You have the contacts in Vice. We need to know if one of the working girls has disappeared recently.'

'That's a hard one,' Davidson said. 'A lot of the women are organised by pimps, who themselves may belong to one or other of the gangs, but there are also a lot of freelancers. Someone disappearing off the street could mean that they're taking a break from the business. That's especially true of some of the older women because there are a lot of teenagers out there at the moment.'

'It's all we've got. See what the guys from Vice can give you and then try some of your contacts in the business. If this woman was on the street, maybe one of the other girls knows her. I might be grasping at straws, but this is the first break we've had.'

'What about the Carlisle business?'

'Where are you on that?'

This was the time to come clean, Davidson thought. But something was holding him back. He could pull the plug on the PSNI anytime and get a fair pension, which he would have to hand over to the previous two Mrs Davidsons. Irene was loaded, but she wasn't the type to have a loafer hanging round. He couldn't jump ship until his relationship with Irene was cemented and that would happen only when he proved useful in ensuring that the life insurance cheque for her dead husband arrived. 'I'm making a little progress but it's tough going. Nobody believes that Carlisle was murdered so I have to tread carefully.'

'Okay, I was hoping we'd be a little further ahead on Carlisle. Either you find something that says we should look deeper or you find nothing and I have to eat humble pie. For the moment, I need you on the torso case. Try Vice and your contacts on the street and for God's sake find me a name.'

Davidson stood up. 'On it, Boss.' He felt like a shit. Sooner or later he was going to have to admit the progress he'd made on Carlisle's death. And when he did, he would have to package it carefully.

21

Chief Superintendent Davis entered DCC Jennings' office with a certain amount of trepidation. The DCC's reputation was not a good one and there were general lamentations when his return to duty at HQ was announced. She was aware that Jennings' return had particular significance for Wilson, which meant it had particular significance for her. Wilson had almost succeeded in having Jennings fired. And Jennings was not known for his forgiving nature. She was intelligent enough to see choppy waters ahead.

A smile sat uneasily on Jennings' lips as Davis entered his office. He stood but did not approach her. He extended his hand across his desk and she took it before sitting in the chair her superior indicated. 'Thank you for coming, I know how busy you must be. I felt we should get to know one another as soon as possible.'

'Happy to oblige, I've always had a good working relationship with my superiors.'

I'll bet you have, Jennings thought. His eyes went down to the file on his desk, the PSNI version of the life and times of Yvonne Davis. Although he had spent the afternoon poring over every word that had been written by Davis's superiors, he still preferred to form his own opinions through direct contact. He believed that he was better than most at looking behind the façade people present as their public face. He rated his ability to read people almost as highly as his ability to ditch his morals if the situation required it. Both powers had served him well during his rise to the higher echelons of the PSNI. Over the past days he had been assessing the warmth of the reaction to his return and, aside from Nicholson and Grigg, the temperature was tepid. The chief constable was pleasant but preferred his own hires beneath him so the ground Jennings inhabited was doubly shaky. 'And how is life at Tennent Street?'

Davis forced a smile. 'Hectic, but I'm gradually getting on top of it.'

'I've been getting myself up to date and I notice that a number of murders are still unsolved.' He put his palms together as though about to pray.

She had expected that Wilson's team was going to be the point of attack and she was prepared to defend. 'There are two major investigations currently under way. The first concerns the body in the burned-out car at Helen's Bay, and the second, which came to light only yesterday, is the naked woman's torso found in Redburn Country Park. The Murder Squad has been under-resourced for some time and I would be very grateful if you would lend your weight to my requests to the chief constable for reinforcement.'

He flicked through Davis's personnel file before opening a drawer and depositing it inside. Nicholson was right. Yvonne Davis had already taken sides. A pity, he thought, she would have been a useful ally. 'In the realm of reinforcement, we are all at the mercy of the politicians. I saw you on television last evening, I thought you performed very well.'

'Thank you, unfortunately there wasn't much I could say.'

'What you did say came across well.' He watched her closely to see how she responded to compliments. She was taking them in her stride. He would have preferred something a little more servile. 'How has the investigation progressed today?'

'We've established that the young woman was more than likely a prostitute. But we still have no idea of her identity, how she died, where she died or when she died.'

'It seems like a mystery wrapped up in an enigma.'

'It is certainly a complicated case.'

He knew that the prostitute angle would have sent Wilson off running like the good gun dog that he was. It also thwarted any chance he had of quickly shutting the investigation down. The one fact to emerge from this day's investigation was the spiciest possibility. The crime was now anchored in sex and sex sold newspapers. He would have to suspend all thoughts of closing down the investigation until the public interest was sated. His input could come only if and when the asset was in danger of exposure. For the moment, he would have to follow the investigation with the rigour expected of a deputy chief constable. He stood and extended his hand across the desk. 'I look forward to working with you. I've heard good things about you and I know that the chief constable is one of your greatest admirers.'

Davis rose and took the outstretched hand. She couldn't wait to get to the ladies' room and wash her hand. She felt somehow soiled. As a young woman, she had hated the way men had examined her as though they were undressing her with their eyes. Jennings was more intense than that, he had tried to look inside her and see how she worked.

22

As soon as Davis left, Jennings stood up from behind his desk and exploded with expletives. Doing nothing and hoping that Wilson would be rooting around without result was no longer an option. The question was how could he usefully interfere to hobble the investigation. The clean-up had been messier than they might have intended but there was no real evidence and so far nothing was pointing in the direction of Icepick. He could almost feel the Sword of Damocles swaying above his head. Rehabilitation had been harsh but he was back where he belonged. But for how long? His whole life was now bound up with keeping Icepick safe. If the sneaky bastard really had protected himself by leaving an account of their previous dealings, then he had no option but to ensure that Wilson's investigation came to nothing. He really didn't like Icepick. He had watched his ascent in the political arena following his transformation from an IRA hatchet man to one of the craftiest politicians in the province. And all the time, Jennings knew that he was a moral degenerate who liked to strangle prostitutes. He looked round his office. He had certainly had substantial help to arrive at the post of deputy chief constable. But it had cost him. He didn't want to think about what life would be like if his job was taken from him. The loss of his life's ambition would be worse than spending a couple of years behind bars. He wanted to take action, but he couldn't see a way forward. It was all down to Wilson. He had been the one responsible for his years in the desert. If only Wilson wasn't there, he would feel safer. Maybe they would have to consider the unthinkable. The lack of evidence had been a good idea at the time but if the idiot who did the clean-up had left some evidence behind it could be planted on the pimp and justice would take its course. Jennings emitted a smile for the first time. The pimp would be the prime suspect. He would have to concentrate on ensuring that Wilson bought completely into that hypothesis. Maybe there was a way out of this infernal mess after all. When it was over, he and his intelligence colleagues would have to deal with Icepick themselves.

23

Wilson woke up on the couch in his sitting room. It was four thirty. He didn't recall falling asleep. He remembered calling Reid as he did every evening. The main elements of their conversation were always the same: how her mother was progressing – as expected; what the weather was like in LA – stonking; what the weather was like in Belfast – cloudy with rain forecast. Technology meant that he could not only talk to her but also see her. And he could tell that, despite the pressure of her mother's impending death, she was happy. That raised more fear in him than he would be willing to admit. He was essentially a loner. Despite his success in the sport, he had never been one of the rugby 'crowd'. Despite his success in his policing career, he had never been part of the PSNI 'crowd' either.

After his call with Reid, he had poured himself a glass of Jameson and sat on his couch looking out at the lights of the city. He had thought about the women who would be walking the Linenhall Street area waiting for a passing motorist to stop. The woman who the naked torso belonged to had probably been one of their number. His mind had then pondered the grubby business that is prostitution. Films such as *Pretty*

Woman give an impression of prostitution that is totally at odds with the truth. The punters generally don't look like film stars and they aren't about to ask a streetwalker dressed in tank top, mini-skirt and thigh boots to join them for dinner at Deane's. No, the transactions take place in the back seats of cars, on litter-strewn alleyways or in grubby bedsits with stained mattresses. And most of the women sell themselves only in order to feed their habit or their children. He wasn't so naïve as to think that there were not some willing participants – indeed, he'd met one or two during his career – but they were few and far between.

His mouth felt furry, indicating that he must have had more than one whiskey before he fell asleep. He walked to the kitchen and saw that he had skipped dinner, again. No dinner and God knows how many glasses of whiskey was a combination best avoided. He ran the water until it was cold, filled a pint glass and downed it in one go, immediately feeling the effect of rehydration. Sleep was out of the question. He would normally run off a hangover, but his game leg was giving him jip, as it always did when the weather turned cold. He filled another pint of water, returned to the couch and drank half the glass. It wasn't just the absence of Reid, nor the headache caused by the whiskey, it wasn't even the jip in his bad leg. Things weren't going well. Ever since Sammy Rice shuffled off to whatever grave had been prepared for him, Wilson had felt the pressure increasing. He'd been here before, feeling like he was losing the reins, but this time he was worried that he might not be able to cope.

Better men than Wilson had wilted under the pressure of years of investigating horrible crimes. Now, presented with two active intractable cases, both with unidentified victims and neither amenable to normal police procedures, he had to start practising what he preached. Investigations didn't always lead to results. Murderers by their nature are devious bastards. They don't just jump up and start shouting 'I did it'. They hide in the corners like the cockroaches they are. It is only when people like him shine a light on them that they begin to squirm. Only then they can't properly remember what they did. The balance of their mind was disturbed. And the friendly judge hands down a six-year custodial sentence. They do their time and rejoin society as though nothing happened. Meanwhile, a body has been rotting in a grave and a family has been destroyed by grief.

Wondering what time it was in LA, he lay down on the couch and started to smile. All he needed was a shrink sitting in a chair beside him listening attentively to all his problems. The thought lurking at the back of his mind made another fleeting appearance. It was associated somehow with the idea of the shrink. He tried to grab hold of it but, like a butterfly, as soon as he came close it flitted away. He drifted back to sleep.

24

Peter Davidson saluted the duty sergeant and sauntered down to the CID section of Musgrave Street station. He was well acquainted with the layout of the place, having been among the first detectives co-opted to the new PSNI Vice Squad when it was set up in 2005. He had spent five years trying to stem the growth of organised vice rings in Belfast. A gig that had cost him his second marriage. Most of the initial squad members were gone, but Davidson zeroed in on one who had remained. He smiled when he saw DS Deric Beattie scoffing a breakfast roll and a coffee at his desk. Beattie waved a couple of greasy fingers in his direction before sucking them and returning them to the breakfast roll. Davidson walked across the squad room and pulled an empty chair close to Beattie's desk. He remembered Beattie when he weighed a trim one hundred and seventy pounds. The DS now topped the scales at about two hundred and eighty pounds. Davidson didn't bother to proffer a handshake as both of Beattie's hands were otherwise occupied.

'Welcome, stranger,' Beattie said through a mouthful of bread roll. He slugged back some coffee to clear the logjam for speech. 'To what do we owe the dubious pleasure?'

Davidson looked round the room. It had been seven years since he'd sat at one of the desks and nothing appeared to have changed. The computers were more modern, but the desks and chairs were the same as the day he had left. 'I need your expertise, Deric.'

Beattie finished the final bite of his roll, bundled up the greaseproof paper that had surrounded it and tossed the paper into a wastebasket beside his desk. 'Not like you to need pointing in the direction of a good shag. You were always able to find your way round the ladies.'

Davidson had already found a good shag and she was still lying in a warm bed in Hillsborough, where he would much prefer to be. He smiled at Beattie, whose twin necks were shaking at his intended joke. 'Still the life and soul of the party, eh Deric? This isn't an old-times visit. I've put my time in this squad well and truly behind me.'

Beattie put on a stern face. 'We're still busy here, Peter, stemming the flow of filth into the city. There are more women on the game than ever before. The big problem is that the Holy Joes who stand up in church every Sunday complaining about the sex trade are its greatest customers.'

Davidson explained about the naked torso.

'I read about it,' Beattie said. 'What can I do for you?'

'The pathologist reckons she was a working girl,' Davidson said.

'But she had no head, legs or arms. How did he work that one out?' Beattie asked.

'He's a Kenyan and it seems that he has spent some time working with the prostitutes in Mombasa. He saw lesions associated with chlamydia and herpes in her vagina. He reckons she might also have had gonorrhoea.'

'Lucky oul' punters then.'

Davidson sighed. Black humour had got the people of Northern Ireland through thirty years of misery, but it seemed to be ingrained in the psyche at this point. 'I can't see her working at the high end. So, my guess is that she was on the street. Any of the usual suspects disappeared over the last week or so?'

'We don't take a roll call every evening.' Beattie smiled at his joke. 'And there are more recruits joining every week. Times are hard in this great new world of Brexit.' He leaned back and nodded in the direction of a young officer sitting near the end of the room. 'Ronnie,' he shouted, 'get your arse over here.' He turned back to Davidson. 'Ronnie is our expert on the streetwalkers. A bit like you in your day.'

Davidson sighed theatrically. 'Enough, Deric, eh!'

'Still touchy?'

Ronnie came over slowly to Beattie's desk. Davidson could see from the young man's face that there was no love lost between the two men. He'd been there himself, DS Deric Beattie was an acquired taste. Davidson introduced himself and gave a quick background. 'Any of the usual suspects missing?'

'Hard to say,' Ronnie concentrated his gaze on Davidson, who got the impression that he preferred not to look at Beattie if possible. 'They come and they go. I'm out most evenings to have a word, but I haven't noticed anyone missing. I'll ask around though.'

Davidson took a card from his pocket and offered it to the young man.

Beattie's hand shot out like the tongue of a gecko after a fly. Intercepting the card, he turned to his colleague. 'You find anything, you tell me and I communicate with DC Davidson, okay?'

Ronnie nodded and started back towards his own desk. How to win friends and influence people, Davidson thought as his gaze returned to Beattie.

'You were on the squad when Dolan was here, weren't you?' Beattie asked.

'He was arriving when I was leaving,' Davidson said.

'You heard about him, I suppose; bloody gamekeeper turned poacher.'

Davidson had heard about Jeff Dolan. A former PSNI vice officer who became an enforcer to a vice ring.

'Could have been you, that,' Beattie said.

Davidson stood up. 'I wouldn't be at all surprised if some day someone turned your lights out, Deric.'

'Just joking', Peter, just joking.'

Davidson started for the door of the squad room. 'Well I'm not.'

On his way out he stopped at the duty sergeant. 'Got an envelope by any chance?'

'Do they not have any stationery at your station?' The sergeant fidgeted beneath his desk and came up with a white envelope.

'Young copper in CID, Ronnie something, I didn't catch his name.'

'Ronnie Foy.'

Davidson dropped one of his cards into the envelope and wrote Foy's name on the front. 'I'd be obliged if you made sure he got this envelope, directly to him, I mean.'

The sergeant took the envelope and nodded. There was a knowing look on his face.

25

Wilson looked at his watch, it was ten past two in the afternoon in Belfast and ten past six in the morning in LA. His day couldn't get much worse. There was negative news everywhere he looked. He returned his gaze to his computer. The report from Forensics didn't do anything to lift the gloom. There were no fingerprints on the torso and, as they had already learned from Dr Muriuki, the torso had been completely cleaned with oxygenated bleach. It was very unhelpful of the murderer not to leave them at least a fingerprint to work with. Samples taken from the burial site had been sifted and tested but revealed nothing. The absence of blood at the site indicated that the woman had been killed in another location and had possibly been dismembered there. Wherever she had been dismembered would be awash with blood. That gave them the whole of Belfast to consider. No, he was wrong, the possibility was much wider than that. Earlier in the morning he had visited Redburn Country Park and was surprised to see that his PSNI search cohort had been augmented to the tune of a platoon of young soldiers. Harry Graham was doing his best to enthuse the searchers, but it was evident to everyone, including Wilson, that they were on a fool's errand. As he was leaving the park, he'd received a call from Davidson reporting on his visit to Musgrave Street. No glimmer of light there either. He didn't know whether it was despondency or a bad stomach, or both, that had caused him to miss lunch. He printed off the forensic report and sent a copy to O'Neill for inclusion in the murder book. He looked at the whiteboard and saw that nothing had been added. It confirmed in a visual way that the investigation was stalled. He should read the file that Davis had circulated concerning new administrative procedures for budget control. It had been sitting on his desk for two days with a red sticker on the front with the words 'For rapid circulation' clearly printed on it. All depends on the meaning of the word 'rapid', he thought as he reached for the file. The phone rang and he emitted a sigh of relief. Saved by the bell, quite literally.

'Detective Superintendent Wilson,' he intoned.

'Dr Muriuki here. I have just received the results of the tests I asked for and I thought I might discuss them with you before transmitting them.'

Wilson noticed for the first time how very precise the pathologist's English pronunciation was. 'Thank you, Doctor, I appreciate your diligence.'

'I am convinced that my initial suspicion that the lady might have been a sex worker was correct. The biopsies I sent to the lab confirmed that chlamydia and genital herpes were present as well as gonorrhoea. There are many cases where the sufferer has chlamydia and gonorrhoea existing together. The torso was very carefully cleaned and the vagina was also flushed with oxygenated bleach.'

'So there's no chance of any spare DNA from the last person who had sex with her,' Wilson said.

'No chance whatsoever I'm afraid. Aside from her STDs, she was a relatively healthy young woman. At least her organs proved to be healthy. There was some evidence on the lungs of significant smoking, but the damage was relatively slight. I sent the contents of her stomach for analysis. You might be interested to know that several hours before her murder she ingested potato, meat and curd cheese.'

'What's that, some kind of Chinese dish?' Wilson asked.

'You're the detective. I've also sent her DNA away. Given the delays in the lab I wouldn't expect any news on that front for a few weeks.'

'Will the DNA tell us what nationality she was?' Wilson knew he was grasping at straws.

'Despite what you may have seen advertised on the television, DNA does not indicate exact nationality. For you it might indicate some Irish, Scottish and Scandinavian ancestry. For me it would be African and Arab, like much of East Africa.'

'So what will the DNA tell us?'

'Nothing directly, but we could use it as a match if we could find some of her relatives. I'm afraid that's all I can offer you.'

'What about time of death?'

'The larvae I took from the body at the site are being examined in the lab. The forensic entomologist will undoubtedly be in touch as soon as there is some information. My autopsy report should already be on your computer.'

'Thank you, Doctor.' Reid couldn't have done a better job, but Wilson wasn't going to tell her that.

There was a chink of light at the end of the tunnel. It wasn't enough to illuminate the wall, but it was something, and in a barren landscape even a small plant stands out.

26

The team gathered at the whiteboard for a debriefing at five thirty. The lights in the room were blazing and the rain was hammering on the windows with a cadence reminiscent of the drumming of an Orange Lodge band. The mood was not uplifting. O'Neill had brought the whiteboard up to date with the results of the forensic and autopsy reports. On the face of it, and in terms of real evidence, they were no further ahead than they had been in the morning. Wilson ran quickly through the latest elements, including his conversation with the pathologist. The faces that he stared into probably reflected his own. They were experienced detectives and they knew a stalled investigation when they saw one. There had been complete silence during his exposition. He looked at Graham. 'Harry, anything at all on the search of Redburn?' He already knew it was a negative, but he needed to get some discussion going among the team.

'Washout, Boss,' Graham began. 'Thanks to assistance from the military we've managed to cover every inch of the park. No freshly dug ground and nothing of a suspicious nature. Lots of used condoms though.'

'So, we're finished in Redburn?' Wilson asked.

'Pretty much,' Graham said.

'And only the torso was buried there,' Wilson concluded. 'We'll leave the crime scene tape up for another couple of weeks, just in case.'

'Won't matter, Boss,' Graham said. 'We'll have every rubbernecker in Belfast up there as soon as the park is opened. It's been a monumental waste of resources, but it had to be done, I suppose.'

'You suppose right, Harry,' Wilson said. 'People don't like the idea of picnicking in an area where their children might come across decaying body parts.'

Browne nodded at the window. 'I think there's very little chance of that, picnicking season appears to be well and truly over.'

That brought smiles to the faces of the team.

'Peter, any news from our friends in Musgrave Street?'

'They're not exactly beating down the bushes on our account. I made the request, we just have to wait and see whether they come up with something. I've been trying to get information from the working girls but so far nothing.' Davidson was being economical with the truth, which was that he couldn't find a single prostitute willing to speak to him. The word had gone round that the last person who had given him information had spent a month in hospital recovering. He didn't like to be the source of someone's misery.

'We have very little evidence to go on,' Wilson began. 'So, I'll start with what we don't know but need to find out. We need the name of the woman associated with the torso, we need her address and we need the names of her friends.' He stopped as a particularly heavy squall hit the side of the building. 'And that's only for starters. Ideally we'd like to have the rest of her body parts so we can find out how the hell she died. We'd also like to know where the crime scene is so that we can process it and collect some evidence.'

'Even Santa would baulk at that list,' Graham said.

'Any ideas?' Wilson looked round the team.

'How about a profiler?' Browne offered.

It was inevitable that someone would come up with that suggestion. Wilson didn't believe in profilers, but there was no way he was going to put down any idea. 'Maybe when we get a bit more evidence, right now a profiler would have little or nothing to work on. But it's not a bad idea. Anything else?'

'Have you thought about the possibility of a serial killer, Boss?' O'Neill said.

Wilson was both surprised and delighted. O'Neill was the quiet one, she preferred to listen and didn't normally contribute. 'It has crossed my mind, but so far we haven't found any similar crimes. I'm open to that idea if we do. In the meantime, we don't want to set off an alarm bell that every woman in Belfast is at risk.'

'Maybe we have our own Peter Sutcliffe!' Browne said. Peter Sutcliffe aka the 'Yorkshire Ripper' was convicted of murdering thirteen women in Britain and attempting to murder at least five others. Many of the women were prostitutes.

'We have one murder, not a crime wave,' Wilson said. He turned to O'Neill. 'Siobhan, plug into the National Crime Agency computer and see if any similar crimes have been committed in the UK. Harry, wind the search down and preserve the burial site. Peter, continue trying to identify this woman. Someone out there knows who she is. We need to find that person. Rory, continue to liaise with Forensics and Dr Muriuki. Hopefully a lead will evolve.' He knew that was a forlorn hope. 'See you all in the morning.'

The troops slunk away, their shoulders down like a defeated army. They chatted among themselves while Wilson returned to his office. Something about this murder was bothering him. People who murder prostitutes generally have disdain for them. They tend to toss them aside like broken dolls for someone to find. He could understand the murderer washing away DNA that might identify him in the future. Or perhaps his DNA was already on file and he feared instant identification. But dismembering the body and dispersing the parts, that was something new.

It was getting late and he should have already contacted Reid. He was sure she would understand. He brought up Skype and saw that she was listed as away. He decided to give her a call anyway. It rang until a disembodied computer voice told him that she was not available. He felt instinctively that something was the matter. There would be no drinking tonight. He would grab a takeaway and watch a movie. And continue calling Reid until he reached her.

27

The lights were blazing in Jennings' office and the rain made streaks as it ran down his windows. He was reading a copy of the autopsy report on 'Jane Doe', the woman whose torso had been found in Redburn Country Park. In a folder on his desk were the photos taken by Forensics at the burial site. They were gruesome to say the least and would make striking exhibits for the jury if the case ever got to court. That was an eventuality that he would do almost anything to avoid. As he examined the photos, he felt nothing for the victim. He saw the torso with the jagged cuts at the neck, shoulders and groin simply as a threat to him and his position in the PSNI. What idiot came up with the plan to dismember this woman? He smiled as he imagined some Oxbridge graduate hacking away at a dead woman's limbs. That would never happen of course. The man with the chainsaw had been a former squaddie who had probably done things much worse than dismembering a dead body. It all came back to their old friend Icepick. His problem was that he liked to see the light fade from her eyes while he was inside her. This he accomplished by putting both of his hands round her neck and squeezing until she passed out. The victim generally came round later but sometimes the inevitable happened. Strangling is not an exact science. Those who did come round received a higher payment than agreed. And since the strangler was a valuable asset of MI5, those rare instances where the victim simply expired had to be covered up. After all, the women were only prostitutes. They were at the disposable end of the human ladder, just above or below junkies, he wasn't quite sure. He put the autopsy report aside, smiling as he did so at the disquiet it must have caused Wilson.

There was not a shred of evidence, no cause of death, no time of death, no indication of where death had occurred. Lessons had obviously been learned since their last experience with the ever-valuable Icepick. In the long run, he may not have to play any part in the cover-up. He can simply use Wilson's inability to solve the crime to flay him professionally and publicly. He wondered whether he should also use the failure to stick a pin in Chief Superintendent Davis's rising balloon. The chief constable hated his guts and he had tried to disguise the fact that the feeling was mutual. But Baird was astute and probably knew that he was waiting for the slightest trip by his rival to pounce. Baird had already marked Davis as a protégé. Working on the basis that my enemy's friend is my enemy, perhaps he would destroy Davis simply to demonstrate that he was not the spent force everyone assumed he was. The thought gave him an almost sexual pleasure. Nailing Wilson, Davis and Baird in one fell swoop was probably impossible. But one could dream.

28

Wilson was walking up and down his living room. The detritus of a half-eaten Chinese meal was on his kitchen table beside a half-empty bottle of red wine. He had tried to contact Reid a dozen times without success. Skype showed that she was away, and her mobile went straight to voicemail. He was not one of those people who wouldn't admit that he was worried when he was. And at this point, he was damn worried. Belfast could be dangerous sometimes, but Los Angeles was something else. The current murder rate had to be over one per day if not considerably more. But it wasn't only about murder. Recently the son of one of his colleagues had visited the US and ended up being the victim of a vicious attack. A man had got out of an SUV that pulled up beside the youngster and hit him across the back of the head with a baseball bat. What if something similar happened to Reid? Her mother was dying. Would she be sufficiently compos mentis to call him if something untoward happened? He doubted it. Mind you, Los Angeles was more than five thousand miles away. What the hell could he do even if Reid was in trouble? He knew he wasn't being rational. Reid was a grown woman. She'd worked with Doctors Without

Borders in the Congo, which was generally considered to be a place many times more dangerous than LA. Why the hell was he so worried? The answer was simple and had everything to do with the new turn in their relationship: he couldn't bear the thought of losing her. He sat down and stared at the bottle of wine. He wasn't about to go there again. The phone rang and he pulled it from the cradle.

'Ian.'

A wave of relief ran through his body. He wanted to scream, Where were you? Why did you put me through so much worry?, but he restrained himself. 'Steph, is everything okay?'

'God, Ian,' her voice was strained. 'It's been a terrible day. My mother collapsed mid-morning and I had to get an ambulance to take her to hospital. The people who complain about the National Health Service should come here and try to deal with the hospital administration. I had to sign my life away just to get her admitted. I know you must have been worried, but there was no opportunity to contact you.'

'I'm okay now that I know you're not lying somewhere hurt. How's your mother?'

'She's all right now, but it was touch and go there for a while. This kind of thing has to be expected. Her own doctor was with her just now and I spoke to him before he left. It's a matter of days, maybe a week or so.' She broke down in tears.

He waited silently to allow her to compose herself. Finally, the sobbing stopped. 'You don't sound okay,' he said.

'It's been quite a traumatic day. Although maybe I should be getting used to those. Discovering that my mother isn't the fiend I always thought she was, and is in reality a vulnerable human being was difficult enough. But throw in a certain and impending death and it's no wonder my emotions are heightened.'

Once again his first reaction was to head for Belfast International. All she would have to do was ask. He needed the confirmation that it would be helpful. 'What happens next?'

'They're keeping her in overnight, but she's anxious to get home.' Her voice was clear and strong.

'And what about you?'

'I'm sorry for blubbing. It's probably just as well you're not here, people have been known to kill their partners in this kind of emotional turmoil.'

'You only have to ask.'

'I know that, but quite honestly this is something that I prefer to go through on my own. I'm going home now and I'll try to get some sleep. It must be nine o'clock where you are.'

'Something like that.'

'How's your case going?'

'Good.' He wasn't about to burden her with his problems. 'You go home and rest. Your mother is where she should be and getting the care she needs. There's certainly more trauma ahead so you need to build up your reserves and that means more sleep.'

'I miss you, Ian.'

'I miss you too, Steph.'

'What's with the Steph thing? I was just getting used to being called Reid.'

'It seems right.' He wanted to continue to hear her voice, to reassure himself that she was coping. But she needed sleep. 'I'll call tomorrow.'

'I'm picking up my mother at ten in the morning so I'll be leaving the house at nine. Call me before I leave.'

'I promise.'

29

While Wilson had extolled the virtues of sleep to Reid, he didn't manage to get off to sleep himself until the early hours of the morning. When he did sleep, his rest was disturbed by dreams full of chopped-up bodies, Gorgon faces and dark shadows. He awoke feeling more tired than when he had gone to bed. There was no possibility of running off his negative feelings. Sitting at his breakfast bar, cradling a cup of strong coffee, he wondered why he wasn't rushing to Reid's side. He could justify his reluctance with the excuse that he didn't like the idea of interjecting himself into the mother–daughter dynamic. But he was having a hard time convincing himself that he wasn't just creating a pretext that would keep him in Belfast and at work.

The murder book was lying open on the coffee table. He had spent much of the evening and the early hours of the morning reviewing the material. It was rare for a case to have so little direct evidence. He was beginning to believe that the killer might well be a serving or retired police officer. Without doubt there had been a determined effort to remove any possible evidence. Because of Muriuki's past experience they had learned that the torso most likely belonged to a prostitute.

But without a name, without an address and basically without a life, they were precisely nowhere.

THE MOOD at the morning briefing reflected the lack of progress. As soon as they had rehashed the information of the previous evening's briefing, Graham left for Redburn Country Park to finish the search before closing it down. Two days and a mass of searchers had produced exactly nothing. Davidson also left to follow up with the Vice Squad. Wilson remained in the office twiddling his thumbs. He needed to develop some action but didn't know how to go about it. And his old friend McDevitt wasn't helping. He'd picked up a copy of the *Chronicle* on his way to the station and the naked torso murder was still front and centre. McDevitt's article was a mass of speculation. Were they dealing with a serial killer who could strike again at any moment? It was the kind of sensationalist crap that was light on detail and sells newspapers. He didn't appreciate the pressure that articles increasing fear in the female population would put the team under. His thoughts were interrupted by a call from Davis. Their presence was required at Headquarters.

WILSON COULDN'T SAY that much had changed on the fourth floor since Jennings' sabbatical. As he entered the DCC's office he saw that Jennings still looked down on the chairs directly before his desk. Walking beside Davis, he was aware of her nervousness. As was his usual practice, Jennings ignored their presence while he worked on some highly important papers. Finally, he closed the file and put his signature on the circulation slip stapled to the cover. He looked up and locked eyes with Wilson.

Davis could almost smell the testosterone as Wilson and Jennings stared at each other like a pair of rutting bulls. 'You asked to see us, sir,' she said, attempting to break the strained atmosphere.

'Yes indeed, chief superintendent, please take a seat.' Jennings ignored Wilson.

Davis sat and turned towards Wilson who had already taken the seat beside her.

Jennings removed a copy of the *Chronicle* from a plastic tray on his desk and laid the front page facing Davis and Wilson.

'We've seen it, sir,' Davis said.

'And what do you suggest we should offer as our excuse for the lack of progress?' Jennings asked.

'McDevitt's article is full of wild speculation,' Davis began. In the car on the way to HQ, they had decided that she should make an effort to keep the conversation between her and Jennings with Wilson contributing only when required. 'There is no serial killer and as far as we can ascertain the women of Belfast can sleep soundly in their beds.'

'And what will we do if we announce that this is a one-off event and a second body turns up?' Jennings was pleased to see that Davis's desire to protect Wilson might leave her vulnerable.

'We follow the evidence,' Wilson said. He could see where Jennings was going and he wasn't about to allow Davis to be skewered on his behalf. To hell with the deal he'd made with her in the car. They were at HQ because Jennings wanted to gloat over the lack of progress. Jennings was simply using the article in the *Chronicle* to ratchet up the internal pressure. 'And for the moment there's precious little of that. The killer has been meticulously careful, in fact he's been almost too meticulous. The use of the oxygenated bleach to clean the body, the removal of the head to disguise the cause of death, it's almost as if he is one of us. Despite his best efforts, however, we have some leads.'

Jennings smiled, even under the cosh, Wilson had come out fighting to protect his superior. He wondered whether something was going on between them. That would be typical of Wilson and he knew from Davis's file that she had been divorced for several years. It was another avenue to pursue. 'It's more than forty-eight hours since the torso was discovered. I have looked at the file and I notice that there are no suspects, that no interviews have been held and, as you so rightly point out, that there's a dearth of evidence. I have spoken to the chief constable about the possibility of seeking help from the Met. Perhaps a fresh approach might lead to better results.'

'That would undermine the reputation of the PSNI,' Davis said.

He doesn't give a fig for the reputation of the PSNI, Wilson thought, this is payback time.

Jennings nodded sagely. 'It would be a most unfortunate situation. Of course, the CC is loath to take such an action, but unless there is some significant progress in the next few days I fail to see any other alternative. I suggest that you go back to work in order to avoid that eventuality.' He picked up a file from his plastic tray, opened it and began to read.

Davis and Wilson rose together. It was obvious that they were both on the line.

'Smarmy bastard,' Davis said as they walked to the lift.

'Smarmy, devious and dangerous bastard, ma'am,' Wilson added. 'You'd best not be so closely associated with me. The DCC has a vindictive streak in him and I seriously injured his career. I have to watch out, but there's no reason you should have to suffer.'

'When I took the job to head up the station I was aware of my responsibilities. If that bastard wants my skin, he's going to have to work for it.'

30

Peter Davidson was wandering through central Belfast. He was on the lookout for 'characters', people on the other side of the law who peddled whatever was making money at the time. It was turning out to be a lean morning. He'd met one pimp and two drug pushers so far but, as they say in the movies, 'nobody knew nuttin about nuttin'. There was a vicious north wind blowing and, although the sky had patches of blue showing through the grey, it felt like rain was not too far away. The topcoats had been out of the wardrobes since the end of September and the people of Belfast were beginning to batten down the hatches with the onset of winter. There were a couple of empty tables outside the coffee shops that would remain on station whatever the weather, but in general outside furniture was disappearing by the day. Davidson knew that Wilson was at HQ having his nuts roasted due to the lack of progress on the case, but even the idiots at the top of the tree must appreciate the difficulties they were facing. He was walking along Donegall Square when his phone pinged. He smiled, anticipating a message from Irene. However, the text was from Ronnie Foy, asking for a meeting in the Harlem Café in Bedford Street in half an hour. He didn't know the Harlem Café, but since Bedford Street was less than a ten-minute walk away he would have plenty of time to find it.

Twenty-five minutes later, Davidson was sitting at a corner table facing the door of the Harlem Café. He wasn't surprised that he had never been there before. Davidson had heard about hipsters but he had never visited one of their haunts. He wasn't even sure that he was in one now, but looking at the dozens of framed paintings on the walls and the lights disguised as skulls above his head he thought this has to be such a place. A large white cup of coffee sat on the table in front of him. He was watching the door when DC Ronnie Foy of the PSNI Vice Squad walked in, casting a quick glance over his shoulder as he did so. Foy walked across the café and sat down facing Davidson, who immediately waved at the waiter. He could see that Foy was nervous. 'What can I get you?'

'Cappuccino.'

Davidson took a sip of his coffee, it was excellent. 'Great coffee, you chose well. I doubt if any of your colleagues use this place, especially DS Beattie.'

'That bastard, he hates your guts, you know that?'

'Do I look surprised?'

'He told us to forget about you when you left. The duty sergeant gave me your card and tipped me the wink that you were one of the good guys.'

The waiter arrived with the cappuccino and placed it in front of Foy.

'What have you got for me?' Davidson asked.

Foy sampled his coffee. 'Maybe something or maybe nothing, I've been asking around the last few nights and none of the regular girls are missing. But last week we picked up this Lithuanian pimp, guy by the name of Valdas Kapas. We got word that he was pimping a group of Eastern European women through various cities in the UK. The NCA database shows that this guy is no stranger to the police interrogation room, so we expected him to play the game and then leave town. But the guy did not behave like he'd done this a hundred times before. He was almost pissing himself. At the time, we put it down to him maybe thinking that we still use rubber hoses in Belfast, but now I don't know.' He finished his coffee. 'Look, I 've got to get back. Beattie has a thing about me. I think he wants to get me tossed out.'

Davidson was taking notes. 'You have a photo of this guy Kapas?'

'We didn't photograph him. Beattie took him aside and then cut him loose. Beattie'll have my arse if he finds out I talked to you.'

Davidson could imagine that money changed hands during Beattie's quiet conversation with the Lithuanian. 'Don't sweat it. Beattie is all piss and wind. If he bothers you again, give me a call. There are some things in his past that he wouldn't like to be made public. How many women did Kapas have in tow?'

'Between three and five.' Foy finished his coffee. 'As soon as we cut him loose, he and his women split.'

'Any idea where to?'

'Back to the mainland.' Foy stood. 'I gotta go. Keep me in mind if there's ever a vacancy in your squad. I need to get out of Vice before I plant one on Beattie.'

Davidson stood up and extended his hand to the young police officer. 'You did the right thing.'

'And you're not going to tell Beattie?'

'You have my word.'

They shook hands and Foy hurried out of the café.

Davidson took up his coffee and drained the cup. Might be nothing, he said to himself. But it was still something that Wilson would definitely need to know about.

31

The news that the search of Redburn Country Park had terminated came in about noon. What little evidence there was had been collected and would probably lead nowhere. Wilson had then spent half an hour in Davis's office debriefing their meeting with Jennings. They resolved to not give Jennings ammunition to fire at them. Neither of them had any idea how to accomplish this objective. They were in the hands of the gods and they knew it. On his return to the squad room Wilson had tried to focus on his administrative work but had failed miserably. His mind was flitting between the torso case and Reid's situation in LA. He felt powerless in both situations.

Davidson knocked on the door of his office before entering. Wilson was leaning back in his chair and he allowed it to return to the stable position. He could see that Davidson was hyped. He pointed at a chair. 'Tell me.'

Davidson gave him a briefing of how he had met Foy and the information that Foy had given him in the café.

Wilson listened while Davidson talked. Perhaps there really was a God after all. 'What do you think?' he asked when Davidson had finished.

'The kid is certainly on the up and up. Beattie is a gold-plated arsehole. My guess is that he tapped the pimp for part of the earnings and then sent him on his way. He must have known it might be a lead but didn't want us on the Lithuanian's trail in case we asked some embarrassing questions.'

Wilson tapped on the glass partition separating his office from the squad room. Browne and O'Neill both looked up from their computers and Wilson signalled to O'Neill.

'Siobhan,' he said when she arrived at the door. 'Valdas Kapas.' He spelled out the name looking for verification from Davidson as he went. 'Lithuanian national and pimp, get on the NCA database and see what we have on him. Also find out whether there's a Lithuanian liaison officer at the NCA.'

'Any way we can find out whether the torso belongs to an Eastern European?' Davidson asked.

'The pathologist took some DNA and I was thinking along the same lines but apparently we're out of luck there.' He hoped this was the break they were looking for and not just another wild goose chase like the search of Redburn Park. 'Let's suppose she was one of the Lithuanian's girls. Any idea where she might have plied her trade?'

'Could be anywhere, Boss. The street, a small hotel, an apartment rented by the day on Airbnb.'

Something important surfaced again in Wilson's subconscious, he tried to grab it but failed. He'd asked O'Neill to find out about similar cases on the NCA database. Was it something to do with that request? He looked at Davidson and smiled when he saw the quizzical look on his face. 'I was away with the fairies there for a minute. Something has been bothering me since I first saw the torso. I've been trying like mad to put my finger on it, but every time I get close it seems to drift away.'

'It'll stick one of these days.' Davidson knew that he was going to have to tell his boss what he had learned from Carlisle's neighbour. He also knew that the sooner he did it the better. 'Boss, I've been holding out on you a bit.'

'A bit?' Wilson leaned forward.

'You've been so busy lately what with the guy in the torched car and the woman's torso.'

'Spill it, Peter, for God's sake.'

Davidson shuffled uneasily in his seat. 'It's about the Carlisle investigation, Boss. I've found out a few things that might confirm your suspicions. I got the phone records from the hospice and tracked down the number of the phone that cancelled Carlisle's appointment. It was a mobile. I tried calling it, but it's dead. My guess is that the sim has been dumped. Maybe even the whole phone. I think that we need to get a court order to find out whether there's a name on it and what other calls were made from it.'

'That's good work, Peter. I thought you might have been coasting on this one, but clearly you've been on the ball.' The question was did he need this right now. There was no possibility of getting a court order. To do so would mean exposing the fact that he was carrying out an unapproved investigation. And if HQ ever got wind of the name of the victim, there would be hell to pay.

'That's not all, Boss. One of the neighbours saw some men parked outside Carlisle's house on the day he died. One of them was wearing a white jacket like the male nurses do at the hospice. They seemed to be waiting, and as soon as Mrs Carlisle left, the man wearing the white jacket entered the house.'

Wilson could see the action in his mind's eye. The man with the white jacket was the one charged with giving Carlisle the hot shot. 'You'll need to get a statement from this neighbour. We'll start building up a murder book, but we've got to keep it under wraps for now.' His mind was racing. There was now concrete evidence that all was not well with Carlisle's supposed suicide. But it took a lot of power to arrange the death of a major political figure, even one whose day in the sun was over. If one word of this investigation got out, it would be curtains for him and possibly for Davis too. He could see stress lines on Davidson's face. 'You don't like it, do you?'

'I've been at this job a long time and no, I don't like it at all. It's the kind of investigation that can get a bomb put under your car or maybe get you shot by accident. The coroner has decided that Carlisle was a suicide. I imagine there are some people very happy with that conclusion. And I think that anyone going round asking awkward questions is putting their own life at risk. I don't think the two guys in the car were the usual suspects, which means that they were either spooks,' he stopped for a minute, 'or maybe even the police.'

'We keep all this to ourselves.' Wilson saw the look on Davidson's face. 'Who else have you told?'

'Harry.'

'I doubt Harry was happy to have been taken into your confidence,' Wilson said.

'No, Boss.'

'Any other bombshells that you'd like to drop on me?'

Davidson wondered about admitting to his affair with Irene Carlisle but thought better of it. 'No, Boss.'

Wilson looked into the squad room as Harry Graham walked in. He motioned Graham towards his office.

Graham stood at the door. 'All members of the search team have been returned to their previous duties.'

'Come in and close the door,' Wilson said. He waited until Graham had complied. 'Peter and I have been having a little chat.'

Graham looked from Wilson to Davidson and back to Wilson again. He didn't have to guess what they had been discussing. 'Sorry, Boss, I told Peter to tell you.'

'It's all right,' Wilson lied. It very definitely wasn't all right. 'This really needs to be kept in house.'

'Okay by me,' Graham said. 'I've been shitting myself since Peter confided in me. The people who do this kind of thing don't stop at people like us. We're expendable.'

'All the more reason to keep this information between us three for the moment,' Wilson said. 'Peter, see how Siobhan is getting on with the NCA.'

'Sorry, Boss.' Davidson stood.

Wilson smiled at Davidson. 'Sorry, my arse, you've done a great job.' He turned to Graham. 'Harry, write up the search report and have it added to the murder book. And close the door on the way out.'

He watched the two police officers leave the small office. He needed to be alone and he needed to think. He should have been pleased that he'd been right about Carlisle's death not being a suicide. But instead he wished he'd never had that revelation. It might just have opened Pandora's box. A tingle passed along his spine. It was the same feeling he used to have when he was about to run out on the field against what most people considered to be superior opposition. As a rugby player, he'd always welcomed that tingle because it meant he was up for the game. Did that hold true in this case? If Peter and Harry were scared, then he had every reason to be also. Whoever was hiding under the rock was only safe as long as the coroner's conclusion was accepted by all. Perhaps that tingle hadn't been excitement, maybe it was just plain fear.

32

Wilson tossed the remnants of his lunch, a tuna salad sandwich that contained an inordinate amount of sweetcorn kernels, and a coffee from the new dispensing machine that tasted of equine pee into the wastebasket. He wanted desperately to call Reid but knew she would be on her way to the hospital to pick up her mother. He tried to focus on work. Did he need to start looking into a death that had already been accepted as a suicide? He sometimes wondered whether people were right about him. Perhaps he really did attract trouble. Wasn't a charred body in the boot of a BMW and the naked torso of a young woman found in a public park enough to be going on with? He spent much of the afternoon pondering these questions and wondering how the hell he was going to proceed on each of these three problematic investigations. It was sometime after four o'clock when there was a knock on his door and he looked up to see Siobhan O'Neill waiting for approval to enter. He waved her inside.

She placed a file on the desk in front of him. 'Everything the NCA has on Valdas Kapas, and it's a lot. They do have a Lithuanian liaison officer, but he's out on an operation today and won't be back at the office until tomorrow. You'll find his phone number on the front of the file.' She stood back preparing to leave.

'Well done.' Wilson pulled the file towards him. 'How is your mother?'

'Up and down. She remembers a little less every day and she's able to do a little less. We're rapidly reaching the point where she'll have to go to a care facility.'

Wilson saw a tear at the corner of her eye. 'Won't that be easier on you?'

'I'm all she has.'

And she's all you have, Wilson thought. Freedom is very much a matter of mind not of body. 'Won't she feel better being cared for?'

'Probably, but she has moments of lucidity, although they're becoming few and far between. What will she think if she doesn't recognise her surroundings or the people taking care of her? I don't want her to go into care until it's absolutely necessary.'

'If I can help in any way, you only have to ask.'

'Thanks, I appreciate it.'

'There's nothing more you can do today, go home. We'll see you in the morning.'

'You're a kind man, Boss.'

'Get off with you.' He watched her collect her coat and leave the squad room. Why is it always the women who accept the responsibility of caring? It must have something to do with the extra leg on the chromosome. He picked up the file and opened it. Valdas Kapas stared back at him from a small black and white photo. He had close cropped receding hair on a head as round as a bowling ball set on top of a gym-worked neck and frame. In the photo, he wore a white silk scarf over a designer quilted jacket with the collar turned up. His face was pale and Slavic and he had an insolent Putinesque look. Wilson recognised the face of a dangerous man when he saw one. His official address was in the English town of Wisbech, at a house well known to local police as the headquarters of the Lithuanian mafia in the United Kingdom. Kapas had begun his life in Britain as a gangmaster picking up migrant Eastern European workers in the morning and selling their labour to farms in Cambridgeshire. He progressed into renting property to migrants and then into the more lucrative area of setting up accounts in workers' names and running up debts and money laundering. Financial fraud led him into protection and prostitution rackets. The catalogue of crimes that Kapas was suspected of ran the full spectrum, the most serious was the murder of a female migrant worker. Despite several efforts to put him behind bars, evidence always managed to vanish and witnesses retracted their statements.

It was getting dark when Wilson finally closed the file. At last he had a prime suspect. From what he had read Kapas was certainly capable of murdering a prostitute. Dismembering her body and scattering the body parts was another matter. He had been a stranger in Belfast. How would he have found a place to cut up the body? How would he know where to bury the pieces so that they would not be discovered? Perhaps he'd had help from his new friend in the PSNI Vice Squad? The first task in the morning would be to launch a nationwide request to have Kapas picked up and returned to Belfast for questioning. Wilson put the file away in his desk drawer. It was time to find out what was happening in Los Angeles.

33

Reid's mother had been discharged from the Ronald Reagan UCLA Medical Center at ten o'clock in the morning. The medical team felt there wouldn't be many more trips to the hospital. Mother and daughter had discussed whether a hospice would be preferable to home for the impending demise and they had decided together on a home event.

Reid no longer viewed her mother as the cruel person who had abandoned her family but simply as someone who had felt trapped in a loveless marriage and saw a way to escape it. Unlike the majority of women in the same position, she had taken the chance. Of course, there were casualties, and Reid and her brother were the main ones. Reid would never forget the pain her mother's departure had caused, but she had found that she, unlike her brother, was able to forgive. She had been psychologically injured, but she had survived. Perhaps she would have survived better if her mother had stayed, but who knew, perhaps the opposite would have been the case. Certainly her time with Doctors Without Borders might be seen as an attempt at self-harm. Nobody who valued their life, and was in their right mind, chose to spend three years in the

Kivus. Post-traumatic stress disorder wasn't confined to soldiers returning from war. Their family was their war zone. And so much of what she was today was a product of that one decision by her mother to pack her bags and run away with a man who professed to love her more than her husband did. That love proved to be only skin deep.

And now there was a man in Reid's life who professed to love her. How deep would that love prove to be? Her mind went back to the night before she left Belfast. Standing on Donegall Street outside the Redeemer Central Church she had used the word that she knew would change their relationship forever in one way or the other. Their love-making that night had been the tenderest she had ever experienced. Now they were five thousand miles apart and, much as she loved her job in Belfast, Venice Beach was growing on her.

She looked over at her mother as they drove away from the hospital. She could see the ravages of the cancer on her face and recognised the destruction the rapidly dividing cells were doing to her mother's body. After all, she had spent half her life dealing with the effects of disease on humans. Her mother's body had turned on itself and was destroying itself from the inside. A tear forced itself from her right eye as she envisaged her mother lying on the steel table. This was the reason that she had become a pathologist. She hated the look on a patient's face when they received the bad news. Her clients' faces were already frozen. And yet, she had to respect the bravery her mother was showing. Only once, this last time she was in hospital, had she let her guard drop. The tears came, and she saw that she admitted to being terrified. Reid had hugged her and told her that it was alright to cry, and that she would always be there Reid understood fear.

Her mother looked over and smiled. 'Take me for breakfast.'

Reid wanted to be home. She was expecting a call from Wilson. 'But you had breakfast at the hospital.'

Her mother ignored her. 'Somewhere nice, where I can see the ocean.'

Reid turned onto Santa Monica Boulevard and headed for Ocean Avenue. It was a beautiful sunny October day. Back in Belfast the first chill of winter would be biting, but here she could sit outside and enjoy a breakfast with her mother while they looked out over the Pacific. She just wished that Wilson was here with her. She'd been on the *Chronicle's* website and read McDevitt's articles on the finding of the naked torso. She knew that there would be no surprise visit to LA while Wilson was fully engaged in the hunt for this murderer. She turned onto Ocean Avenue and parked at the first restaurant that had outside tables facing the sea. As soon as they were seated, she sent Wilson a text indicating that they would talk later. She signed off with love.

34

Wilson had chosen the sensible option and gone straight home after leaving the station. The desire was there to spend an hour or so in the Crown but, since the path to hell was paved with good intentions, he dismissed what seemed to be a good idea. His inability to contact Reid was bothering him. It undoubtedly had something to do with her mother and the hospital. Should he have taken the chance of flying to LA? Perhaps Reid had given him the wrong message. The call from McDevitt came just as he entered his apartment.

'I'm sitting in your booth at the Crown,' the journalist began, 'and directly in front of me is the creamiest pint of Guinness I've seen in many a long day.'

'I'm sorry, Jock. No can do this evening. I'm looking forward to chilling out and a film on Netflix.'

'Pining for the beautiful pathologist no doubt. Anyway I was lying about being in the Crown. I'm downstairs and I've got a nice bottle of red.'

Wilson didn't know whether to believe him. 'If you're downstairs, press the bell.'

The bell sounded.

'Okay, come on up.' Wilson felt it might be a mistake to invite McDevitt in but with Jock you never knew. He was delighted that they were beginning to make progress on the case and maybe a few glasses of wine and a chat might invigorate what was left of his brain. He opened the door and then moved to the kitchen where he removed two glasses from the upper cabinet. He turned just as the door closed and McDevitt appeared holding a bottle of red wine up for approval.

'Saint-Émilion Grand Cru,' McDevitt said, opening a drawer and removing a corkscrew. 'Your favourite.'

'What's the occasion?' Wilson set the two glasses on the breakfast bar and watched McDevitt struggle with the cork. 'Give me that.' He pulled the corkscrew out of McDevitt's hand. 'I thought that the doctors told you that you wouldn't be able to open wine bottles for at least six months.'

'You were sorely missed at the opening of Club 69 this evening.' McDevitt watched Wilson withdraw the cork and pour two glasses. 'Davie Best didn't mention you by name, but I could see he was devastated that you didn't turn up, and so I took advantage of the arrival of some semi-naked ladies on the stage to liberate that bottle of red.' He raised his glass. 'To Belfast's newest money laundry.'

Wilson clinked glasses. 'Cheers! My invitation must have gotten lost in the post. Other than filling me with cheer at the expense of Best, what the hell are you doing here?'

McDevitt sipped his wine. 'Bloody nice vintage, Davie's not slow to spend his money. Especially on his friends, both new and old.'

'Tell me.'

'Davie's moving with a better class of villain these days. The bullyboys in the jeans and bomber jackets are a thing of the past. If the Rices and McGready could see what their true-blue organisation has morphed into they'd roll over in their collective graves. Lots of guys in sharp suits, a couple with strong southern accents would you believe, and a good few continentals. I thought you might have Davie in the frame for the naked torso lady?'

'I don't see it.' Wilson sipped his wine. He wasn't about to admit that Davie Best was the first name he had written on the whiteboard.

'Are we still in the information-sharing business?' McDevitt asked.

Not for the first time Wilson thought that if McDevitt hadn't been a top-class crime journalist, he would have made a more than decent copper. And while he wasn't adverse to information exchange, he always felt that he came out on the wrong side of the exchange process with people like McDevitt. 'It all depends. What do you have to offer?'

'I'm well acquainted with several ladies of the night, in a professional capacity of course.' He smiled when he saw the look on Wilson's face. 'I scratch their backs and they scratch mine, metaphorically.'

'Peter Davidson's been down that road.' Wilson held out his glass for a refill.

'Peter Davidson is yesterday's man as far as the vice scene is concerned. There's a new breed of sex worker out there. The brasser of old has been pensioned off and the new model can flay the skin off a man.'

'And your information?'

'You know the name of the game, Ian, you show me yours and I'll show you mine.'

'What if I don't have anything to offer?'

'Then there'll be no exchange.'

'The search of Redburn Country Park came up empty. Clearly you already know that the woman was most probably a prostitute. We have no idea of her identity or where the other body parts might be found. We have no cause of death and we're waiting on the bug man to give us the time of death. So I can't see what you would like me to share.'

'That's good enough. It appears that your corpse is almost certainly not one of the regular ladies.'

'Davidson already established that.'

'I'm going to break with one of my ethical principles here.' McDevitt shared the remnants of the bottle with Wilson. 'I'm going to give you a piece of information and accept nothing in return.' He saw the smile on Wilson's face. 'Well, not exactly nothing. I want you to make sure that I'm kept abreast of the investigation.'

'The last person who made that request turned out to be the killer, I'm sure you remember the case?'

'Secondly, I hear that some of your people have been asking questions about Jackie Carlisle's death by suicide. I know that there's no way you'd hold out on me on something like that.'

'The information sharing is over. There is no ongoing investigation into Carlisle's death.'

McDevitt realised that he had touched a raw nerve. If Ian Wilson wasn't his only friend, the speculation on Carlisle would be in tomorrow's *Chronicle*. But he sensed that reporting the story would be hanging his friend out to dry. 'I'm going to share anyway. One of my contacts informed me that a very unsavoury character was in Belfast recently pimping a string of Eastern European women. The boys in the Vice Squad put a flea in his ear, but I also heard that he received a visit from one Eddie Hills, who suggested that the climate in Belfast was bad for his health.'

'Who's your source?' Wilson asked.

McDevitt tapped the side of his nose. 'I'd be breaching the journalistic code if I told you that.'

'It wouldn't have been a fat bastard called Beattie, would it?'

McDevitt smiled. 'You really are a detective.' He picked up the empty bottle of wine. 'You don't happen to have another bottle of wine handy, do you? By the way, did I tell you that I've been invited to Hollywood to meet some head honchos in some studio or other?'

Wilson went to the sideboard that acted as a bar and started opening a bottle of wine. It was going to be a long evening.

35

Wilson finally made contact with Reid in the wee hours and they spent the best part of an hour exchanging the news of their days. He envied how laid back she had become. Despite the stress of caring for her dying mother, she seemed a lot more relaxed than she was when she'd left Belfast. It struck him that this was probably connected with her ability to forgive her mother for what she had done.

It was raining cats and dogs when he padded into the living room just past seven o'clock in the morning. There would be no run today. He made himself a cup of coffee and plonked himself on the couch. He was concerned that the Carlisle investigation had leaked out. McDevitt was better at unearthing a story than any other journalist he'd ever met, which probably meant that the leak was limited, but only for the present. It's impossible to keep a secret and it was inevitable that Davidson's ferreting around would come to light. He would have to ensure that it would reach the ears of his superiors later rather than sooner. He could cross that bridge when he came to it but that wasn't his way. He wanted to have plenty of real evidence when he was called to account for what the hell he was up to, which meant he would have to put Davidson back on the case. The evidence they had already collected was substantial but certainly not enough to convince his superiors. He finished off his coffee and headed for the shower. It was one of those days when he couldn't wait to get to the office.

AT EIGHT THIRTY the team assembled at the whiteboard and Wilson gave a potted history of the criminal activities of Valdas Kapas. He had already written 'Valdas Kapas at the top of the board along with the words 'Prime Suspect'. Kapas wouldn't be the first pimp to have murdered one of his stable and he certainly had the track record that would lead eventually to the ultimate crime. He turned to Harry Graham. 'Siobhan has the contacts at the NCA. We need to get in touch immediately and find out whether they know where Kapas is at the moment. Then we need to alert the local force and have him picked up. We probably don't have enough to have him brought back to Belfast, so we'll travel to wherever he is. Get on it straight away.'

O'Neill and Graham peeled off and went to O'Neill's desk.

'Rory, for Christ's sake find me something in the forensic report or the autopsy report that I've overlooked. Peter, I need to speak with you in my office.' Wilson led the way and closed the door when they were inside. He motioned Davidson towards a chair.

'What's up, Boss?' Davidson was apprehensive. He wondered whether Wilson had found out about his relationship with Irene Carlisle.

Wilson explained the content of his conversation with McDevitt the previous evening, highlighting the exchange on the unsavoury character who was obviously Kapas and the leak on the Carlisle investigation.

'It was that fucker Beattie,' Davidson said when Wilson had finished. 'I'd bet my pension on it. Foy told me that Beattie had insisted on having a private word with Kapas before he set him free. I'll bet money changed hands. Then when the body turned up and none of the regular working girls had disappeared, Beattie earned an extra few quid by passing the information on to McDevitt. I'll wring that bastard's neck if I ever get the chance.'

'And Carlisle?'

'On my mother's grave, Boss, you and Harry are the only two I told about the guys in the car and the guy with the white jacket.' This wasn't true, as pillow talk included Irene in the select band. Carlisle's insurance policy was worth two hundred and fifty thousand pounds. His widow had been denied a claim when her husband's death was ruled a suicide. She had a substantial motive, therefore, in ensuring that the PSNI proved it was murder. Davidson was sure that the crafty old biddy was the source of the leak, but there was no way he was telling Wilson that. He vowed to keep his big trap shut in future, especially after sex with Irene.

'If Jennings finds out about the investigation into Carlisle's death, I'm toast. He's just looking for a chance to stamp my card.'

'I know, Boss. You, me and Harry are the only ones in the loop.'

Wilson leaned back in his chair. How the hell had McDevitt got hold of the information? The answer was that someone else knew. 'What about Carlisle's widow? Would she have leaked your visit?'

Relief flooded through Davidson. 'I was thinking that myself. She could have told McDevitt that we'd been by and the little prick put two and two together.'

'And floated the idea past me to see how I would react.' The devious bastard, Wilson thought.

'If McDevitt has even a hint of a story like Carlisle being murdered, he's going to start digging and there's no knowing what he'll come up with. What are our chances of tracing that phone?'

'Nil.'

'What about the call log? We could get the tech guys to pinpoint the location of the people who were called from the phone.'

'It's worth a try.'

'You're back on the case. I don't want to be caught with my trousers down when HQ ultimately finds out what we've been up to.' He noticed that Davidson didn't appear too happy. 'Something wrong?'

'I'm three years away from retirement. If you're right and Carlisle was murdered, we're not dealing with the ordinary criminals we encounter on a day-to-day basis. Jackie Carlisle was a somebody in this province. For God's sake, he was a major player. The people who murdered him needed to cover up something big. They're still out there and I'm poking at their cover-up with a stick. Can you see where I'm coming from?'

Wilson could definitely see where he was coming from. 'It's what we signed up to do, Peter. If things get too hairy or if you feel at any moment that your life is in danger, we'll have to go another route.'

Davidson was about to say that he already felt that his life was in danger but held his tongue. 'The guys in the car were professionals. There aren't a lot of people in the province who could pull off a murder like that. I'm afraid that I won't have time to tell you that I'm in danger before I find myself on a slab in the Royal.'

'Point taken, Peter.' Wilson could see that Davidson was genuinely scared and he agreed that he probably had a reason to be. He looked at his watch. He was expected in Davis's office for a briefing on the naked torso case. 'Go gently, Peter, go very gently indeed.'

36

'We have him, Boss,' Graham burst into Wilson's office.

'Calm down, Harry.' Wilson pointed towards a chair. 'Take a deep breath and start again.'

Graham pulled in a gulp of stagnant air. 'I just got off the phone with the NCA. They actually have an ongoing investigation into Kapas and his gang. They've amassed enough evidence to put them behind bars and they're just about to arrest the whole bloody lot of them.'

'Do they have any idea where our man is at the moment?'

'He's in Liverpool. They've been keeping tabs on him and it seems that the bugger has been pimping his way round the UK. He hits a city for a few days or maybe a week until he upsets the locals and then he moves on with his girls in tow.'

'Hence his interview with Eddie Hills, which must have put the shit up him. We need to get to Kapas before the NCA grabs him. Get on to the local force and ask them to pull him in. You and I will head over to Liverpool as soon as they have him.'

'The NCA has a Lithuanian liaison officer with them at the moment. It might be an idea to ask him to come along if we're going to interview Kapas.'

Wilson thought for a minute. The NCA was charged with investigating organised crime and would claim precedence over his murder investigation. They needed to act quickly. 'Okay, have him on standby. Where is he now?'

'In Wisbech. He could be in Liverpool in a few hours.'

'Get on to Merseyside Police first. When we have Kapas we'll contact this Lithuanian guy.'

'On it, Boss.' Graham was already out of the office.

Wilson watched the team through the glass partition. There was a different ambience in the squad room now that they were making progress. It was odds-on that they would have their murderer in the next forty-eight hours. Wilson seldom counted his chickens before they hatched, but if the victim turned out to be one of Kapas's women, his violent past would put him firmly in the frame for her murder. All going to plan, in just over forty-eight hours he could be winging his way to the city of the angels. The thought lifted his spirits. A result and a chance to be of assistance to Reid would be the perfect package. The best way to show Reid that he cared deeply for her would be to be there for her when she needed him most. The phone on his desk rang and he picked it up. 'Detective Superintendent Wilson.'

'It's Doctor Muriuki.' The Kenyan lilt came over the phone. 'May I call you Ian and you should call me Andrew. I never liked Andy.'

'How can I help you, D..., Andrew?'

'I received the lab report on the samples I took from the organs. The lungs show that there was evidence of pulmonary oedema.'

'Which is?'

'In layman's terms, fluid on the lungs. The victim was probably strangled.'

'And I suppose the head and neck, if they were not missing, would be evidence of the crime?'

'Yes, there would possibly be injuries on her face, eyes, ears, nose, mouth, chin, neck, head and scalp, including redness, scratches or abrasions, fingernail impressions in the skin, deep fingernail claw marks, ligature marks, thumbprint-shaped bruises, blood-red eyes, pinpoint red spots called petechiae. And on the hands, blue fingernails. A whole spectrum of medical evidence would have been available to confirm my conclusion.'

'It's safe to assume that someone tried very hard to conceal the cause of death.'

'You have dealt with strangulation before?'

'Most of our murders have been crimes of violence with a weapon. However, just recently, we had a case of erotic asphyxiation that turned out to be an old-fashioned hanging. And some years ago I worked on a case where a prostitute was strangled with a ligature.' The little bell was ringing loudly in Wilson's head before he finished the sentence. They had not found that murderer. It was the one case that he should have remembered before now.

'I did a thesis on strangulation for my final-year project,' Muriuki continued. 'I'm considered quite an expert in the area. Strangulation is an ultimate form of power and control, where the batterer can demonstrate control over the victim's next breath. Sober and conscious victims of strangulation will first feel terror and severe pain. If strangulation persists, unconsciousness will follow. Before lapsing into unconsciousness, a strangulation victim will usually resist violently, often producing injuries to their own neck in an effort to claw off the assailant, and frequently also producing injury on the face or hands of the assailant.'

'Does the victim always die?' Wilson asked.

'Good lord no. Very little pressure on both carotid arteries or the veins for ten seconds is all that is usually necessary to cause unconsciousness. However, if the pressure is immediately released, consciousness will be regained within ten seconds. To completely close off the trachea, three times as much pressure is required. Brain death will occur in four to five minutes, if strangulation persists.'

Wilson made a note to get O'Neill to research strangulation in the UK. 'So the murderer might have made a mistake?'

'Quite possibly. There are men who cannot perform sexually unless they have complete control over their partner, and there is no more complete control than the power over life and death. I should introduce a caveat before we go further. I have concluded that the victim was strangled from the slightest of medical evidence. You must not take it for the gospel truth.'

'Don't worry, Andrew, I won't, but I think it holds up as a working hypothesis.'

'If that is your decision. I have one further piece of information. The forensic entomologist has issued his report. The body was in the ground for approximately thirty-six hours.'

Wilson did the math. The murder was committed during the period that Kapas was in Belfast. It was all coming together.

'How is Professor Reid getting on?' Muriuki asked.

'Her mother is poorly, unfortunately that's all I can say.'

'It's a very difficult time for both of them. I will pray for them.'

'Thank you, Andrew. I'll be in touch.'

37

Valdas Kapas was enjoying a post-coital cigarette when there was a commotion at the front door of the house he was renting in the Bootle area of north Liverpool. Kapas had become an avid user of Airbnb. There were no hotel forms to sign, which meant no trace of where he had been. He was totally unaware that his every movement was under observation by the National Crime Agency. He jumped out of bed and looked down into the street. There were four men at the front door, two in police uniforms and two wearing stab vests over normal clothes directly behind them. He started dressing quickly and shouted at the woman in his bed to get her backside out of there. What was he being rousted for? It wasn't prostitution. They didn't send four men to ask him if he was running a couple of girls. The knocking became louder and the shouts of 'Police, open up' more strident. There was a back exit and he was heading for it when one of his girls told him there were two policemen at the rear of the house. There would be no escape. 'Šūdas!' he exclaimed. He opened the front door just as one of the uniformed police officers was preparing to hit it with an enforcer.

'Valdas Kapas?' the first policeman said.

'No,' Kapas tried to smile. 'My name Markas Zubas.'

One of the policemen at the rear came forward and took a photograph from his pocket. He held it up beside Kapas's face. 'I'm Detective Sergeant Pierce of the Merseyside Police and we are taking you to Walton Lane police station for questioning.' He turned to the uniformed officers. 'This is him. Put him in the van.'

'Wait,' Kapas protested. 'You make a very big mistake. You ask my wife, she tell you that I am Markas Zubas.'

'I'm sure she will, mate,' Pierce said. He turned to the two police officers, one of whom had already taken out a set of handcuffs. 'In the van, now.'

Kapas was handcuffed and led towards a waiting police van.

'I need lawyer,' Kapas said over his shoulder to Pierce and his colleague.

'We're not arresting you,' Pierce said. 'We are simply requesting you to help us with our enquiries.'

Pierce watched as the uniforms bundled Kapas into the rear of the van. He turned to his colleague. 'The Paddies will be happy.'

'Offed one of his girls,' Pierce's colleague said. 'Looks like a proper thug, silly bugger.'

Pierce started walking towards their car. 'Innocent until proven guilty, my son. Try to remember.'

38

Wilson and Graham were on the evening flight from Belfast International to John Lennon Airport. They walked straight over to Pierce as soon as they exited the baggage area. Pierce wasn't holding a card with their names, but they recognised one of their own.

'DS Pierce.' He held out his hand.

Wilson took it. 'Detective Superintendent Wilson and DC Graham.' He towered over Pierce, who was about five feet eight, of slight build, and had short brown hair and a pale open face. He looked young to be a detective sergeant and Wilson surmised that he was a graduate entry like his own sergeant, clever little buggers in a hurry.

Pierce and Graham shook hands. 'We have a car outside and your friend Kapas is awaiting your pleasure at Walton Lane.' The accent was pure Liverpool. 'I looked you blokes up,' Pierce said as they walked through the concourse. He looked at Wilson. 'I hope you don't mind, superintendent. You were some sort of rugby player?'

'All in the past,' Wilson said.

'You got knackered by a bomb. What was that like?' They

exited the building and Pierce walked towards a parked car with a 'Police on Duty' sign in the window.

'Not very pleasant. Take my advice and never stand close to a bomb.'

The trio laughed.

HALF AN HOUR later Pierce steered the car past a barrier and into the parking lot in front of a large two-storeyed, red-brick building. The station was separated from the pavement by a low concrete-block wall. This was the way police stations had looked in Belfast when Wilson was a child. Thirty years of terrorism changed all that.

'The chief super would like a word,' Pierce said as he signed Wilson and Graham in at the desk. 'Stickler for protocol is our chief.'

'Don't worry, we've been there before,' Wilson said. 'And I know the drill.'

Pierce nodded at the duty sergeant, who came out from behind the desk. 'Harry and I will grab a cup of tea and Sergeant O'Connor will see you up.'

THE CHIEF SUPER turned out to be a rugby buff and Wilson had had to go through a couple of his stories before signing an autograph and being released for the real reason he was in Liverpool. O'Connor picked him up and brought him to the canteen, where Pierce and Graham were seated at one of the tables along with a third man, who stood as soon as Wilson approached.

'Detective Sergeant Lukas Skeria from the Lithuanian Criminal Police Bureau, currently on assignment as liaison officer in the UK.' He bowed as he held out his hand.

Wilson took his hand and introduced himself. The Lithuanian was a shade shorter than Wilson but had the frame of a body-builder. His head was shaven and he had a few days' growth of beard on a round open face that was notable only for a pair of striking blue eyes. Wilson guessed that he was in his late twenties or early thirties. Graham went to the coffee machine and procured a cup for his boss. Wilson sensed there was to be a short conference before the interview with Kapas and he sat down just as Graham put a cup of coffee on the table in front of him.

'As I understand it,' Skeria took the lead, 'you want to interrogate Kapas about the torso of a young woman that you have found in Belfast.'

Wilson sipped his coffee. It compared favourably with the brew available at the station in Belfast. 'Your English is excellent, sergeant.'

'I studied English at university and I've had plenty of practice. My wife is English and doesn't speak a word of Lithuanian.'

Wilson was struck by the fact that most of the foreigners he met spoke enough English to get by while English-speakers tended to have only their own language. 'Our pathologist has established that owing to the cocktail of STDs in the body, the torso possibly belonged to a prostitute.' Wilson nodded at Graham, who produced the murder file from his satchel and opened it at the photographs of the torso at the burial site.

Pierce and Skeria leaned forward to examine the photos.

'Although we can't be certain,' Wilson continued, 'it doesn't appear that any of the local working girls are missing. The fact that the head, arms and legs haven't yet been found means that, aside from DNA, we have no means of identifying the victim. Also, we have no cause of death. Our working hypothesis is that she was strangled prior to being dismembered. We've established that Kapas and his ladies were present in Belfast at the time of the murder.' He saw a frown cloud Skeria's face. 'You have a concern, Sergeant Skeria?'

The Lithuanian scratched his right eyebrow. 'I'm sorry,

superintendent, you are obviously much more experienced in these matters than me. Having said that, our team has been working for six months on taking down Kapas and his partner. In that time, we've had a chance to examine every part of their lives. Kapas is a thug, there's no doubt about that. I have seen him beat migrant workers until they've bled. He is also a liar and a cheat, but I don't see him strangling the life out of a woman. I may be wrong, of course, but I don't even see him as a murderer. And I definitely do not see him dismembering a body in the way it has been done here. The murderer of this woman is a monster.'

Wilson finished his coffee. 'I respect your assessment, Sergeant Skeria, and I will do the interview.' He turned to Pierce. 'Do you have a room where you and Harry can observe?'

Pierce nodded. His face didn't hide his disappointment at not being in the room.

Wilson stood. 'Then let's not keep Mr Kapas waiting any longer.'

39

Valdas Kapas was sitting back in his chair drinking a Diet Coke when the door opened and Wilson and Skeria entered the room. They were impressive figures and he thought they would both make acceptable recruits for the Russian mafia. The Russians like them big and strong. They sat across from him and the older one put a file on the table.

'I am Detective Superintendent Ian Wilson from the Belfast Murder Squad,' Wilson spoke slowly and clearly.

'*Aš esu Lietuvos policijos seržantas Skeria. Žinau, kad tu kalbi angliškai.* I am Sergeant Skeria of the Lithuanian police and I know that you speak English.'

'I don't understand,' Kapas said, grinning.

'We can have this interview in English,' Wilson said, 'or we can have Sergeant Skeria translate and it will take twice as long, in which case I am going to get very pissed off and you are going to be very sorry. Do you understand that?'

Kapas looked into the eyes of the big policeman and knew that he meant what he said. 'Okay, I understand.'

'No more bullshit,' Wilson said, 'and maybe you'll get out of here quickly.'

Kapas was very sure that this interview wasn't simply about prostitution. 'No bullshit.'

'I'm going to do this interview under caution,' Wilson said. He switched on the recorder and gave the time and had each participant give his name. He issued the usual caution. 'Six days ago you were in Belfast, is that correct?'

'Yes.'

'And you had several young women with you?'

Kapas looked at Skeria, who nodded. 'Yes.'

'They were all prostitutes servicing clients in the city, is that correct?'

Kapas sighed. 'Yes.'

'Working from apartments?'

'Some from apartment we share but others on street.'

'Give me the address.'

Kapas gave them an address in central Belfast.

Wilson knew that Harry Graham would check that out immediately. 'One of your girls went missing, is that correct?'

Kapas scowled. 'Rasa, the bitch. She ran away.'

Wilson opened the murder file and showed the photos from Redburn Park. 'Could this torso belong to Rasa?'

Kapas looked at the photographs, turned and emitted a stream of dark-coloured vomit onto the floor.

Wilson closed the file and picked it up. The chief super wouldn't appreciate having his interview room messed up. 'Let's finish now and have the room cleaned.' He looked at Kapas, who was wiping spittle from his mouth. 'What's Rasa's surname?'

'Spalvis,' Kapas said. 'Rasa Spalvis.'

Wilson looked at Skeria, who nodded and left the room.

Wilson took Kapas's arm and led him to the door, where a uniformed officer took charge of him. 'Put him in a cell until we get this place cleaned up. And get him a cup of tea.'

Pierce and Graham were waiting in the corridor. 'I've

arranged to have the room cleaned,' Pierce said. 'You can resume in fifteen minutes.'

They retired to the canteen and occupied the same table as before. Wilson was pleased with the first session. They now had a name for the victim and Skeria would be in contact with the authorities in Vilnius. By the time they resumed they would have Rasa Spalvis's charge sheet. It was significant progress. It looked like Skeria's instincts had been right about Kapas. Either the man could bring up vomit at will or the photos had affected him. If he couldn't look at the photos of a woman that he had murdered and butchered without vomiting, then it was unlikely that he had been capable of dismembering her. Wilson would have to develop a new narrative. One that didn't involve Kapas as either the murderer or the dismemberer. The trip to Los Angeles was receding into the distance. It was nearing eight thirty in the evening. He had already messaged Reid and told her of his trip to Liverpool and that he would contact her when he had an opportunity.

FIFTEEN MINUTES later they were back in the interview room facing a very pale-faced Valdas Kapas. The photographs in the file had had a sobering effect.

Wilson turned on the recorder and did the preliminaries himself. He laid the file on the table and was about to open it when Kapas put his hand out to stop him.

'I can't be sure, but it maybe is Rasa,' Kapas said.

'And you genuinely thought she had run away?' Wilson asked.

'Yes. She went out to work and didn't return. What could I think?'

'And you did nothing about it?'

'What was there to do? I couldn't go to police. We had passport. Where could she run? Sooner or later she make her way home. They always come home.'

'So you weren't worried?'

Kapas shrugged his shoulders. 'Rasa was big girl, very experienced.'

'Was she working the apartment or the street when she disappeared?'

'She work street on night she vanish.'

'Were you and Rasa good friends?'

Kapas smiled, exposing a mouth of small sharp teeth. 'Valdas big friend with all the girls. I keep them very happy.'

Wilson turned to Skeria. 'Please check out with the other girls whether there was any animosity between Ms Spalvis and Mr Kapas.'

Skeria nodded and made a note.

'You think Valdas do this?' Kapas pointed at the file.

Wilson and Skeria remained silent while Kapas looked from one to the other.

'Did you?' Wilson asked.

Kapas stood. 'No, you no do this to Valdas. Yes, I am bad man. I do many bad things, but this I do not do.'

'Please sit,' Wilson said. Kapas's outrage seemed genuine. He doubted that the Lithuanian was their man, but there was always a possibility that he was just a very fine actor. He decided to push the envelope. 'You have to see this from our perspective. One of your women is murdered, dismembered and buried in Belfast. You don't look for her and after a few days you go on your merry way. We're policemen, we know that there is often friction between prostitutes and pimps. Maybe you argued over money. You fought and by accident you killed her. Then you dismembered her and buried the pieces. If you admit it, things will go better on you.'

Kapas banged both of his fists on the table. 'No, I do not do this thing. I think now I need lawyer.'

'That might make us think that you're guilty.' Wilson could see the confusion on the Lithuanian's face.

Kapas's body collapsed across the table like a deflated

balloon. '*O, Dieve!* This cannot happen. I not kill Rasa, I not kill anyone.'

'Okay,' Wilson said, 'if you didn't kill Rasa, then who did?'

Kapas lifted his head slowly from the table and looked directly at Wilson. 'I don't know. This is nightmare. I think Rasa has run away and will soon come home. She need passport for return to Lithuania.'

'When you were in Belfast did you have any problems?'

'Police interview me but after I pay money I can go.'

'What police?' Wilson asked.

'Vice police. Fat sergeant ask me for two hundred pounds.'

'Any other problems?'

'We get visit from local criminal, man like Valdas. He tell us to leave. If no leave, there will be much trouble. I have seen such men working for the Russians. They are bad men, they have no respect for life.'

'Can you describe him?' Wilson asked.

'Big. Blond hair cut very short, like military man. I take his advice and we leave Belfast next day after visit.'

'And Rasa was already missing when you had this conversation?'

'Yes. For maybe one day.'

Wilson closed the interview and called the uniformed officer into the room. He motioned for Skeria to follow him.

40

Pierce and Graham were waiting in the corridor.

'Is there somewhere we can talk other than the canteen?' Wilson asked.

Pierce nodded and they followed him to an empty office.

'What do you think?' Wilson asked Skeria as soon as they were seated.

The Lithuanian policeman thought for a moment. 'I'm waiting for information on Rasa Spalvis to arrive. If it is her, then I don't think it was him.'

'I think he's good for it,' Graham said. 'Look at the guy, look at his hands. That pair of mitts could easily choke a woman. He has the means and he certainly had the opportunity. All we need to nail him is the motive.'

'On the face of it,' Wilson said, 'he looks good for it, but why do it on our patch? We'll have to check whether he rented transport in Belfast and have Forensics look at the place they were staying in. We also need to interview at least one of the women to see if there was any antagonism between Spalvis and Kapas. However hard I try, I can't see a Lithuanian who doesn't know Belfast dismembering a body and burying the pieces God knows where. We're going to hold Kapas for twenty-four hours. In that time Sergeant Skeria will interview the women and my sergeant in Belfast will check whether Kapas hired a car during his visit. By this time tomorrow we should have the question of motive cleared up and Forensics will be able to tell us if a body was dismembered in the place Kapas stayed in Belfast.' He turned to Pierce. 'Can you organise to hold Kapas?' Pierce nodded. 'And maybe you can arrange for some uniforms to pick up Kapas's women.'

Pierce stood up. 'On it.' He left the three men sitting in the room.

Wilson looked at Graham. 'Looks like we're here for the duration, Harry. You'd better call home.'

'I already squared it with the missus,' Graham said.

'What about you, sergeant?' Wilson asked Skeria.

'No problem. In the UK I'm a single man. My wife and children are in Vilnius.'

'Then let's ask the duty sergeant to book us into a local hostelry and suggest a decent Indian restaurant. I don't know about you guys, but I'm famished.'

'IT SOUNDS PROMISING,' Chief Superintendent Davis said after Wilson had given her a briefing on their interview with Kapas. The duty sergeant had located Wilson, Graham and Skeria rooms at a local Premier Inn and the best Indian restaurant in the area had been booked. There was silence on Wilson's end of the line. 'Are you still there, Ian?' she said finally.

'Yes, ma'am.'

'But something is wrong?'

He could hear the exasperation in her voice. It was nine thirty and he was obliged to call her at home as per her instructions. He had a feeling that she had had a few drinks. 'I'm not sure that he did it.'

'For God's sake, Ian, it's got to be him. Don't overthink the bloody thing. He's perfect for it.'

'It could be him, but there are too many holes for a good defence team to exploit.'

'The court case isn't our business. Close the bloody holes and get Kapas over here tomorrow. And that's a bloody order. If you screw this up, it won't be just you that'll get flushed down the toilet.'

'Understood, ma'am. I'll call again in the morning.' He put down the phone.

It had probably been a mistake to call, but he had promised before he left Belfast to do so. He liked Davis and he had no desire to be the reason that her career went south. But she herself might end up being the cause of her own downfall. Trying too hard to please was sometimes worse than not trying to please at all. He didn't give a damn what his superiors thought of him. A quick result might look like the way to go from Davis's perspective. It would be another notch on the pole that she could grip onto to pull herself closer to her goal. But for Wilson, rushing in to arrest Kapas would be like ignoring a patch of quicksand directly in front of him. He was almost sure that a case against Kapas would finally collapse and the weight of that collapse might crush both him and Davis. His stomach rumbled to remind him that he hadn't eaten since breakfast. Tomorrow morning they would either close the holes in the case against Kapas or they would have to develop an alternative narrative. He hoped like Davis for the former but feared the likelihood of the latter.

Kapas had been placed in a cell for the evening and Wilson had contacted Browne so that he and O'Neill could handle the investigation into Kapas's stay in Belfast. Knowing he couldn't do much more this evening, he finally headed out to dinner.

41

Wilson, Graham, Pierce and Skeria met in the interview room at Walton Lane station. 'Let's start with Sergeant Skeria, if that's all right.'

'Fine by me,' Skeria said. 'The very competent Detective Sergeant Pierce and his colleagues at Merseyside Police picked up three women from the address where Kapas was staying. I interviewed them separately before leaving here last night. There was no indication of any friction between Kapas and Rasa Spalvis. All three are agreed on that point. Also, they all stayed in the same apartment in Belfast and, considering that the body was so completely dismembered, I think that at least one of them would have been aware if something had happened there or involving Kapas. In the meantime, I received a communication from Vilnius concerning what we know about Spalvis. Unfortunately, I haven't had time to prepare a translation. I can, of course, give you the main points now. It is not a pleasant story.'

'Please proceed,' Wilson said.

Skeria opened a file and removed a photograph and a sheaf of paper. He put the photograph on the table where everyone could see it. It was a mug shot showing a slight, blonde-haired pretty woman. Wilson had seldom seen such sadness in a face. The story of how that much sadness got into a young woman's face was certainly going to be an unpleasant.

'Rasa Spalvis was born near the Lithuanian–Latvian border,' Skeria began. 'Her parents were alcoholics and incapable of looking after her so she was sent to a state-run children's home. Her seven brothers and six sisters were also sent to homes throughout Lithuania. She made several attempts to run away and was punished. According to herself, she started smoking opium at thirteen years of age. She was visited at the home by a man who claimed to be her godfather. It was a lie and he raped her when she was thirteen. At fifteen, she left the home for good. The next years were very difficult for her, but she gradually built a life, getting a job and moving into an apartment with three other girls. Then she had another unlucky break when a woman claiming to be her sister turned up. Of course, she was really a procurer for a group of criminals who force young girls into prostitution at home and abroad. We first had notice of her when she was twenty and had already been a prostitute for three years. One year later she disappeared and the word was that she had been sent to England, presumably straight into the hands of Kapas and his friends. When you found her torso, assuming that it is her torso, she was twenty-three years old. I have requested my colleagues to locate one of her siblings and take a DNA sample so that you can confirm her identity.'

'Is there anything in there about her being in Belfast previously?' Wilson asked.

'No, as far as we know this was her first time leaving the UK since arriving here two years ago.'

Wilson didn't bother to remind him that Northern Ireland was in the UK. 'Thank you, Sergeant Skeria,' he said, 'not a pleasant story but one we hear many times. Can I keep that photo?'

'Certainly.' Skeria pushed the photo towards Wilson, who put it in his own file.

'The holes are opening wider.' Wilson's mobile rang and he answered it. 'Rory, I'm putting you on speaker. Where are you?'

'I'm at the apartment that Kapas rented. Luckily, it's vacant for the moment. I've managed to pull two forensic technicians off their job and they'll be able to tell whether anyone was murdered here and certainly whether anyone was dismembered here. There would have been a fountain of blood and it would have been impossible to get rid of it all.'

'Good job, Rory. What about Siobhan?'

'She's running down all the car hire companies as you suggested.'

'Any idea when you guys will be finished?'

'We only have the forensic guys until midday, but they assure me that if there's blood in the apartment they'll have found it by then. Siobhan should have contacted all the car companies by then as well.'

'Okay, Rory, get back to us as soon as you can.' Wilson turned to the other men at the table. 'Is there something useful we can do between now and midday?'

'Anybody got a deck of cards?' Graham asked.

42

Royson Jennings was elated, but he was so practised at hiding his emotions that Yvonne Davis, who was sitting across from him, would never have guessed. She had just finished briefing him on the advancement of the investigation into the torso. He had steepled his hands in front of his face and listened intently to her report. 'Excellent,' he said when she finished. 'Another feather in your cap if I'm not mistaken. An altogether excellent result.'

Davis shifted uneasily in her chair. She had tried not to be too positive about the outcome of the investigation. She had a great deal of respect for Wilson and if he had reservations, it was wise to take them into account. She contemplated saying something at this point but decided not to unleash the DCC's legendary temper.

'When can we expect to announce the arrest of this Lithuanian fellow?' Jennings asked.

'Superintendent Wilson is trying to close some of the holes in Kapas's statements. You're aware of how thorough the superintendent is in all his cases. He doesn't want to present a case to the DPP that will be thrown out.'

Jennings knew very well how thorough Wilson was, and

how bloody lucky he was too. The man was the equal of Harry Houdini in extricating himself from sticky situations. 'I'm totally in agreement with checking all the facts, but the citizens, and particular our female citizens, need to be reassured that they can walk the streets in safety. This was simply a falling out among criminals. A situation that is altogether too common. I want this case closed as soon as possible and the suspect transferred to Belfast. Do you understand?'

Davis nodded. She had got the message.

Jennings opened a file from the desk in front of him and began to read. Davis sat for a minute awaiting a sign that she had been dismissed before realising that she had already received it. She rose slowly from her chair and, without speaking, made her way to the door. She could understand why Wilson and the DCC hated each other so much. They were polar opposites.

Jennings held his glee in check until the door closed behind Davis. He then smiled broadly and clapped his hands. He wasn't as stupid as Davis thought he was. He had picked up on the fact that Wilson was unsure about the guilt of the Lithuanian. But it was still a win-win situation for him. If they decided to let the pimp go, he would have a stick to beat them with. If they referred the case to the DPP, it would most probably be thrown out and, again, he would have a reason to flay both Wilson and his chief. God was certainly good, to him at least.

Jennings had to admire Wilson in a certain sense. From nowhere and with virtually no evidence, he had discovered the name of the victim. That was a major achievement. Then he had identified a possible suspect. Jennings was confident that the current line of enquiry would muddy the waters and keep the real culprit safe. And best of all, he hadn't had to lift a finger to make it happen.

He thought about passing on the good news to his

collaborators but decided against it. He liked the idea of them stewing in their own juices. From his point of view the whole plan to protect the very valuable intelligence asset Icepick had been a mistake. The man was a degenerate and a murderer. However, they had already made their beds and now they were going to be compelled to lie in them.

43

Some days the time just drags interminably. Pierce had provided a couple of daily newspapers and they had been read from cover to cover. Kapas had been given breakfast and then spent the morning in a cell except for a short visit outside for a smoke. Wilson watched him through an upstairs window as he prowled round the yard at the rear of the station, pulling hard on his cigarettes. He was behaving like a guilty man but was he guilty of Rasa Spalvis's murder? Wilson doubted it and everything they had learned pointed to that conclusion. But if there was even one scintilla of a chance that Kapas was guilty, Wilson would have him. The trip to Liverpool and the interrogation of Kapas had made Wilson think more deeply about the crime itself. If the cause of death was strangulation, it would have been a bloodless death. But the mutilation of the body would have been a very bloody affair, and whoever dismembered the body would have been bathed in blood. Yet, there was no blood in the soil at Redburn Park. They needed to locate the site of the dismemberment. It was approaching midday and the interview room containing the four men was beginning to smell like a locker room. There was tension in the air as they waited for Wilson's phone to ring.

When it did, Wilson grabbed it and opened the call. The phone was still on loudspeaker.

'Hi, Boss,' Browne's soft mid-Ulster accent came over the phone. 'Bad news on the apartment. The few splashes of blood found were consistent with a small cut and a lot older than the past week. The technicians have packed up and gone back to their normal job. Siobhan has exhausted the list of hire car companies and it's a bust there as well. Anything else you'd like us to do?'

'No, if anything else comes up I'll call.' He turned to the three other men. 'That does it for me.'

'Shit,' Graham said. 'He looked good for it. But you're right, there are too many holes. What are you going to do with him?'

Wilson looked at Skeria. 'I think you're the best one to answer that question.'

'The case against Kapas and his partner is almost complete. We have his passport, so he's not going anywhere. The hammer will drop on them next week at the latest. He'll always be findable.'

'Get him into an interview room,' Wilson said to Pierce. 'I want Harry to interview him about paying the money to Beattie and I want a signed statement to that effect. I don't like bent coppers.'

Pierce stood up. 'Then I'll cut him loose?'

Wilson and Skeria nodded in unison.

Wilson looked at Pierce. 'I'll send a message to your chief super commending you,' he said. 'And I won't forget to thank the NCA for lending us Sergeant Skeria. Despite this setback, we've at least identified the victim and you've both been a big help.'

'Thanks,' Pierce started for the door. 'I'll get Kapas.'

Harry stood up and followed him. 'Are you sure about this, Boss? We're not going to be flavour of the month with the Vice Squad.'

'They'll get over it.'

Skeria extended a hand to Wilson. 'It's been interesting seeing you work.'

Wilson took his hand. 'How long more will you be in England?'

'As soon as we put Kapas and his gang away I'll be returning to Lithuania. I miss my wife and children.'

Wilson watched Skeria leave. This job eats people, he thought. Maybe it had eaten him. He was on his way back to Belfast because there was a crime to be solved. There was no wife or child to return to. He thought about Davis and the slur in her speech the previous evening. Maybe loneliness was the copper's lot.

44

Wilson and Graham were booked on the ten to five evening flight from Liverpool to Belfast. They left Walton Lane just after Graham had collected the statement from Kapas and the Lithuanian had been set free. They ate a lunch of club sandwiches and Guinness at the airport and discussed where they could go next with the investigation. The trip hadn't been a complete waste of time. They now knew the name of the victim and also that she had no connection to Belfast, which meant that she wasn't targeted. Unless the blond man with the military bearing, no doubt Eddie Hills, had something to do with her death. That line of enquiry hadn't been entirely thrown out. It was one thing to throw a scare into a pimp by visiting him, it was quite another to disappear one of his working women, kill her and dismember her body. Was Hills capable of such a crime? Hell yes. A good deal of progress had been made but they were still some distance from having any of the answers that really mattered. If the selection of the victim was totally random, then they would have the devil's own job in developing a motive. Wilson had no idea how many punters there were in Belfast who regularly used prostitutes, but he reckoned there were several thousand and they weren't exactly broadcasting it. Hills or a punter? He would prefer it to be Hills. Finding the punter and pinning the crime on him would be a bigger task.

THEY LEFT Belfast International just after six o'clock. Graham went directly home and Wilson went to the station. The squad room was empty. He walked straight up to the whiteboard and scrubbed out 'Jane Doe', replacing the words with 'Rasa Spalvis'. He pinned the photo he had taken from Skeria beside her name and stared again at the face of the young woman.

Some people are born lucky and some get the really shit end of the stick. Despite her brothers and sisters, Spalvis was alone in this world. Everyone that she'd met had let her down or abused her. Anger rose up from inside him. She had a crap life and then Hills or some local punter had choked the life out of her and mutilated her body. He was going to make someone pay. He heard a noise and turned to find Davis standing behind him.

'Is that her?' she asked.

'Yes.'

She came closer and stood beside Wilson. 'An attractive woman, but she sure doesn't look happy.'

Neither do you, Wilson thought. 'She had a shit life. Perhaps death was a pleasant release.'

'It wasn't up to someone to make that decision. You're certain it wasn't this Kapas character?'

'Pretty certain, it's too much of a cliché, the prostitute murdered by her pimp. It might have been a fit if it wasn't for the dismemberment and the hiding of the body parts. He knew that she was a nobody. If he'd killed her, he would simply have left her for us to find while he disappeared back to where he came from. We might never have found out who she was.'

'Just another woman found on the heath months after her death. Isn't that another cliché? But I'm sure you would have found out who she was.' She looked at the whiteboard. 'Maybe Rasa Spalvis has finally got a piece of good luck. You're going to go to bat for her.'

Wilson had been here many times before, perhaps too many times before. Two lonely people looking for something that wasn't really there. He could suggest a drink or dinner, and he knew where it would end up. He also knew that they would both regret it almost as soon as it happened. And it would change their relationship forever. He was in control of what happened next. They stood silently staring at the photo on the whiteboard, waiting for their moment to pass.

When it did, Davis spoke first. 'DCC Jennings is going to have our skins.'

'That's been tried before.'

She returned his smile. 'Sleep well, Ian.'

'Thank you, ma'am.' He watched as she walked out of the room. There was a hint of disappointment in her gait. The old Ian Wilson wouldn't just have watched her leave. What had happened to that version of himself? It was eleven o'clock in the morning in Los Angeles and he needed to hear Reid's voice. He headed to his office to make the call.

'YOU LOOK ROUGH,' she said as soon as he put on the camera. 'You want to tell me about it?'

He gave her the short version of what had happened in Liverpool. 'Back to square one,' she said when he'd finished.

'Not quite, we have a name and more importantly we have a face.' He was tired and he knew that what was ahead was more slog.

'It's not easy for you these days.'

'You're a one to talk. How's your mother?'

'She's perked up a bit, but that's to be expected. They pumped her full of some pharmaceuticals and handed her a bag of pills on the way out of the hospital that would have got them prison in the UK. There was enough opioids in the bag to knock out an army.'

'How long do you reckon?'

'She's a strong lady. I'm learning to appreciate her more as we're getting to know each other. You know, people save themselves in very different ways. She did what she did to save herself from a lousy marriage, but she wasn't aware of the price we would all pay for the way she did it. She was asleep on the sofa yesterday and she called out for Peter. So my brother is clearly on her mind. In contrast, she hasn't mentioned her husband's name since I got here and he hasn't called once to find out how she is. Go home, Ian, and go to bed, you look all in.'

He didn't feel all in and he wasn't going home to bed. His mind was on Rasa Spalvis and women like her. Someone had to speak for them. 'Till tomorrow,' he said.

'I miss you. Sometimes I feel like just flying home.'

'I know. I really wanted Kapas to be our man so that I could join you.'

'Love you,' she said as the picture went blank.

He switched off the desk light and sat in the darkened office.

45

Wilson left his car in the station and picked up a black cab outside for the short trip to Great Victoria Street. His snug was available and he was halfway through his first pint of Guinness when McDevitt arrived.

'You're paying one of the staff here,' Wilson said and pushed the bell summoning the barman at the same time.

'Thirty quid a week.' McDevitt took a seat across from him.

'I've known these guys for years and they'd sell me out for thirty quid a week?' He ordered a pint for McDevitt and a refill for himself.

'Very biblical, everything in Northern Ireland has religious overtones. Like Protestants not being able to use RIP anymore because of the Catholic connotations. You look like you need a shave and a shirt. The rough look isn't your brand.'

'I had to stay overnight in Liverpool.'

'Any news? The editor bumped me from the front page because you guys have been swinging the lead.'

The barman deposited two pints and Wilson paid him. He passed a pint to McDevitt. 'You'll be back on the front page very soon.'

McDevitt took a slug of his pint. 'Time to share.'

'We have the woman's name and a photo. There'll probably be a press conference tomorrow.'

'But my good friend will slip me both in advance.'

'How much is thirty pieces of silver in real money?'

They both laughed. 'Nobody in the frame?' McDevitt asked.

Wilson thought about Eddie Hills. He was capable of it, but what was the motive. Throwing a scare into Kapas, maybe. But to kill a woman to throw a scare into a pimp? Even for a low life like Hills, it just didn't compute. Wilson shook his head.

'No other juicy little titbits for your old friend?'

'When are you off to LA?' Wilson asked.

'Subtle change of subject, so there probably is something that you could divulge to Jock, but you're afraid that Jock will somehow manage to throw you under a bus. Let me guess.' Jock leaned forward and whispered in Wilson's ear. 'Something to do with Jackie Carlisle.'

'Any chance that you'll have time to give Reid a call when you're over there?' Wilson didn't flinch at the mention of Carlisle's name. 'I'm sure that she'd welcome a friendly face from Belfast.'

McDevitt pushed the bell and ordered refills. Wilson didn't protest. He had planned several drinks, which was why his car was sitting outside the station.

'My agent and I are flying to LA next week,' McDevitt said. 'Waste of bloody time, of course, but we're going through with it anyway. There might just be a few pound in selling an option. Chances are nothing will ever come of it. If Reid is still there, we'll have her out to dinner.'

'It appears that Reid will still be there.' The barman arrived with the two pints. 'And two Jamesons to chase them,' Wilson ordered.

'It's going to be one of those nights,' McDevitt said. 'Things in Liverpool must have been really bad.'

'You have no idea.'

46

Wilson had spent another night on his couch. He remembered that McDevitt had deposited him at his apartment but that was it. He had a faint memory of waking in the middle of the night to go to the toilet or drink some water or get sick or maybe all three. He'd been visited by several spectres from his past, including his father and his wife. Sammy Rice had even made an appearance and he thought that Mickey Duff and Rasa Spalvis might have been in there too. The whole dream had been a mishmash of the past and the present. He woke up as dawn was breaking over the city. His head hurt and would probably hurt for the whole day. He didn't know whether it was from the drink he had consumed in the Crown or the pressure he felt from the torched man and the dismembered woman. The fact that both had wandered through his dream concerned him. He remembered something Shakespeare had written about the dead having their revenge, then he wondered how he remembered that quote. It was something he'd learned at school eons ago. He staggered into the bathroom and removed his clothes before going to the toilet and then showering in water so hot that it reddened his skin. It made him feel marginally more human. He looked at his hand and decided that he needed several cups of coffee before he could trust it to shave him.

An hour later he had drunk three cups of coffee, consumed an omelette with difficulty and washed down several strange looking pills with a pint of water. He remembered that Reid suggested this action the last time he had overindulged. He made himself a fourth coffee and went to sit on the couch to watch the city wake up. There was a full hour before he would have to present himself at the station and he wanted to be at least alert when he got there. He sat lamenting his irregular lapses with regard to drink. The answer to any problem is not to be found at the bottom of a bottle. But there was always a chance. As he set down his cup, he noticed a small piece of paper beside a pen on the coffee table. There was a semi-legible scrawl on the paper. He had no memory of writing it so it must have been left by McDevitt. He picked up the paper and read a name, 'Bridget Kelly'. Something exploded in his head. He felt like he had been kicked by a horse. As soon as he composed himself, he picked up his phone and called McDevitt. He received the voicemail message three times before a sleepy McDevitt answered the phone. 'I thought you'd still be out for the count, just like I was,' McDevitt said.

'What the fuck are you up to Jock?' Wilson asked.

'Hold on a second there, Ian. What are we talking about?'

'The piece of paper you left on my coffee table.'

'What? My memory of last night is hazy, but I know I didn't leave a piece of paper on your coffee table because I wasn't in your apartment last night. You bade me goodnight outside your apartment and I travelled on with the taxi to my place. What the hell was on the paper?'

'Nothing, I had a bad night and I must have woken at some point and written myself a message. I'm sorry for waking you. Back to sleep with you.' Wilson cut the line before Jock could reply. He picked up the paper and tried to recognise his own writing in the letters. A shiver ran up his back. How did he drag that name up from the recesses of his mind and have the sense to write it on a piece of paper while lying senseless on his couch? He folded the piece of paper and put it in his wallet. Maybe the little bell in his head could stop ringing now. He went to his computer and typed in the line about the dead seeking revenge. On the screen in front of him he saw the quote from Macbeth.

THERE'S AN OLD SAYING: *the dead will have their revenge. Gravestones have been known to move, and trees to speak, to bring guilty men to justice. The craftiest murderers have been exposed by the mystical signs made by crows and magpies.*

47

The explosion was inevitable and all the more painful for the man with the sore head. Wilson's attempts to tune out Jennings' rant were largely unsuccessful due to his lack of control of his brain functions. The DCC was famous for his tirades, but today he was outdoing himself. The word apoplectic didn't come anywhere near describing his present disposition. Davis and Wilson sat stoically while Jennings dragged their professionalism through the mud. They had a perfect prime suspect within their grasp and they had freed him. Why hadn't he been brought back to Belfast? What the hell were they doing ruining the investigation? ACC Nicholson and Grigg had been invited to the meeting to witness the dressing down and no doubt to be a Greek chorus, spreading the news of Davis's and Wilson's disgrace. Jennings spewed invective and spittle at the two police officers until he eventually ran out of steam and permitted the defendants the opportunity to speak.

'I should point out,' Davis began, 'that before the visit to Liverpool we had no idea of the victim's name or what she looked like. That situation no longer exists and we now have an opportunity to find her on CCTV and follow her movements.

Also, Kapas has surrendered his passport and will in any case be arrested by the NCA along with his accomplices in the gangmaster case. He is still an active line of enquiry in the investigation, which will now concentrate on Spalvis's movements on the day of her death. We would appreciate if HQ would agree to a press conference at which we might enlist the help of the public.'

Wilson looked at his superior. He was very impressed. Maybe she would make it after all.

'This investigation has been botched from day one.' Jennings' normally pale face was streaked with red. 'Now you want me to go on television and beg the help of the public because we can't do our job. Well you can go and whistle for that one.' Inside he was churning. It had all looked so easy. The Lithuanian would go down, and even if he didn't, the investigation would have lost months pursuing him. That scenario was now in the toilet. 'I am considering moving the investigation to another station.'

Wilson cleared his throat to speak. 'I'm afraid that would be in direct contradiction to the terms of reference developed by the chief constable for my squad. You should have received a copy of the CC's paper. If not I can always send you a copy by email.

'Get out.' Jennings shouted. 'All of you.'

Davis stood. 'I assume that even if there is no press conference we can release the woman's name and the photograph to the press. They're howling for details of our progress and we have made a significant amount.'

'Do it,' Jennings said. 'Now get out, and if this Kapas character does a flit then there will be consequences.'

Davis led the way out of the office, followed by Wilson and Grigg. Nicholson lagged behind.

'Not now,' Jennings said, and Nicholson joined the queue exiting the office.

Davis didn't speak until they were in the rear of the car heading back to the station. 'What the hell was that about?'

'Your guess is as good as mine.' Wilson sank back into the seat. An early morning rant from Jennings was the last thing he'd needed when he was nursing a hangover. 'McDevitt is straining at the leash to get back on the front page. I think that if we give him the photo and the name he might be convinced to word his article as a request for the public's help.'

'It's just as well we have a friend in the press. I'm surprised that Jennings made it as far as he did. The DCC job calls for diplomatic as well as organisational skills. The man back there was out of control.'

'I was thinking that too. Why is Jennings so interested in this case? There's not a word about the charred body in the boot of the BMW. That's more local, possibly involves drugs, murder and gang violence. And he just lets it slide by while he goes ballistic over the Rasa Spalvis case. Interesting.'

JENNINGS WAS PROWLING UP and down his office, trying to regain control of himself. Ian fucking Wilson, always creeping out of the woodpile to screw up a perfectly good situation. How in heaven's name had he got from a naked torso to a name and a photo of the woman? The man had the luck of the devil. If his luck continued, Jennings and his collaborators might very well end up in jail. That was not going to happen. He would take whatever steps were necessary, with whatever consequences, but he was not going to jail.

48

Wilson and Graham briefed the team on the result of the trip to Liverpool. 'Although we've made huge progress, we're still a long way from a result,' Wilson said. 'Kapas remains a line of enquiry, but my gut tells me that we're through with him. Now we're going to try and find out Spalvis's movements for the time she was in Belfast.' There was a collective groan from the team. Nobody relished the prospect of hours watching CCTV footage. 'According to Kapas, Spalvis was working the streets when she disappeared. Let's concentrate on the area round Linenhall Street on the twentieth and twenty-first of October.' He took down the photo from the whiteboard and handed it to O'Neill. 'Scan it and get it out to the uniforms. Tell them to find out if anyone saw her around the time of her disappearance. Send me the scan too, I'm going to get it out to the press. Somebody in Belfast saw her over those two days. We just have to jog their memories and then we can start establishing a timeline. We're going to get the bastard that killed this young woman and we're going to put him away.' He strode towards his office. 'Siobhan, come with me.'

'I want you to do me a favour, Siobhan,' Wilson said as soon as they were inside the office.

O'Neill nodded.

'I want you to get on that machine of yours and get me the file on Bridget Kelly, a prostitute murdered in Belfast in 2002.'

O'Neill swayed a little and Wilson put out his hand to steady her. 'It's all right, Boss, no breakfast. Bridget Kelly, 2002, the computer file, is that it?'

Wilson thought for a moment. It would do for a start. Fifteen years was a long time. He needed to refresh his memory. 'Yes,' he said almost absentmindedly. And get yourself down to the canteen and eat something. Go on.'

O'Neill forced a smile and left.

Wilson knocked on the glass partition and motioned Browne inside. 'Find out where Eddie Hills can be located,' he said as soon as Browne entered. 'You and I are going to pay him a visit.'

He sat down at his desk and switched on his computer. The machine had just warmed up when he received an email from O'Neill with the scan of Rasa Spalvis's photo attached. He picked up the phone and called McDevitt. 'Where are you?'

'The office.' McDevitt was chewing on something crunchy.

'Put down the apple for a minute. It's your lucky day, I'm about to share.'

'What was that weird shit you were up to this morning? You almost gave me a heart attack.'

'Nothing to concern you, get out your pen, her name was Rasa Spalvis and she was a Lithuanian prostitute.' He gave McDevitt a potted version of her background. 'She was part of a troupe of women brought to Belfast to service punters with a bit of exotic. You could emphasise the uglier side of the business as she was trafficked.' He forwarded O'Neill's email. 'I'm sending you a photo for the front page. It'll be in your email any minute now. When you write it up, you can mention that we'd like to speak with anyone who saw this lady on either the twentieth or twenty-first.'

'Got the email. This stuff is gold. I won't forget the next time I have something to share. By the way, our meeting in LA has been moved up. We're leaving the day after tomorrow. Inform the little lady and send me her number. I'll give her a slap-up meal and let her know that you're pining for her.'

'Have a good trip.' Wilson cut the communication.

Jennings would have a canary when he saw tomorrow's *Chronicle*, but Wilson didn't give a damn. He looked at Browne working the phones. Things seemed to have settled down in his sergeant's life and it was just as well. The squad had never been stretched so thin. He needed everyone giving one hundred per cent.

How easy would it have been if Kapas had been the murderer? It certainly appeared that Jennings would have been happy. And probably Davis too. He was pleased that she had stood up for him. He had suspected that her allegiance was shifting to HQ and he wouldn't have blamed her. Kapas in jail would also have meant that he would have been on his way to LA, which would have made him and Reid happy. If all that was true, then why the hell hadn't he arrested Kapas and dragged him back to Belfast? The answer was simple. The nasty bugger didn't do it.

Browne came to the door. 'I called the manager of Club 69 and told him that we were looking for Hills. He told me to hold on while he checked. When he got back he said Hills is having breakfast with his boss at the Harbour Café. He also asked me what you like to have with your bacon and eggs.'

THE HARBOUR CAFÉ was a ten-minute drive from the station and was located, as the name would suggest, on the edge of Belfast Harbour. As Wilson and Browne entered, they saw Davie Best and Eddie Hills sitting at a corner table. The two men were sitting on the same side of the table and two plates of bacon, eggs and pancakes were already set across from them.

Best pointed at the chairs. 'Glad you could join us for breakfast.'

Wilson looked at the plate in front of him. It looked good, especially in his current state of hangover. A full Irish breakfast of bacon, eggs, sausage and black pudding was the perfect cure for a hangover. 'Thanks, Davie, I believe I will.' He started forking egg and bacon into his mouth.

Best smiled, he had expected Wilson to refuse the food. 'How can we help you?'

Browne reluctantly started to follow his boss's example.

'It's Eddie really that I want to talk to.' Wilson was enjoying the food. 'It appears that Eddie had a run in with a Lithuanian pimp called Kapas.'

Best looked at Hills. 'Answer the man, Eddie.'

'Who told you that, Mr Wilson?' Hills said.

'Kapas himself.' Wilson mopped his plate with the pancake. The food was beginning to prove its worth as a hangover cure.

'Now why would I have done something like that?' Hills asked.

'No idea, Eddie. You tell me,' Wilson said, sipping the coffee.

Hills was about to answer when Best put a hand on his arm. 'Where are we going with this?'

'Kapas was in Belfast with four female prostitutes on a hit-and-run visit,' Wilson said. 'That could very well have pissed off someone who runs their own prostitution racket. That someone could have had a word with Kapas, but maybe the Lithuanian's Russian connections gave him the balls to resist. Next thing one of his girls turns up dead and dismembered.'

'The woman in Redburn Country Park was a Lithuanian?' Best asked.

'It'll be in tomorrow's papers, along with her photo and name.' Best's jocular mood had changed.

'That's a very serious allegation, Mr Wilson,' Best said.

'I've alleged nothing. I only laid out a hypothesis that might end up as a line of enquiry.' Wilson pushed his cup away. 'This place is good. I'm glad you introduced us to it.'

Best stared into Wilson's eyes. 'Let's say that a friend of Eddie's asked him to have a quiet word with this bloke Kapas in relation to interfering with a local enterprise. Let's say that it ended there. Murder is bad for business.'

'Tell that to Mickey Duff,' Wilson remarked.

Best looked at Hills. 'Do you know this Mickey Duff character?'

Hills smiled. 'I heard about him, but I never met him.'

'If I want a Chuckle Brothers impersonation, I'll go to the theatre,' Wilson said. 'Eddie's in the frame for the woman until we learn otherwise. I hear he was a dab hand with a chainsaw in Iraq, or was it Afghanistan?'

'You've got a bad mouth, Mr Wilson,' Best said. 'It's not good to poke a sleeping bear.'

Wilson stood up. 'I'll pay for our breakfasts on the way out.'

'Hey, Browne,' Hills called as they left the table. 'See you down the Kremlin.'

Wilson felt Browne tense beside him. 'Keep moving.' They went to the till and Wilson paid.

'They know,' Browne said as they hit the sea air outside. He was shaking.

'It's their business to know.'

49

As soon as they were seated in the car, Wilson turned to Browne. 'You can't keep anything hidden when you deal with the criminal fraternity. We keep files on them and they keep files on us. They know where we live and they know about our family connections. It's like a balance of power.'

'I'm quitting,' Browne said. His hands were shaking. 'They're going to hold it against me.'

'Only if you give them the power. And you are certainly not quitting. The day is long gone when gay men were not accepted in the force. You're a damn fine policeman and you're not going to allow yourself to be pushed out of the job because a couple of criminals know your sexual orientation. Having a sexual preference for men isn't a criminal offence.'

Browne started the car. 'I'm not cut out for this job. I know it already. Quitting has been on my mind since I took the job here and saw how Nicholson used my private life to manipulate me.'

'Don't give them the power. Be who you are and stand up to them. Nicholson and Hills are both scum, albeit in different ways. I'm giving you the job of following up the Hills line of enquiry. You have my authority to harass the hell out of him. Get him into the station this afternoon. Let him cool his heels in an interview room for four or five hours and then grill him on his whereabouts on the day of Spalvis's murder. Take an official statement from him. Then check every minute of it. Show him that you can put his life under the microscope any time you feel like it.'

'That does sound like harassment, Boss.'

'Hills is a valid line of enquiry in the investigation into the murder of Rasa Spalvis. You will not be doing your duty if you do not examine the possibility that Hills is the killer.' Wilson noted a distinct change in Browne's body language. Exiting from the Harbour Café he had been deflated. His confident self had not fully returned, but it was almost there.

WILSON HAD ONLY JUST ARRIVED BACK in his office when O'Neill knocked on his door. He beckoned her to enter.

'Problem, Boss,' she shuffled uneasily. 'There's no computer file for Bridget Kelly.'

'Not surprising,' Wilson said. 'The exercise of computerising the old files is still ongoing. They should have already done 2002 though, but I heard that there's a backlog.'

'There is, but that's not the problem. They're up to 2006 on the old files. The problem is they never had an old file for Bridget Kelly.'

'Bullshit, I worked on the case myself. I examined that file on lots of occasions. It must be downstairs in the archives at Musgrave Street.'

'I've asked. There is no file, either digital or on paper. If there was a file, then it's disappeared.'

'Okay, Siobhan, don't worry about it. I'll look into it myself.' What were the chances that the very file he needed was the file that was missing?' He called for a car and put on his coat.

. . .

MUSGRAVE Street station covered the Falls Road and much of the Catholic area of Belfast. Wilson checked in with the duty sergeant and started downstairs to the part of the station containing the archives. Wandering through the basement area brought back memories, not all of them pleasant. Nothing ever seemed to change in the bowels of the station. Wilson almost expected to come across a skeleton dressed in an old RUC uniform and covered in cobwebs. He pushed open the door to the archives and saw that the reality wasn't so far removed for his imagination.

'Jesus, Archie,' Wilson said on seeing the man behind the desk outside the archives. 'I thought that you were retired.' Archie Muldoon was already an old man when Wilson had joined the force and that hadn't been today or yesterday. Muldoon was that rare creature who had found his calling on his first day in the job and had never left the small room in which they now stood. Wilson thought that perhaps he even slept in the station. Whether he did or not, nobody above ground cared.

'Ian Wilson, what brings you back into my world?' Muldoon looked up through a pair of glasses with lenses as thick as bottle tops. If people could be said to resemble animals, then Muldoon would have been a mole, which would have been totally appropriate given his subterranean life. His skin was so white it could only be likened to alabaster.

'I set one of my young coppers the task of retrieving a file and she can't find it either in the archives or on the computer.'

'And a detective superintendent comes down here himself to locate a file. It must be bloody important.' He pulled out a ledger from under his desk. 'This is my own personal ledger. Nothing to do with the official stuff. What file are you looking for?'

'Murder case from 2002, Bridget Kelly.'

Muldoon flicked through the pages of his ledger. There was

a computer sitting on his desk, but Wilson surmised that it had probably never been switched on.

'Wait here,' Muldoon disappeared into a deep room with filing cabinets ranged along the walls. He fiddled in a filing cabinet and then returned to his desk to consult the ledger one more time. He went back to the filing cabinet and spent ten minutes or more searching. He finally returned to his desk. 'I'll be damned. It's not where it's supposed to be. Some bugger must have misfiled it.'

'How could that be, Archie, you're the only bugger who does any filing? Perhaps someone has made off with it.'

'Don't be daft. People rarely come down here. When they do, they stand where you are now and I retrieve the file. They sign a chit if they're taking the file away and when they bring the file back I mark it in my ledger. My book says that the file is still here.'

'Who was the last person to take the file out?' Wilson asked.

Muldoon looked up his ledger. 'That would be Detective Superintendent Spence in April of 2003. He had it out for two weeks and returned it early May the same year. According to the ledger, I refiled it myself.' Muldoon scratched his head. 'Twenty-five years and I've never lost a file.'

'Don't dwell on it, Archie. I doubt you lost this one either.'

'What do you mean?'

'I think some clever bastard has stolen it.'

'But the ledger says that it's still here and I have the only set of keys to the archives.'

'Nobody in this world has the only set of keys to anywhere.' Wilson started to leave. As he moved down the subterranean corridor, he could hear an echo of Muldoon repeating 'twenty-five years'.

50

Wilson sat alone in his office at the station. He usually had a modicum of control over the direction of an investigation, but he was unsure what was happening with the latest one. His befuddled mind had eventually made a connection between the murder of a prostitute by strangulation with a ligature in 2002 and the murder of a Lithuanian prostitute most likely by strangulation in 2017. He could have accepted that the combined effect of Guinness and Jameson had conjured up that connection if it wasn't for the fact that the murder file of the earlier victim had somehow vanished. It was time to make a call.

'It's Ian,' he said as soon as the phone was answered.

'Aye, Ian, how are ye?' Miriam Spence replied. 'He's pottering in the garden. I'll get him for you.'

Wilson could hear the noise of a door opening and a name being called. Eventually the phone was picked up.

'Ian, how are ye?' Donald Spence's voice was as strong as ever.

'Great. I need to see you.'

'Of course, when do you want to come?'

'Is now a good time?'

. . .

PORTAFERRY IS a small town located at the southern end of the Ards Peninsula near the narrows at the entrance to Strangford Lough. It has become a magnet for senior citizens with a desire for the quiet life away from the hectic pace of Belfast. Former Chief Superintendent Donald Spence had exchanged his suburban Georgian dwelling for a magnificent modern bungalow overlooking the shore and the small ferry port. Wilson parked his car in the driveway and found the front door already open. 'Anyone about?' he shouted as he stood on the threshold.

'Come on in, man,' Spence called from the interior. 'We're in the kitchen brewing up some coffee.'

Wilson went through and found Donald and Miriam Spence setting the table for what looked like afternoon tea. A tiered stand with a selection of cakes was on the table and three plates had been set out. As soon as Wilson entered, Spence approached him and the two men hugged. Then Wilson hugged and kissed Miriam on the cheek. 'You both look great.' He wasn't lying. The Spences were sporting a tan that they hadn't got from the Irish summer.

'We're just back from a small consulting job with the Jordanian police,' Spence said, tapping the side of his nose. 'We managed to work in a trip to Petra and a couple of weeks at the Red Sea. Sit yourself down, lad. We're wild to hear all the news from the big city.'

The next hour was spent drinking coffee and eating cake while Wilson and the Spences exchanged news. Wilson told them about Reid's mother but didn't go into any of the details of the investigation of Rasa Spalvis's death.

'I'm sure you boys have some business to talk about.' Miriam Spence had been here before. 'Why don't you go to Don's study? The two of you will be more comfortable there.'

Spence's study was a homage to his time in the force. There

were the photos showing the stations where he had worked, the citations and the frame containing his medals, the only thing missing was the frame containing the uniform. Perhaps that was under construction. The one picture of Miriam and the children looked out of place. Donald Spence had given his life to the RUC and the PSNI and he wanted anyone who entered his study to know it. Spence had picked up two bottles of beer from the fridge in the kitchen and they settled into two comfortable chairs.

'The torso in Redburn Country Park or the charred body in Helen's Bay?' Spence asked.

'Not just a visit with an old friend?' Wilson tipped his bottle to Spence and drank.

'Not your style! Tell me which one it is and run me through where you are.'

Wilson started at the finding of the woman's torso and proceeded through Liverpool before finishing at the interview with Best and Hills. There was an intermission while Spence had a toilet break and returned with two fresh beers.

'You've done well,' Spence said when Wilson finished. 'To get where you are now from where you started is nearly a miracle. And, of course, it wasn't supposed to happen that way. Whoever killed and mutilated that poor woman was pretty damn determined to make sure that there was sod-all evidence to go on. The fact that it was probably random makes motive difficult to establish. So you're between a rock and a hard place at the moment.'

'That's why I'm here. Do you believe in messages from the grave?'

Spence stared. 'Don't tell me you got religion?'

Wilson explained what had happened. When he said the name 'Bridget Kelly', Spence started and had to catch his bottle when it slipped from his hand.

'Lord God! If I were a Catholic, I'd bless myself. That case has been on my mind for fifteen years.' Spence said.

'The same here. Funny thing is though, when I went looking for the file it seems to have disappeared.'

'Is Archie Muldoon still alive?'

'Aye, still at Musgrave Street, still in the catacombs, I was there this morning.'

'I was afraid something like this would happen.' Spence stood up and went to a filing cabinet. He opened the bottom drawer and took out a thick six-inch file before returning to his seat and laying the file on his desk. 'That was one fucked-up investigation. I was upset that we didn't get a result and I'm sure that we were interfered with. Although I don't know why. I must have had a premonition though because I withdrew the file and made a personal copy.' He flipped the file open. 'I copied every piece of paper, every memo, every report and every photograph. Then I returned the file. I suppose we can assume that all the physical evidence has also disappeared.'

'The file would hardly be disappeared and the physical evidence have been left. I didn't even bother to look. But we have to assume whoever did the clean-up was at least that competent.'

Spence took a slug of his beer. 'I've read this file off and on over the years. Despite that, I have no great insight to offer you. I'm as much in the dark today as I was fifteen years ago.'

'Maybe someone meant us to be in the dark?'

'And that someone would have to be on the inside. If the file was made to disappear, it needed someone with the keys to Muldoon's archives.'

Wilson picked up the file and flicked through the contents. Spence was as good as his word. Everything appeared to be there. 'Can I borrow this?'

'You asked me whether I believe in messages from the grave. Well, I've certainly had some experiences in my life that I can't explain. So I can't rule out the possibility that Bridget Kelly has reached out to you after fifteen years to seek revenge for her murder. If I were you, I would ask me to put that file back where it belongs, in the bottom of my filing cabinet. I sometimes wish I had let this one go, but I just couldn't.'

'Since I looked at Rasa Spalvis's torso in Redburn Country Park something has been niggling away at me. Events seem to have been pushing me to look back. So, if you're agreeable, I'll take the file, but I'll return it if it comes to nothing.'

'You're a stubborn bastard, Ian. Take it and I hope that you won't be sorry. That file is like a stick of gelignite. Handle it with care. And if you do break that case, come to me first.'

Wilson closed the file and picked it up. 'Thanks, Donald, I appreciate it.'

They both stood and there was an awkward moment before they hugged. 'Go carefully.'

'Aye, tell Miriam goodbye and thanks for the tea.'

WILSON SAT into his car and put the file on the passenger seat. Spence waved goodbye from the front porch. He didn't look happy. Wilson waved back. He would trust Donald Spence with his life. If Spence was worried, there had to be a good reason.

51

The three men sat in the hut at the rear of Thiepval Barracks in Lisburn. None looked particularly happy. Jennings had taken the seat facing the other two men as though by common consent the focus would be on him. He had spent the day reviewing the situation on the Spalvis case. Wilson still had no idea of the cause of death or who the murderer might be. That knowledge gave Jennings some comfort. However, the report from Musgrave Street that Wilson had been to the archives in search of the Bridget Kelly file had caused his bowels to loosen. He had ensured that the file had disappeared, along with the box from the evidence locker. So he was secure in that area, but how the hell had Wilson made the link between Kelly and Spalvis?

'The situation has become more serious since we last met,' Milan took the lead. He looked up from the table into Jennings' eyes. 'You assured us that there would be very little advancement in the case. Apparently, you were mistaken.'

'I'd like to point out,' Jennings wasn't going to kowtow, 'that it was your man's sloppy clear-up that put us in this position in the first place. If the torso had been buried properly, none of this would ever have come to light.'

'We're not here for recriminations,' Black Bob Rodgers said. 'If Icepick goes down, we go down with him. That fact should be enough to focus our minds.' He looked at Milan. 'Have you been able to confirm that Icepick has safeguarded himself by leaving an incriminating statement with different individuals?'

'We're working on it,' Milan said.

Rodgers looked at Jennings. 'Then we have to depend on you, Roy.'

Jennings shifted uneasily in his chair. 'I really think that it's time to consider other options.'

'We have already looked at most of the options open to us,' Milan said. 'The majority are unpalatable. But if you wish to share something?'

'What about removing the lead detective?' Jennings said.

'Frying pan into the fire,' Rodgers said. 'It would have to be a natural death. Anything else would be a can of worms.' He knew about the enmity between Jennings and Wilson and there was no way he was playing into Jennings' hands.

'We'll let you think on it and perhaps you'll present an option to us.' Milan looked at Jennings and smiled. He knew the DCC had the most to lose. And just recently back in his job. How inopportune for Icepick to go off the rails at this particular point in time.

'Inaction is not an option,' Jennings said. His stomach was gurgling and he knew the others could hear it. They had to stop Wilson, but aside from killing him, he couldn't think how.

WILSON FINISHED his call to Reid. She'd seen the tiredness in his face and once again expressed her concern. He'd complained that he had been working too hard and said that he would be on the first plane to LA when the current case was either solved or shelved. The latter was much more likely than the former. He made himself a cup of coffee and sat down with the murder file on Bridget Kelly. It was going to be a long night.

BOOK 2

Belfast, 2002

52

Detective Sergeant Ian Wilson slipped out of the storeroom in the basement of Musgrave Street police station. The young female police constable he'd just had sex with would delay five minutes before she exited. Wilson had been back on duty for one month following eight months of hospital and rehabilitation. Proximity to a bomb blast had sent shards of shrapnel into his right thigh. The surgeons had removed the metal and repaired the damage it had done as best they could, but it was apparent to even a blind person that his sporting career was over. He had been passed fit for duty by the psychologist he had been required to attend for a minimum of three months. She had diagnosed him as having post-traumatic stress disorder. The question was which trauma had caused the condition: his father's suicide, his mother running off with his father's best friend, having half his arse blown off by a bomb planted by an idiot who thought it might be the way to achieve a united Ireland, or the realisation that his glittering rugby career was over? The psychologist had tied his PTSD into his sexual addiction, which dated from his father's suicide. He didn't much care about the original cause, but the diagnosis might have been enough to lose him his job, which was why he'd had a three-month affair with his psychologist. There was no diagnosis of PTSD on his record. Being back at work was all he cared about. His injury had dozens of black clouds but one silver lining. The injury compensation cheque went into buying his wife the house she desired. He wasn't thinking about his wife as he climbed the stairs towards the CID squad room on the first floor. He had married in haste and was already regretting it.

'Where the hell have you been?' Chief Inspector Donald Spence met him on the stairs. 'Get your arse in gear. We have a call out.'

Wilson fell into step behind his boss. 'What is it?'

'Young woman found dead in a flat in Divis Tower.'

'Shit,' Wilson said. Divis Tower, a twenty-storey tower block, had two thousand four hundred inhabitants who were exclusively Catholic and mostly committed Republicans. Catholics still almost universally distrusted the newly formed PSNI and were not inclined to be cooperative.

WHEN THEY ARRIVED at Divis Tower thirty minutes later, a large crowd had already assembled. On their way they passed a couple of burned-out cars. Two police Land Rovers were pulled up at the entrance, with an ambulance parked between them. Four uniformed policemen in full crowd control gear stood at the entrance door. The crowd did not look friendly. A heavy police presence in this area usually foreshadowed a riot. The two detectives descended from their vehicle and started for the entrance. On the way, they were jostled by the crowd and the uniformed officers were obliged to open a path for them.

'This could get hairy,' Wilson said as they entered the vestibule.

'What do you mean could get?' Spence said. 'This is already hairy. We need to get done here as soon as we can and get out.'

'Tenth floor, sir,' one of the uniformed policemen said.

'Is the lift working?' Spence asked.

The uniformed policeman nodded.

Wilson pushed the button and they ascended to the tenth floor. When the door opened, they saw a small crowd standing outside the door of one of the flats. A uniformed policeman barred the door. Wilson pushed his way through and he and Spence showed their warrant cards. 'Get rid of them,' Spence said, indicating the crowd.

'They're residents,' the uniformed policeman said.

'Then get them back inside their flats,' Spence said in his most authoritative tone.

They slipped on plastic overshoes and surgical gloves before entering the flat. They walked along a small hallway into a kitchen whose cleanliness would have done credit to the kitchen at the Europa Hotel. The whole flat was scrupulously clean and Wilson wondered whether this was its normal condition. Arriving at a door at the rear of the flat, Spence pushed it open. A naked woman in her mid-twenties lay sprawled on the bed.

Spence walked to the bed and examined the body. He didn't touch her but scrutinised her from the top of her head to the tips of her toes. There was no blood and no sign of injuries.

'Overdose?' Wilson said from behind Spence. He nodded at a syringe on the bedside table.

'Maybe.' The absence of an overt injury meant that they would need the pathologist to confirm the cause of death.

'What's that smell?' Wilson asked.

Spence's nose twitched. 'Bleach?'

'In the bedroom?'

'Have a quick look round,' Spence said. 'There's nothing much we can do here until the pathologist arrives and the forensic team processes the scene.'

Wilson checked out the room, noting the packet of condoms on the bedside table. Perhaps the woman had been having sex and things had gone too far. That would be up to the pathologist to decide. He picked up a handbag and fished around inside, producing a packet of cigarettes, a box of matches, a purse containing two five-pound notes and some loose change, a used bus ticket and a lipstick but no piece of identification. He picked up the syringe and dropped it into a plastic evidence bag. Then he dumped the contents of the handbag into a series of plastic bags. He picked up the condoms and bagged them. Spence was searching the other rooms of the flat. He found a letter from Social Services behind a clock on a shelf in the living room. It was addressed to a Bridget Kelly. He took a plastic bag from his pocket and put the letter inside.

They reassembled in the small living room. 'Could have been a sexual encounter that went wrong,' Wilson said. He displayed the bags to Spence, who handed over the bag with the letter.

'Her name was Bridget Kelly, that's the name on this letter in any event. You're probably right about the sexual encounter. But how did a romp leave the woman dead? Was it by accident or by design?' Spence said. 'I want Forensics to go over this place carefully. If Bridget was on the game, the place will be full of fingerprints. Sorting that out is going to be a nightmare.'

'Looks like Ms Kelly was a bit of a clean freak. This flat is as neat as a pin. Maybe she wasn't on the game, maybe it was a boyfriend.'

'Instant prime suspect, wouldn't that be nice for a change? Find out what's happened to the forensic team. We need them here now. The sooner we have this place processed and are out of here the better. The longer we have a presence here, the uglier that crowd outside is going to become. I don't envy the job of the uniforms who have to do the door-to-door.'

Wilson took out his mobile phone and called the station. 'Forensics are on the way.'

'That's a relief.'

There was a commotion outside the door and Dr Richard Campbell, Chief Pathologist, pushed his way into the flat. 'Where is she?' he said brusquely. 'Had to leave my car outside. I'm worried it might not be there when I get through.'

'In the back bedroom,' Spence said. He had no great love for Campbell, who thought himself a cut above the police.

Wilson followed Campbell into the bedroom and watched as he examined the body and took it's temperature. Within five minutes Campbell had finished and was on his way to the door of the flat.

Spence intercepted him. 'Well?' he said.

'Dead as a doornail, no apparent injuries. I won't know the cause of death until I examine the body at post-mortem. Probably been dead between twelve and sixteen hours. Some minor bruising on the inner thighs could have been caused by rough sex. I'll tell you more when I've had a proper look. Now, I'd appreciate it if you get out of my way so that I can rescue my BMW.'

Spence stood aside and the pathologist hurried past. 'Arsehole,' he said when Campbell was out of hearing. 'Where the hell are Forensics?' We need to get the scene processed and get the body out of here. Haul your bum downstairs and see if there's any sign of them.'

Wilson exited the flat and could see that the crowd outside the door hadn't been dispersed but had grown in number. The rubberneckers were arriving in force. There was a general push in his direction as he exited. The single constable at the door had been reinforced by a colleague, but they were struggling to control the crowd. Wilson managed to forge a path to the lift. The uniforms at the entrance to the tower were barring new arrivals, but there must have been several hundred people who were already in their flats and were making their way to the action on the tenth floor. Wilson pushed the button to summon the lift and waited patiently for it to arrive. When it did, it disgorged three men already suited and booted in white plastic suits and carrying a number of boxes, which Wilson knew contained their camera and other evidence-gathering equipment. He led them back to Kelly's flat.

'Thanks be to God,' Spence said when they pushed their way into the hallway. He recognised the leader of the team. 'Hi, Denny, she's in the bedroom. Best get going because the sooner we get her out of here the better.'

'I'm with you on that, Donald,' Denny said. 'There's a nasty mood down below. We'll start with the photos so that they can get her out. Maybe that will calm the situation a bit.'

'I doubt it,' Spence said.

Wilson and Spence stood aside and watched the forensic team at work. One member concentrated on taking photos of the bedroom while Denny started to search for fibres, hairs and other pieces of evidence. The third man was dusting for fingerprints.

'How was it called in?' Wilson asked.

'Friend tried to contact her,' Spence said. 'When she didn't respond, the friend called in and the uniforms broke the door.'

Denny came out of the bedroom. 'Was this lass a cleanliness nut or what?'

Spence said. 'Yes, it's like an operating theatre in here.'

The man who had been photographing the body exited the bedroom and went into the living room, shooting photos as he went.

'You can get her out now,' Denny said.

Spence nodded at Wilson, who made for the front door.

The crowd at the door of the flat had grown by almost fifty per cent since the forensic team arrived. 'Get some more men up here and disperse this crowd,' Wilson said to one of the policemen. 'And tell them below that the ambulance team can come up. We're ready to take her out and I don't want any trouble when we do.' He ducked back inside.

After a few minutes there was more commotion at the door

and two ambulance men entered carrying a black plastic body bag and a stretcher. 'She's in the bedroom,' Spence said. He pointed at the stretcher. 'How the hell are you going to get that thing into the lift?'.

'That's our secret,' one of the ambulance men said and he and his colleague laughed.

53

Wilson and Spence exited from the lift and walked through the main doors of the tower. The crowd had grown to riot proportions and it was considerably more aggressive than when they had arrived.

One man emerged from the crowd and approached them. 'Chief inspector Spence,' he called. 'A word, please.'

Spence spoke under his breath to Wilson. 'Councillor Noel Armstrong, Sinn Féin.'

Wilson looked at the new arrival. He was short and squat with a full head of black hair and a round undistinguished face.

Armstrong extended his hand. 'Noel Armstrong, I don't know if you remember me.'

Spence shook his hand. 'Of course, Councillor Armstrong, this is Detective Sergeant Wilson.'

Armstrong shook hands with Wilson. 'You're the rugby man. I read about your injury in the papers. It's a crying shame. I'm a GAA man myself.'

'What can we do for you, councillor?' Spence asked.

'What's the situation in the tower?'

'A young woman has been found dead in a flat on the tenth

floor. She will be removed in the next few minutes and I'd be grateful if you'd ensure that it all goes off peaceably.'

'There's a rumour that she was murdered,' Armstrong said.

'As of this moment the cause of death is unknown. The pathologist will let us know when he's done the autopsy.'

'So, it might have been a natural death?'

'Yes,' Spence replied. 'Or even death by misadventure. Maybe you could pass that information along to the crowd. It might encourage them to disperse.'

Armstrong looked relieved. 'Thank you, chief inspector.' He started moving back towards the crowd.

'That man should be behind bars,' Spence muttered under his breath.

'How so?' Wilson asked.

'He's suspected of being involved in several punishment killings, but there's no real proof against him. Now, he's morphed into a politician like most of the former combatants on both sides of our sectarian divide. I hope to God that that poor wee lass did die from natural causes.'

BACK AT THE STATION, Wilson and Spence went immediately to the squad room. The two other members of their team, DCs George Whitehouse and Eric Taylor, were at their desks. Spence told them what had transpired at Divis Tower. He moved to Taylor's desk. 'Bridget Kelly, Divis Flats, I want to know everything about her and I want to know it yesterday.'

'Yes, Boss.' Taylor immediately fired up his computer.

'George, you're in charge of the door-to-door. Get over to Divis with half a dozen uniforms and start knocking on those doors.'

'Useless exercise,' Whitehouse muttered. He heaved his heavy body out of his chair. 'It's Divis Flats, Boss, we'll be wasting our time. The Fenians will clam up.'

'I love your optimism and tolerance,' Spence said. 'Now, on your bike, George.'

The duty sergeant stuck his head round the door. 'The woman who called in the body in Divis is downstairs and wants to talk to the investigating officer no less.'

Spence turned to Wilson. 'You deal with it.'

'Boss,' Wilson said and followed the duty sergeant out the door.

'You're in luck, man,' the duty sergeant said. 'She's a very good-looking Fenian.'

As they entered the reception area the duty sergeant nodded in the direction of a woman seated beside a young girl on the bench facing the front desk. Wilson walked over and stood before them. 'I'm Detective Sergeant Wilson, and you are?'

The woman stood up. Her head came to Wilson's shoulder, her long dark hair was pulled back in a ponytail. She had perfectly clear blue eyes and her skin was sallow. The only blemish in her otherwise perfectly symmetrical face was her nose, which Wilson reckoned had been broken at some point.

'I'm Marie O'Neill, I'm Bridget Kelly's friend and the one who phoned in earlier.'

'And who is this wee lass?' Wilson asked.

'My sister Siobhan, I'm taking care of her today. Is there somewhere we can speak in private?'

Wilson turned to the duty sergeant. 'We'll be in number one, keep an eye on the wee girl like a good man.' The duty sergeant nodded and Wilson led the way through a door on the left-hand side of the reception area. It led into a long corridor. He pushed open the first door on the left and motioned for Marie O'Neill to enter before him. The room contained only a table and four chairs arranged two by two on either side of the table. O'Neill sat down on one of the chairs and Wilson sat opposite her.

'We were just going to start looking for you,' he said.

'Well I've saved you the trouble.'

'You were worried for your friend, why?'

'Because men are bastards.'

He smiled. It seemed to him a good enough reason. 'Would you like to expand on that?'

'Bridget was a prostitute. She'd been beaten and tortured by some of her clients. So I suppose it was natural to assume that someone had hurt her.'

Wilson took out his book and started to write. He would get Eric to look up Ms O'Neill. 'You say you were friends, how so?'

'We worked together.'

'You're a prostitute?' His tone betrayed his astonishment.

'Surprised I don't look like a skank? We don't have it stamped on our foreheads you know. A lot of the women in Belfast who hit the streets as soon as their kids have their tea don't look like prostitutes either. In my case, it's my job. How did Bridget die?'

'We're not sure yet. She's been moved to the Royal and I suppose the autopsy will be tomorrow. Then we'll know.'

'And if she was murdered?'

'We'll get whoever killed her.'

'Really?' She tossed her head back. 'You mean to tell me that you'll put in the same effort to find Bridget's killer as you would if she was some doctor's wife from the Malone Road?'

'Absolutely. Especially if you can help us.'

'Liar. To you lot, we're the dregs of society. The first chance you get you're going to bury this investigation before it exposes the rotten underbelly of our society.'

'What do you mean?' Wilson knew exactly what she meant but thought he'd like to hear it from his feisty interviewee's perspective.

'There are almost twenty thousand men out there who use prostitutes on a regular basis. They're doctors and dentists and accountants. They're members of golf clubs and the Orange Order. They are regular attendees at church, respectable members of society. And you won't touch them. You'd rather see us as the problem.'

'If she was murdered, I promise you we'll do our best to put the killer away. When did you last see Bridget?'

'I haven't seen Bridget since last week and I don't know any of her regular clients. If one of them killed her, I'd deal with him myself.'

Looking at the set of her jaw, he didn't doubt her. 'Was Bridget particularly houseproud?'

She looked surprised. 'God no, sure her place looks like a tinkers' camp.' She watched Wilson write in his notebook. 'I need to get back to Siobhan.'

'Give me your address.'

She gave an address off the Falls Road and Wilson wrote it in his notebook.

'Does Bridget have any family?'

'She didn't speak much about them. She received her sexual initiation from her father and left home as soon as she could. She's twenty years old. Her whole life was in front of her and some bastard has taken it away.'

'How long has she been on the game?'

'I don't know, probably as long as she could remember.' She stood up. 'I've got to get my sister home. You know where to find me.'

Wilson closed his book. 'We want to get the person who killed your friend as badly as you do.'

She started for the door. 'Then prove it.'

54

Since his return to duty, Wilson had developed the habit of passing through the Crown on Great Victoria Street on his way home. Technically, the Crown wasn't on his way home but that didn't deter him. As an athlete, he had neither smoked nor drank. With that life now firmly behind him, he had launched himself into both vices. He told himself that his evening ritual of a few drinks in a convivial atmosphere was simply an antidote to the rigours of his chosen profession. But deep down he knew he was simply delaying his return home. He wasn't the only young policeman whose home life was experiencing difficulties. It was part and parcel of the job. He was sitting at the bar cradling a pint when Spence sat down beside him.

'Thought I'd find you here.' He signalled to the barman for a pint of Guinness and a refill for Wilson. They sat in silence for a few minutes until the barman placed the drinks in front of them. Spence paid and then lifted his glass. 'Cheers!'

Wilson raised his glass but didn't look too cheerful.

'Tough being back?' Spence sipped his drink.

'A lot has changed in the past few months. This time last

year everything was rosy. Just shows how ephemeral the whole thing is.'

'You could tell that to Bridget Kelly if she was around to hear it.'

Wilson looked at Spence. 'I'm sick of having it pointed out to me that there are lots of people worse off than I am.'

A man came down the bar and stood behind them. 'You're Ian Wilson, aren't you?'

Wilson turned to face him. Being recognised had been a usual occurrence. 'I used to be in another life.'

'I saw you play. You were a force of nature. Can I buy you fellas a drink?'

'No thanks,' Wilson said. 'We're leaving after this one.' He turned back to the bar and the man drifted back to his friends. 'One drink buys you an evening with the late great Ian Wilson,' he said when the man was out of hearing.

'All things come to an end,' Spence said. 'Some kids get injured at nineteen and never kick another ball. Think of the great times you've had and be thankful for them. Now, why don't you go home?'

Wilson liked his boss, who was one of the few coppers at the station with a stable home life. So if he wanted to be like Spence so much, why didn't he go home? Because if he did, he would be confronted with a woman he once thought he loved and who had convinced him that she was pregnant. The child had failed to materialise after they had married. Susan claimed to have had a miscarriage. Then lying in hospital had given him too much time to think, and to wonder whether she had been honest with him. He took another mouthful of Guinness and waved at the barman.

Spence shook his head and the barman retreated. 'This isn't the solution.'

'It'll do for now.'

Spence finished his drink and stood up. 'You'll have to learn to roll with the punches. Lying on the ground isn't an option, so

I'll see you bright and early in the morning. Campbell has scheduled the autopsy for nine o'clock and I told him you'd be attending.' He nodded at the pint on the bar. 'You'll stop at that one if you're interested in holding on to your breakfast when he starts cutting.'

Wilson watched Spence walk slowly through the door of the pub. He turned back and was about to call the barman when he changed his mind.

55

It wasn't Wilson's first autopsy. The naked body of Bridget Kelly lay on the steel table in the centre of the room. Her head had been shaved and she looked like she was asleep although the pallor of her skin was consistent with death. Campbell, Wilson and Campbell's assistant were suited and Campbell was taking the last puffs on his cigarette before starting his work. He crushed the cigarette into an ashtray, pulled down his helmet. then walked to the table. Wilson and the assistant stood back as Campbell picked up the small circular saw and started to remove the crown of Kelly's head.

An hour later, Wilson sat in Campbell's office smoking with the great man while the assistant had been sent to fetch two cups of coffee. Wilson didn't know why he had accepted Campbell's offer of a cigarette as there was sufficient nicotine circulating in the office air to satisfy his need. The assistant deposited the cups of coffee and left the office, coughing as he went.

'Little bastard never touched a fag in his life,' Campbell said. 'Every time he comes in here he coughs up his lungs. Anyone would think that fags are not good for you.'

Wilson crushed out his cigarette and sipped his coffee. 'So, she was strangled?'

'That is my conclusion. I spent some time examining all the tissues of the neck, superficial and deep, in an attempt to track the force vector that produced the injuries.'

'But there were no external marks on her neck?'

Campbell took a slug of his coffee. 'Oftentimes, even in fatal cases, there is no external evidence of injury. While patterned abrasions and contusions of the skin of the anterior neck are typical of strangulation, some cases have no externally evident injury whatsoever. Injuries not at all apparent on the day of death may actually become visible the next day, as the skin begins to dry and become more transparent.'

'But you're sure that she was strangled?'

Campbell didn't reply but looked at Wilson as much as to say that he was mad to doubt the conclusion.

'And she had recently had sex?'

'Just prior to death. I would also say that the strangulation took place during coitus.'

'Was semen present in the vagina?'

'No.' Campbell finished his coffee and lit up another cigarette.

'Can we get fingerprints from the neck? Surely the indents caused by the fingers can be dusted and photographed.'

Campbell shook his head. 'It's a very rare case where the latent fingerprints of the assailant can be recovered from the skin of the victim's neck. You and your forensic colleagues are quite at liberty to try, but I doubt that you'll have any success.' An inch-long piece of ash fell from Campbell's cigarette onto the reports on his desk. The pathologist didn't bother to remove it.

Wilson wrote a note in his book. No semen, no latents, although they would try to raise some. They would have to depend on the forensic team to find something at the flat that might point to the perpetrator. The problem there would be that they would find too much. Carrying out eliminations on the fingerprints followed up by interviews on possible alibis would be the way to go. Wilson finished his coffee. 'Anything else I should know?'

'The puncture mark from the syringe was made post-mortem. Toxicology will tell us what was in it, but it didn't cause her death.'

'Are you sure?'

Campbell put on his harsh look. 'I've been doing this for longer than you've been alive. She was strangled and then injected with a substance that is at the moment unknown.'

'Sorry,' Wilson said. 'Injection post-mortem doesn't fit.'

'Whether that fits or not, those are my conclusions.'

'One last thing, in the bedroom at the flat I got the smell of bleach.'

'Good man, sergeant, I should have mentioned that someone washed the body in bleach. Obviously an attempt to wipe away any evidence of bodily fluids.'

Wilson thought for a moment. 'So the murderer knew what to do. Perhaps it wasn't his first time.' He stood up.

'How are your injuries going?' Campbell asked.

Wilson was taken aback. Campbell rarely strayed into the personal. 'I'll walk with a bit of a limp for the rest of my life.'

'Twelve inches higher and you would have been one of my clients.'

'Must be grateful for small mercies, eh!'

'For me, the difference between life and death is the most stark difference that there is.'

56

The team gathered at the whiteboard to hear Wilson's debriefing on the results of the autopsy. He had already added the important points to the board. He also gave a rundown on his interview with Marie O'Neill.

'Eric,' Spence said.

Eric Taylor stood forward. 'Nothing much to add to the DS. Her parents are still living in Andersonstown. I checked in with them. The local lads had already informed them of her death. The father didn't appear overly bothered. It seems they disowned her years ago.'

'What about Ms O'Neill?' Wilson asked.

Taylor referred to his notebook. 'Born on the Falls, nothing in childhood, started a sociology degree at Queen's but flunked out, rumours of drugs, never been arrested, married to Patrick Quigley but keeps the name O'Neill, one child: a boy, Seán.'

Spence looked at Wilson. 'Are you sure that she's a prostitute?'

Wilson shrugged his shoulders. 'Like she said herself, it's not printed on her forehead, but that's what she told me. I think that maybe she's a part-timer.' He realised that he was going to have to improve his interview technique. Maybe he had been too taken by her looks and her spirit.

'George, the door-to-door,' Spence said.

Whitehouse eased forward. 'As we expected, Boss, no one saw anything. The women were pretty harsh on her – blokes arriving at all times of the day and night and that sort of stuff. Some of the men said she was a pretty wee thing who kept herself to herself.'

'No special boyfriends?' Spence asked the team.

All three shook their heads.

'The best chance would be O'Neill,' Spence said. 'Ian, you and George check the parents out. The father sounds like a bit of a prick so don't go too gentle. Victims of abuse sometimes go after their abuser years down the line. See if there's been any recent contact. If so, we put the father in the frame.'

'What about Forensics, Boss?' Wilson asked.

'Report due later today,' Spence said. 'Ian, my office, now.'

Wilson followed Spence into his office. As soon as they were inside, Spence indicated that Wilson should close the door.

'Take a seat,' Spence said. 'While you were at the autopsy, I had a visit from a Chief Inspector Jennings from Intelligence Division. I've never run across this bloke, but I do know his boss, Superintendent Gilligan, and I don't particularly like him.'

'I know Jennings,' Wilson said. 'He was at the college when I was there. He's a graduate entry with bells on. I had no idea that he was advancing in the organisation so fast.'

'It's the old story, who you know is a lot more important than what you know. He was here to find out where we were on the Bridget Kelly investigation.'

'What's the Kelly investigation got to do with Intelligence Division?'

'On the face of it, nothing, but the fact that Gilligan sent his boy nosing around here this morning has set my antennae twitching.'

'Maybe Kelly was one of their touts?' Wilson suggested.

'Could be, that's the simple explanation and I hope to God it's the reason. But if Gilligan is mixed up in her death, there could be some devious work ahead. Now, away with you, we're on the clock on this one.'

57

Whitehouse parked outside a small apartment building on Roosnareen Avenue. Wilson could see he was uncomfortable just being in the Catholic suburb of Andersonstown. The detective constable was a true-blue Orangeman. They climbed the stairs to the second floor, a task that required an effort from Whitehouse, who habitually carried fifty pounds more than he should. Wilson knocked on the door, which was eventually opened by a woman in her mid-forties. The two police officers produced their warrant cards and introduced themselves.

'Are you Mrs Kelly?' Wilson asked.

'Aye, I'm Margaret Kelly, you'd best come in.' She led them through a small hallway and into a living room.

'It's about your daughter, I'm sorry for your trouble,' Wilson said.

Margaret Kelly burst into tears and Whitehouse remained silent. He didn't commiserate with Fenians.

'They said she was murdered. Who would do such a wicked thing? She was such a wee lass.' She took a handkerchief from her pocket and dabbed at her eyes before blowing her nose. 'Patrick has gone to talk to the funeral people. They say it costs three thousand pounds to bury someone and we don't have that kind of money.'

'When did you last have contact with your daughter?' Wilson asked.

'She called by two months ago while Patrick was out. We had a cup of tea together. It was nice. I felt that we could become mother and daughter again.'

'How long had she been gone?'

'She left on her sixteenth birthday. Said she was going out to buy a packet of cigarettes and never came back. She phoned two days later to say that she was all right, that she was living with a friend and we were not to bother trying to find her.'

There was a noise of the front door opening and closing. Wilson noticed Margaret Kelly stiffen. 'That'll be Patrick.' There was a tinge of fear in her voice.

The man who entered the living room was small and as rotund as Whitehouse. His paunch hung over his belt. His face was pudgy and his nose was purple. His head was topped with a mop of grey-flecked brown hair. He looked Wilson and Whitehouse up and down. 'Fucking peelers, it's about time.'

Wilson took out his warrant card and showed it to the new arrival. 'I'm Detective Sergeant Ian Wilson and this is my colleague Detective Constable George Whitehouse, and you'll be Patrick Kelly.' Wilson extended his hand. 'I'm sorry for your trouble.'

He looked at the extended hand but didn't take it. 'I always said that silly wee bitch would get herself killed.' He brushed past the two policemen and sat in an easy chair.

'I understand that you haven't had any contact with your daughter for about four years,' Wilson said.

Patrick Kelly looked at his wife. Wilson could see fear in her eyes. He had no doubt believing that this man was an abuser of both his wife and his daughter.

'She walked out of this house one day and didn't bother to come back,' Patrick Kelly said.

'And you haven't seen her since?' Wilson asked.

'No.'

'I wonder if you wouldn't mind accounting for your movements on the day before yesterday,' Wilson said.

Patrick Kelly rose out of his chair with an ease that belied his bulk. He crossed the room and stood directly in front of Wilson. 'I do mind.' He spat the words out. 'You think that I had something to do with my daughter's death?'

'We have information that there was an issue of sexual abuse between you,' Wilson said.

Patrick Kelly balled up his hand into a fist. 'Who have you been talking to? I never laid a hand on that child.'

Wilson looked at Margaret Kelly and saw that he had just been lied to. It was a pity that Patrick Kelly had escaped justice through the death of his daughter.

'Get out! I'm not going to have you make insinuations about me interfering with my daughter. I've nothing else to say to you.'

Wilson put on his hardest policeman face. 'Then I'm afraid that I'm going to have to ask you to accompany DC Whitehouse and me to the station, where we can carry out a full interview.'

Patrick Kelly stared at the two policemen. They were two big bastards. They could probably take him with one hand tied behind their backs. The bravado seeped out of him like air escaping from a balloon. 'Look, I'm disabled. I went to physio the day before yesterday, then I came home and spent the rest of the day in front of the box. The snooker was on from Sheffield. Ronnie O'Sullivan beat Robert Milkins thirteen frames to two. She'll tell you that I was here all day.'

'You're referring to your wife, Mrs Margaret Kelly?'

'Yes.'

'Then please refer to her properly.'

'Okay, Mrs Margaret Kelly can vouch for me,' Kelly spat back.

Wilson looked at Mrs Kelly and she nodded.

'That'll do for now,' Wilson said. 'We may need to speak to you again.' He walked across to Margaret Kelly and handed her his business card. 'If you ever need me for any reason, my number is on that card. If you lose the card by accident, you can get me at the station, Detective Sergeant Ian Wilson.'

Margaret Kelly took the card and put it in her pocket. 'I want to see my wee girl.'

'She's in the mortuary at the Royal. I'll make the arrangements. We'll need you to make an identification.'

'I'll do that,' Patrick Kelly said.

His wife stared at him. 'No, you will not.' She turned back to Wilson. 'When can we bury her?'

'There'll have to be an inquest, but as far as we're concerned, the body can be released as soon as your arrangements are made. DC Whitehouse will be in touch when the visit to the mortuary has been arranged. Once again, I'm truly sorry for your trouble.'

'HE'S GOOD FOR IT,' Whitehouse said as they walked back to the car.

'Maybe. I opened the door for his wife. If his alibi is rubbish, we'll hear from her.'

58

The forensic report was on Wilson's desk by the time he returned to the station. It made interesting reading. The flat was almost totally clean. In fact the forensic team concluded that it had probably been cleaned post-mortem. The dust bag was missing from the vacuum cleaner and every surface looked like it had been recently scoured. The search had turned up four latent prints on the underside of one of the bedside units. None had yet been identified. Wilson made a note to invite Patrick Kelly to the station to have his prints taken for elimination purposes. There were no hair follicles. There was no evidence of recent sexual activity. None of Bridget Kelly's clients had left behind a scrap of evidence that would identify them. Either she was fastidious in her cleanliness or she had the neatest clients in Belfast.

There was something very wrong with the whole scene. There were passages in American movies where the killer suited up in a plastic overall before killing but that generally happened when there was going to be a lot of blood spatter. Here, the killer had suffocated the victim, then washed the body in bleach before giving the flat a good clean.

It was going on thirty-six hours from the finding of the body and the only one they had in the frame for the murder was the victim's father. Wilson wasn't convinced in that direction. For one thing, he didn't seem like he'd be much of a cleaner. They could, of course, put out a general request for all those who had sex recently with one Bridget Kelly to please come forward. He doubted that the police phone lines would be inundated with calls in response to such an invitation. And yet, they needed to know who was the last person to see Kelly alive. As Whitehouse had surmised, the door-to-door had produced precisely nothing. Kelly was a known prostitute who plied her trade on the tenth floor of Divis Tower and none of her neighbours took a blind bit of notice of the comings and goings from her flat. Wasn't Northern Ireland just the greatest country?

Wilson walked to the whiteboard. Everything they knew about the crime was encapsulated in crime scene and autopsy photos and the autopsy and forensic reports. It was time for Bridget Kelly's little black book to turn up, but he feared that if such a book had ever existed, it no longer did. The murderer has already displayed meticulous attention to detail. He thought about Marie O'Neill. She was typical of the people of the Falls in her cynicism about the PSNI, but really her cynicism derived from a different spring. She thought that they wouldn't bother with Kelly's death because she was a prostitute. It was part of the theory of policing that said it was all right for paramilitaries on both sides to murder each other. It was only a problem when they started killing well-meaning civilians. Well, whatever other people might think, for Spence and him at least, a murder was a murder and all victims had equal value. Someone had gone to a lot of trouble not to leave evidence behind. The flat and the victim had been sanitised by someone who knew what they were doing. And then there was the appearance of CI Royson Jennings out of nowhere. If Kelly had been a tout working for the PSNI, what was the harm of saying so? It would simply open up another line of enquiry. Wilson knew the man he needed to talk to next.

59

Wilson parked his car in one of the side streets off the Falls Road. Whereas the Shankill Road is a blaze of royal blue with almost every shopfront sporting the colour that represents the Protestant religion, the Falls has a more eclectic look. Shopfronts and public houses are painted in a range of colours with the notable exception of royal blue. There is, of course, the more or less obligatory flying of the green, white and orange flag of the Irish Republic. Wilson's destination was a public house flying not one, but two, tricolours. It was a small establishment with a road front of perhaps twenty feet. He pushed open the door and found himself in a small front room with a bar against the wall on the left-hand side. Bench seating was set along the other three walls of the room with a series of tables and stools. There were perhaps a dozen men present and the conversation stopped dead as soon as he entered. He walked to the bar and ordered a pint of Guinness. The barman looked over Wilson's shoulder before beginning to dispense the drink.

Wilson sat on a stool at the bar while the drink was put in front of him.

A man left one of the tables and sat beside him. 'I heard the Crown is your pub of choice these days, Mr Wilson.'

Wilson turned and looked into Frank Cahill's rheumy eyes. 'I like to spread the joy of my company around.'

'Always happy to see you too. I heard you had a confrontation with a bomb.'

'Nothing personal, I'm sure.'

Cahill nodded at the barman, who pulled a pint of Guinness and put it on the bar. 'We're done with it, Mr Wilson. The armed struggle is over. We're committed to bringing about a united Ireland through the ballot box.' He picked up his pint and sipped the black liquid. 'But I'm sure you didn't come here to discuss politics. What can I do for you?'

Wilson smiled when he looked at Cahill. Was this man really one of the most dangerous terrorists that the island had produced? Cahill was seventy if he was a day and he looked like everyone's idea of a kindly grandfather. He was an accomplished musician and could hold a tune with the best of them. A couple of years previously Wilson had watched Cahill give a stand-out performance on television as he begged forgiveness for his part in the violence that had blighted so many lives. 'The wee girl that was found dead in Divis.'

'Aye, I heard about it. Shocking business.'

'We're having a bit of difficulty putting someone in the frame and I want to close off some avenues of enquiry. Was she a tout?'

Cahill smiled. 'Don't your own people talk to you?'

'I think they may not trust me.'

'I can believe that. Be a good man and finish up your drink and go somewhere you're welcome. That wee lassie was no more a tout than I am. And you mark my words, if I knew who the bastard was that murdered her, it would be the worse for him.'

'I tend to believe that.' Wilson finished his drink and stepped down off his stool.

'Take care of yourself, Mr Wilson. I really was sorry when I heard about your injury. There are a lot of stupid beggars out there these days.' He extended his hand and Wilson took it.

He walked back to his car. It had been a shot in the dark, but it was important to check it out. Wilson hated politics because he hated crimes that were committed to further some ideology or agenda. When he had stood in Bridget Kelly's bedroom, he was sure that he was looking at a good old-fashioned case of murder. Men have been killing women since the dawn of time. But then why the hell was Jennings sticking his nose into their case?

WILSON HAD THOUGHT about going to the Crown but had decided that he better head home. Now, he sat facing his wife across the dinner table. Their conversation was stilted and of the variety common between strangers. She asked about how the case was proceeding and he told her between bites of their shop-bought steak and kidney pies. Although Susan didn't cook, in the three years of their marriage she had amassed a small library of cookbooks. He found it strange that they were her favourite bedtime reading. He asked how things were at school, not because it was of any interest to him, but because it seemed polite to feign interest. He wondered why they were still together. They rarely talked and, despite his diagnosed sexual addiction, they rarely made love. Their relationship was developing a complexity that he hadn't envisaged when he'd first seen her in the bar of the rugby club.

The death of his father had been a watershed in Wilson's life. Pulling open the door of the garden shed and finding your father's brains plastered to the wooden planks while he lay dead in his favourite chair is not recommended to anyone. From that day he was looking for something that wasn't easy to explain or to find. He thought for a time that it was a wife and family. They weren't the only couple in Belfast to have made that mistake. Now, he desperately wanted Susan to discover his infidelity while at the same time hiding it from her. He wanted her to make the decision that he knew they should make. He glanced at his watch and saw that it was only half past eight. He thought about making an excuse to return to the station. He was most comfortable with his life when he was sitting at his desk in the squad room or tramping round Belfast prodding its underbelly.

'Would you like a pudding?' Susan broke into his ponderings.

'No. Not for me.'

He glanced at her face as they silently cleared the table. She looked so damn unhappy and he knew he was the reason.

60

Wilson had had a bad night. They had warned him at the hospital that there would be some recurrence of the pain and now he was beginning to believe them. He was limping badly when he entered the station and saw the duty sergeant nod in the direction of the bench in the reception area. He looked over and saw Marie O'Neill sitting there.

'No wee girl with you today?' he asked, sitting down beside her.

'No, she's at home with Ma.'

'She seemed like a nice wee thing.'

'She's so bloody bright, first place in her class every year. I hope she gets the chance to make something of herself.'

Unlike me, Wilson thought she might have added, but she didn't.

Instead she said, 'I wanted to say sorry in person. I came on a bit strong the other day.'

'It's understandable, you'd just lost your friend.'

'I see in today's *Chronicle* that it was definitely murder.'

'She was strangled, and our belief is that it happened during sex.'

She nodded. 'The punters love having power over us. Strangling a woman must be the ultimate thrill for some of them. Do you know who did it?'

'We're pursuing lines of enquiry, but we're not in the habit of discussing an investigation with anyone, even close family members.'

'You're giving me the spiel. It's just like I thought isn't it? She was expendable, only an oul' whore.'

Wilson stood up. 'Let's get a cup of tea in the canteen.'

THEY SAT TOGETHER AT A TABLE. Wilson noticed some of his colleagues exchanging knowing glances. He nodded at the teacups. 'The tea is just about drinkable, the coffee should be on the banned substances list.'

She didn't laugh. Possibly because banned substances weren't a laughing matter for her.

'You're married,' he said.

'After a fashion, my husband kicked me out a year ago. I had a bit of a problem with painkillers. And my tricking, of course.'

'Is there no road back?'

'I wish there was. A life on the streets is no life at all.'

'I know someone who could help.' Wilson was thinking of his ex-lover, the psychologist. 'It's never too late.'

She drank her tea. 'I might take you up on that.'

'Do you talk to the other girls?'

'Sure, you've seen it in the films, after work we all meet up in some late-night greasy spoon and discuss the punters over cups of coffee.'

'I'm serious.'

'My colleagues are also my competitors. If we get a punter who shows us a little respect along with paying the dosh, we tend to keep him to ourselves.'

'What about the bad ones? The punters that put the girls in hospital.'

She laughed. 'Are you asking if there's a sort of whores' most wanted list?'

'Something like that.'

'A couple of descriptions get passed round.'

'Anyone in particular who likes to do the strangling manoeuvre?'

'We've all had something like that happen to us. When they see the light start to fade from your eyes, they usually let go.'

'I think that might have been supposed to happen with Bridget. There were no indents on her neck. He just went too far.'

'That's not an excuse.'

'Can you ask around? Get me a name or a description of anyone who is particularly into strangling.'

'Didn't you listen to what I just said? There are plenty of men out there who like to put their hands round a prostitute's neck. You could be talking five hundred, a thousand?'

'Did Bridget always use her flat for her work?' Wilson asked.

'No, she was young and still near the top of the profession. She sometimes used a small hotel.'

George Whitehouse entered the canteen and walked over to Wilson's table. He looked at O'Neill like she was something with a bad smell. 'The boss wants to see you.'

'Tell him that I'll be along when I've finished interviewing Ms O'Neill.'

'Ms O'Neill is it?' Whitehouse said.

'Off now George, before you say something that you're going to be sorry for.'

'I don't think George likes me,' she said as she watched the corpulent policeman leave.

'There are not many people on George's Christmas card list and vice versa.' Wilson wrote the name and phone number of his psychologist on a paper napkin and passed it across the table. 'I'll give her a call and tell her that you'll be in touch.'

She picked up the napkin and put it in her pocket. 'I'll try to find out whether any of the girls have been almost murdered recently. But don't hold out much hope.'

As they walked out of the canteen, Wilson could hear the sniggers behind them. Arseholes, every one of them. He felt like punching someone's lights out but that might embarrass O'Neill. She'd already made her position on men clear and he was inclined to agree with her. Most of his gender sucked.

61

As soon as Wilson entered the squad room he received a signal from Spence to come into the office. Even through the glass partition he could see that Spence's face was like thunder.

'Sit down,' Spence said. 'We got back a report on the latent fingerprints. Two of them came up with a match. The other two were not hits.'

'Why do I think the result hasn't made you happy?' Wilson said.

'A flat used for tricks and all that Forensics can find is four bloody latent fingerprints. The place should be awash with fingerprints.'

'Not if it was cleaned within an inch of its life.'

'The two hits were guys who were already in the system. Both of them are former members of the IRA and one of them is our old friend Councillor Noel Armstrong. The other is a guy called Cathal McDonald.'

'And that made you unhappy?'

'That and another piece of information I got from my pal Denny in Forensics.' He stopped speaking.

'Are you going to tell me?'

'CI Jennings asked for a copy of the report on the fingerprints and he asked Denny not to tell us. He wasn't aware that Denny and I go back a long way.'

'The slimy little bastard, what the hell is he up to?' Wilson said.

'I have no idea but I suspect it's nothing good. One thing is for sure and that's that he's not going to tell us.'

'Maybe it's because the owners of the two latent fingerprints are men with form and members of the IRA.'

'While McDonald was always up front, Armstrong has consistently denied being a member of the IRA.'

'Guys like Armstrong always do that. They morphed from being terrorists into being politicians. It's happened the whole world over. I can't imagine that there's a political overtone to this crime though. A local prostitute has been killed during some kind of risky sex-game. There's no reason for Intelligence Division to be interested.'

'But they are,' Spence said. 'They most certainly are.'

'What do you want me to do?'

'We need to check these two characters out. There are still two latents unaccounted for. Denny has run some tests on them and both belong to women. We've never considered that the murderer could be a woman. Check whether we have the O'Neill woman's prints on file and, if not, get her fingerprinted for elimination purposes. Run down McDonald and Armstrong, find out if they have alibis for the night in question and see if we can eliminate them.'

'What about Jennings?'

'I'll make some discreet enquiries.'

Wilson left the office and went straight to Eric Taylor. 'Pull me up everything you have on Brian McDonald and Noel Armstrong. And check whether we have Marie O'Neill's prints on file.'

'Councillor Noel Armstrong?' Taylor asked.

'The very same, you know something about him?'

'Nothing, except they're talking him up. He's headed for the Assembly.'

'I need what we have on them yesterday.' Wilson went back to his desk and took out a notepad. He started drawing a mind map of the crime, looking for some way it could be of interest to Intelligence Division. It was often said that all murders in Belfast have some kind of political connection, but it wasn't true. Since the end of the conflict, a good number of killings had been the result of internal warfare within former paramilitary groups. They appeared even more comfortable killing each other than killing combatants on the other side. He remembered his promise to Marie O'Neill and he placed a call to his psychologist to ask for a favour. She agreed to help. He felt good that maybe something positive could come from Bridget Kelly's death.

62

Brian McDonald worked as a mechanic in a garage on the Whiterock Road. Wilson and Whitehouse parked directly outside and walked into the workspace. Wilson recognised McDonald immediately from the photograph on the sheet that Taylor had printed off for him. The complete left side of his face was covered by a pitted purple discolouration, which was obviously a very severe birthmark. The two police officers walked up to the mechanic and produced their warrant cards. 'Detective Sergeant Wilson and DC Whitehouse,' Wilson said as he returned the card to his pocket. 'We'd like to have a word with you. Is now a good time?' The other mechanics in the workshop had stopped work and were staring at the policemen.

McDonald put down the wrench he was holding. 'What's the problem?'

'No problem,' Wilson said. 'We're investigating the death of Bridget Kelly, did you know her?'

The right side of McDonald's face turned red. 'Aye, I knew her.'

'Have you ever visited her flat in Divis Tower?'

'Where are we going with this, sergeant? Lots of guys knew Bridget. How come you're concentrating on me.'

'We're not concentrating on you, Mr McDonald. A latent fingerprint we found in her flat has been verified as belonging to you. We simply want to eliminate you from our enquiries. If it's embarrassing for you to be interviewed here, we can continue at the station.'

'Aye, I visited her at her flat in Divis Tower.' He looked from Whitehouse to Wilson. 'I'll bet you have no trouble getting women, eh sergeant, good looking bloke like you.' He lifted up his hand to his face. 'I was born this way. It's just a whole mess of abnormal blood vessels under the skin on this side of my face. But ever since I can remember people have been treating me like some kind of leper because of it. Well I still have the same kind of urges as you and Bridget was a lovely girl. She was so kind. I wouldn't have harmed a hair on her head.'

'We're not judging you, Mr McDonald, we're investigating a murder,' Wilson said. 'It is not illegal in Northern Ireland to visit a prostitute. It's only illegal to solicit payment for sex. Did you visit Bridget Kelly on the day or the evening of the thirteenth of May?'

'No, I did not.'

'Are you able to account for your movements on that day and evening?' Wilson asked.

'I was at work all day.' McDonald nodded at the other two mechanics who had returned to their jobs. 'The lads and the job cards can confirm that. Then I played a game of five-a-side football, had a few pints and went home.'

'Are there people who can confirm all this?'

'Absolutely.'

'I'd be grateful if you'd write down a detailed account of your movements on the thirteenth and beside each event put the names of the people who can confirm your alibi. DC Whitehouse will pass by tomorrow and collect your statement. And thank you for your cooperation.'

They walked out of the garage and started back towards their car. 'What do you think, George?' Wilson asked.

'I don't like him for it, sarge,' Whitehouse said.

'Now there's one for the books,' Wilson said. 'Finally we agree on something.'

63

Councillor Noel Armstrong wasn't so easy to locate. His office on the Falls Road had no idea where he might be. The councillor was a sort of free electron who wandered round Belfast taking impromptu meetings. Wilson left his card at the office and requested that Armstrong contact him as soon as possible. Wilson declined to give the secretary a reason. He didn't want Armstrong to arrive with a series of prepared answers.

Back at the station, Wilson went immediately to Spence's office. 'McDonald isn't our man,' he said as soon as he entered.

'It would have been convenient.' Spence didn't look happy, the pressure was beginning to tell. 'There must have been dozens of men through that flat.'

'Then there should have been dozens of fingerprints but there weren't. We need to think about the salient points of this case. The forensic report says it all. Either Bridget Kelly was a cleanliness nut or the place had been sanitised. There isn't a hair on the bed or in the bedroom. We've picked up only four fingerprints. The body was washed in some kind of bleach. The murder may have been a mistake but the clean-up wasn't. The murderer did everything to ensure that he wasn't going down. Then we have the interest of our friend Jennings.'

'I've been asking around,' Spence said. 'Gilligan and Jennings run a tight ship. Every time I mention their names I get a blank look. Nobody wants to talk about them.'

Wilson looked through the glass partition and saw the duty sergeant coming towards Spence's office. He opened the door.

'There a Councillor Armstrong downstairs asking for Detective Sergeant Wilson.'

Wilson looked at Spence. 'You want this?'

'Your ball, you carry it. Take George along.'

Wilson left the office and signalled for Whitehouse to follow him.

ARMSTRONG WAS SITTING on a bench reading a copy of the *Chronicle*. He put away the paper and stood up slowly as soon as Wilson and Whitehouse appeared. 'Detective Sergeant,' he held out his hand. 'I received your message and came here immediately.'

Wilson shook the proffered hand. 'This is DC Whitehouse.'

Armstrong didn't offer his hand so Whitehouse nodded.

'How can I help you?' Armstrong said.

'Perhaps this would be better in one of the interview rooms,' Wilson said. He turned to the duty sergeant. 'Is number one available?'

The duty sergeant nodded and Wilson led the way. When they were seated at the table in interview room one, Armstrong immediately took the initiative. 'Is this a formal interview?'

'Not really, but we can make it formal if you wish,' Wilson said.

'I'd prefer to keep it informal if you don't mind,' Armstrong lounged in the chair.

Wilson noted that he was totally comfortable. He looked as though he spent his life in interview rooms.

'Now how can I help you? You didn't tell my secretary what it was you wanted with me.'

'As you know we're investigating the death of Bridget Kelly,' Wilson began.

'A very sad business,' Armstrong said. 'I've met the family and offered them my condolences and whatever help I can give. My office has been on to Social Services to see if anything can be done to defray the costs of the funeral.'

Ever the politician, Wilson thought. 'We have now established that Ms Kelly was murdered.'

Armstrong held up his copy of the *Chronicle*. 'So I see from the newspaper reports. Most of the people in our community were of the opinion that her death was due to some kind of drug overdose.'

'I'm not at liberty to discuss details of Ms Kelly's death,' Wilson said. 'Our forensic team were most thorough in their examination of the murder scene. Perhaps you would like to tell me why one of your fingerprints was found in Ms Kelly's bedroom.'

Armstrong put a shocked look on his face that in Wilson's experience didn't quite make it. He knew about his fingerprint being found. 'I have no idea, Detective Sergeant,' Armstrong's voice was clear and steady. 'I may have visited Ms Kelly's flat while out canvassing, but I have no recollection of being in her bedroom.'

'I'm sure that there is some innocent explanation,' Wilson said. 'I wonder would you be able to furnish us with your movements for the evening and night of the thirteenth. And I would be grateful if you would indicate for each event the name of a person we might contact to confirm your information.'

'You want me to provide myself with an alibi?' Armstrong said.

'You could indeed see it that way,' Wilson said.

'No problem,' Armstrong said. 'I'll have my secretary type it up and deliver it here this evening. I keep a very detailed diary, but I would ask you to keep the contents confidential. I hold meetings with very influential people and I wouldn't like the whole of Belfast to know my business.'

'Thank you for your cooperation, sir,' Wilson stood and extended his hand. 'I'm sure that DC Whitehouse will be very discreet when checking your alibi.'

Armstrong stood. 'Always happy to help the police. I hope you catch whoever killed that poor girl.'

Wilson led the way out of the interview room and back into the reception area. He opened the door and saw Armstrong out.

'I don't like him for it either,' Whitehouse said as they watched Armstrong climb into a red Honda Civic.

'Back to square one, George,' Wilson said, and he wasn't talking about the state of the investigation.

64

Wilson was alone in the squad room. He had grasped two things during his interview with Armstrong. The first was that Armstrong knew in advance that his fingerprint had been found. The second was that his alibi would hold up. Armstrong had made sure of that before he turned up at the station. He knew that neither of these two factors would be enough to conclude that Armstrong was the killer. They had found a latent fingerprint belonging to him in the girl's bedroom. So what? Bridget Kelly was a prostitute who mostly dealt with clients in her home. The existence of McDonald's print proved that point. There was not a shred of evidence against Armstrong, but Wilson found something creepy about the man. He had been too bloody cool in the interview room, so self-assured it actually grated on Wilson. An RUC report on Armstrong was emphatic that he was a high-ranking officer in the IRA and that he had been instrumental in interrogating and punishing traitors. Despite evidence to the contrary, Armstrong always insisted that he had no connection with the IRA and that he was simply a local politician. If the RUC/PSNI file was to be believed, Armstrong's interrogation skills would have come in handy in anticipating

Wilson's questions. The bastard was laughing up his sleeve at them.

Wilson thought about calling Marie O'Neill and asking her to join him for a drink, but did he want to ask her questions, or did he have an ulterior motive? His brain told him that he should go home and have dinner with his wife. But he wasn't thinking with his brain. He was still in two minds when the door opened and Spence walked in.

'You still here?' Spence pulled up a chair and sat beside Wilson.

'I'm finishing my notes on the interviews with McDonald and Armstrong. What's your excuse?'

'I've just been hauled over the coals for our lack of progress on the Kelly murder. Please tell me that there's been some progress.'

'If I worked on intuition alone, I'd say that Armstrong could be our man. But there isn't a shred of evidence against him. Aside from the latent, we have absolutely nothing. George is checking out his alibi, but I bet it's watertight.'

'You go up against Armstrong and you better have plenty of hard evidence in your hand. Nobody saw anyone in the vicinity of the flat on the night in question, there was no murder weapon and there was no motive. So we're light on means, motive and opportunity.'

'Maybe the other working girls will recognise him as a regular punter.'

'You've read his file?'

Wilson nodded.

'Even some of the more brutal members of the IRA are scared shitless of the man. He's ruthless and vicious. I'll bet he came over all cooperative and smarmy in the interview room.'

'I believe he already knew that we'd found his fingerprint. He also knew that his alibi would hold up.'

'Can we break it?' Spence asked.

'I doubt it.'

'Then we're between a rock and a hard place, again.'

'I was thinking of having another word with the O'Neill woman.'

Spence raised his eyebrows. 'I think that you are possibly getting away with your evening forays into the Crown. But I doubt that Mrs Wilson would be too pleased to hear that you're dabbling in forbidden fruit. Go home, eat your dinner and watch television like the rest of us.' Spence turned to leave but stopped at the door. He turned back to look at Wilson. 'You've got the makings of a good detective. The only one who can stop you from becoming one is yourself.'

65

Wilson respected and liked Spence but didn't always take his advice. When he woke the next morning, he wished that he had. He remembered the Crown and talking about rugby with a mass of new friends during the evening. These new friends were happy to ply him with whatever beverage he desired as long as they could be in his company and he continued to regale them with stories from the dressing room. He half-remembered stumbling home and finding that Susan was already asleep. Somewhere in the recesses of his mind he had made the decision to tell her that they were no good together and that they should part. But the resolve the alcohol had created had disappeared by the time he came to a bleary version of himself in the spare room. He lay in bed listening to the sounds of his wife making breakfast in the kitchen. He would wait until she had departed for her job as a schoolteacher before going downstairs.

He had the feeling that this was going to be the decisive day in the hunt for Bridget Kelly's killer. He knew that Brian McDonald's alibi was going to hold up. The only question was would Noel Armstrong's. Many of the citizens of Northern Ireland appeared to have been born with the gift of bilocation.

A gunman seen by several witnesses at the scene of a crime had his presence miles away attested to by a dozen or more friends and neighbours. Alibis were a dime a dozen. McDonald and Armstrong both had hands so they possessed the means to kill Kelly, but then again so did virtually all the inhabitants of Belfast. They probably both had the opportunity, but so did all the other men who visited Kelly's flat but whose fingerprints had been erased. And what the hell motive could someone have for wringing the neck of a pretty twenty-year-old? His head was pounding as he heard the front door open and close and then the sound of a car engine from the street below. He pushed himself up from the bed and stumbled in the direction of the toilet.

An hour later, after a shower, two paracetamol tablets and three cups of coffee, he had managed the journey into the station. He entered the squad room expecting one of Spence's disapproving looks. He had been there before and he would survive.

'Well, look what the cat dragged in.' Spence stood behind Wilson's desk. 'I know that you've been told this before, but you're not going to find the solution to any of your problems in the bottom of a pint glass.'

'Not today.' The pills were wearing off and the headache was returning with double the force. Armstrong's statement on his whereabouts was on the desk in front of him. The local councillor had been true to his word. He had submitted a detailed paper with names and telephone numbers of witnesses.

'George is handling McDonald,' Spence said. 'How are things going with Armstrong?'

Wilson held up the sheets of paper. 'We're only missing his trips to the toilet, that is if he made any trips to the toilet. I looked him up and he's married. I expected his wife to be his main alibi for the evening of the murder, but that isn't the case.' He pointed out a name he had highlighted.

Spence whistled softly. 'Now that is interesting.' The name was well known to members of the PSNI. 'The press would like to have wind of this. Have you contacted her?'

'Not yet, I wanted you to see it first.'

'I wouldn't do it by phone and I don't want you smelling like a brewery when you speak to her. Leave her until the end.'

'This is like using a sledgehammer to crack a nut. He could have listed his wife. I'm sure she would have backed him up.'

'That's the trouble with wives,' Spence said. 'They sometimes harbour a grudge and they are prone to kick you in the balls at just the very moment you don't want them to. Lovers are much more reliable.' Spence looked round the squad room. He and Wilson were alone. Whitehouse was off checking McDonald's alibi and Taylor had slipped out for his morning fag break. 'Marie O'Neill was here this morning looking for you.'

Wilson took Armstrong's paper from Spence's hands. 'She doesn't think we're going to put in the effort necessary to find Bridget Kelly's killer because she was a prostitute.'

Spence frowned. 'She might not be totally wrong. Our superiors at HQ were wetting themselves when they saw that Armstrong might be involved.'

'That explains Jennings' involvement.'

'So naïve,' Spence said. 'Jennings and his boss don't give a shit what the boys at HQ think and they certainly don't act for them unless there's something in it for them. Jennings being involved worries me because I can't even guess why he's monitoring us. But one thing is for sure, he's not doing it for HQ. By the way, Eric told me that O'Neill's prints were on file but don't match any of the latents. She is a good-looking girl. You're not screwing her by any chance?'

'Give me a bit of credit will you, Boss. She's a witness in a murder case. If we ever get someone in the dock, a barrister would use a relationship like that against us.'

'My God, there's a policeman in there after all. I thought that the thing in your trousers did all the thinking for you.'

'That doesn't mean that I haven't thought about it.'

66

Wilson was lucky enough to run across a colleague who was able to supply him with aspirin, vitamin B tablets and a mint mouth spray. Within the hour he felt able to face the world outside the station. Investigating Armstrong's alibi involved a tour of the Catholic areas in West Belfast. Wilson was obliged to take statements from people in Ardoyne, Andersonstown, Divis and the Falls. Everyone that Wilson encountered not only confirmed the alibi but lavished praise on the busy councillor. And yet, the arrogant way Armstrong had approached the interview at the station had raised Wilson's hackles. However, a man couldn't be accused of murder just because of his attitude towards the investigating police officers.

Wilson was in the throes of making a decision never to drink again when he found himself outside Clement's Café in Donegall Square. He bought himself a double espresso and took a seat at a table close to the picture window. There was one more person to interview before he could give Armstrong the all-clear. They would soon have to face the fact that if McDonald's and Armstrong's alibis held up, their lines of enquiry were few and far between. If Marie O'Neill's figures were correct and there were twenty thousand punters in the province, the investigation would be headed for the bin. He looked at his watch. It was time to move. He finished his coffee and started for the northern side of the square before turning right along Chichester Street. He gave himself twenty-five minutes to arrive at his destination, mainly because his newfound limp slowed him somewhat.

The Laganside Courts building had only recently been opened and Wilson had not yet had an opportunity to put his foot inside. He walked to the entrance on Oxford Street and stood before the four-storey building, noting the green glass windows and the Portland limestone. The inside mirrored the outside, a tile floor gleamed and glass and wood predominated. It was a far cry from the conditions in the old courthouse across the road.

Wilson showed his warrant card at the reception and was told to wait. He recognised Margaret Whiticker as soon as she entered the vestibule. She was dressed in a black suit and white blouse and moved with the nervous energy associated with ambitious people. He'd never had the dubious pleasure of dealing with her, but colleagues who had didn't wish to have a second experience. She was well on her way to becoming one of the most prominent solicitors in Belfast.

'Sergeant Wilson.' She switched her briefcase to her left and extended her now free right hand.

Wilson shook her hand. She had beautiful blue eyes, but her face was rather lopsided and her brown hair was mousy and lank. He had checked her out and she was currently single after an acrimonious divorce. 'Thank you for agreeing to meet me at such short notice.'

As soon as he let her hand go, she moved it to his right elbow and applied enough gentle pressure to move him to the edge of the main concourse and away from the flurry of legal eagles rushing to and fro. They eventually settled into an alcove away from the crowd heading for lunch spots close to the courts.

'Now, sergeant, what do you wish to know?'

'We're currently investigating the death of the young lady whose body was found in Divis Tower.'

'I've read about it in the papers.'

'I'm charged with verifying the alibis of several individuals. Councillor Noel Armstrong has given you as an alibi for the evening of the thirteenth. In effect, he claimed to have spent the night with you.'

There was a moment of hesitancy before she spoke. 'That is my recollection.'

Wilson thought that they were a strange pair. 'So you verify that Armstrong spent the entire evening and night with you.'

'Yes, we dined together at my flat and he stayed the night.'

Wilson waited for a further explanation but there was none. 'Are you and he in a relationship?'

Again there was a moment of hesitancy. 'Not exactly, we met casually a few weeks ago and Noel called and I invited him over. I don't think that our relationship is the issue here.'

'I'm sorry if it sounds like I'm prying.'

'That's exactly the way it sounds.' There was an edge to her tone.

Wilson suddenly found himself on the defensive. 'I wonder would you please prepare a statement confirming Mr Armstrong's alibi and sign it.'

'If you think it necessary.' She moved her fingers through her hair.

'I'm afraid that I do.' Wilson noted that she appeared nervous but put it down to them discussing elements of her private life.

'Given the confidential nature of this statement, I'll have to type up something myself. I presume that the PSNI will maintain my confidence. Will this evening be soon enough?'

'Of course, you've already verified the alibi. The statement is only a matter of procedure.'

'If that's all, I have a meeting with a client.' She started to move away.

'You won't forget the signed statement.'

She didn't answer or look back.

Wilson watched her departing figure. Catholic councillor with IRA connections having a fling with a Protestant solicitor known for defending Protestant paramilitaries. Maybe there was hope for Ulster after all.

67

Wilson arrived back at the station just before one o'clock in the afternoon. As soon as he entered, he saw Marie O'Neill sitting in reception with closed eyes. Wilson shook her awake and helped her gently from the seat. 'Not here.' As he turned to leave the station, he saw the look the duty sergeant gave him. O'Neill's constant presence in the station would add fuel to the rumour that he was having his way with her. They stood on the street looking at each other. 'You've got to stop dropping by the station,' Wilson said.

O'Neill bristled. 'I want to know what's going on. My friend was murdered and I don't want her to be forgotten.'

'We're investigating Bridget Kelly's death as we do with every murder victim. We've collected whatever physical evidence there was and we're pursuing a number of leads. Unfortunately, there were no witnesses to the murder, there was no murder weapon and so far we haven't been able to develop a motive. Our best guess is a dangerous sexual game that went too far.'

Her face reddened. 'So she died because she allowed men

to do things to her that they wouldn't do to their wives? It was simply an occupational hazard?'

He sighed. 'If you leave us alone, we might catch a lead that will help us solve this crime. But this dropping by the station day and night looking for a personal update has got to stop.'

'I'm sorry.' Her body relaxed. 'I know that you're doing your best. It's just that people treat prostitutes like shit. Bridget Kelly is dead, so what? There's no word about why she was obliged to sell her body or about the men who took advantage of her. I want the man who killed her to be found, but it doesn't sound like you're going to be able to do that.'

'Don't give up hope. We'll keep plugging away. Sooner or later we'll catch a break.' Wilson could almost taste the lie on his lips. 'When that happens you'll be the first person I'll contact. In the meantime, stay away from the station. My boss had words with me about you. You're married and so am I. Did you contact my psychologist?'

'I'm meeting her this evening.'

'Good, I really hope things work out. You're not cut out for the life. Go back to your husband and child.'

'Forget about Bridget?'

'That's not what I said. A very wise preacher said "let the dead bury the dead". I don't always follow his advice, but I think you should. Think about putting your own life back together. Bridget is gone. Pretty soon she'll be in the ground. You're still here.'

It was the moment for a hug or a kiss or some form of closure but neither of them moved. Eventually he spoke. 'If something breaks, I'll be in contact.' It wasn't quite closure, but it was the best he could do.

68

The evening briefing was a sombre affair. Spence and his small squad knew that they were going nowhere and fast. The lack of physical evidence was crippling the investigation. Wilson had been back over the house-to-house and had seen nothing new. Their initial lines of enquiry were gradually drying up and the instruction from HQ was to bin the investigation as quickly as possible. The *Chronicle* had stopped running stories as, very much as O'Neill had predicted, the death of a prostitute had limited news value.

'What about Whiticker?' Spence asked. Whitehouse had already disclosed that McDonald's alibi was sound.

'Solid as a rock,' Wilson said. 'Do you know her?'

'We've met,' Spence said. 'No chance of breaking her?' He didn't seem to think so himself.

'None,' Wilson said. 'But she's lying. I think he did it.'

The three men looked at him. Spence smiled. 'Messages from above?'

'No,' Wilson said. 'Just a feeling in my bones. There's too many things wrong with this murder. Bridget Kelly wasn't a neatness freak, but her flat was as clean as a whistle. There was a vacuum cleaner in the closet with no bag. The smell of bleach was overpowering. We're supposed to believe that some random punter had the composure to clean up so completely when he'd just murdered a woman, probably by accident. There's a dead body lying on the bed, but he gathers the sheets and remakes the bed without leaving a trace of DNA. Then he meticulously cleans the flat, leaving one of the best forensic teams in the UK with virtually nothing. O'Neill claims that there are twenty thousand punters in the province. How many of those would have had the coolness not to panic and immediately split? Then there's the involvement of our friends in Intelligence Division. What stake do they have in the investigation? Armstrong knew that we'd found his fingerprint before he entered the interview room. Who told him? If you wanted to build a stonewall alibi, who would you use? Your wife? No, one of the top solicitors in Belfast would do nicely. Armstrong claims that he was never a member of the IRA but our people say different. There's even evidence that he might have been involved in the "Nutting Squad" that dug out traitors in the organisation. It all fits. There's no real evidence but it all fits.'

Spence put his hand on Wilson's shoulder. 'It's a nice theory, but if you brought it to the DPP, you'd be laughed out of the room. In order to advance we'd have to crack his alibi and according to you that's not going to happen.'

Wilson went to his desk and returned with a sheet of paper. 'This came from Whiticker's office this afternoon. It's a signed statement that Noel Armstrong spent the evening and the night in the company of Margaret Whiticker. If we break that alibi, this piece of paper would end Whiticker's career as an officer of the court. It's one hell of an enormous risk to take if it's not true. So why is Whiticker taking that risk?'

'Perhaps she's not taking a risk,' Spence said. 'Maybe it's the truth and your well-constructed theory is wrong.'

Wilson laid the paper on the desk closest to the whiteboard. 'I agree that if we don't break the alibi we're done. If it was some cool-as-ice punter who we haven't been able to identify yet, then we're done.'

The phone was ringing in Spence's office. He left the whiteboard and the squad watched as he took the call. He rejoined them and looked at each of them in turn. 'We have a call out, someone just found the body of an indigent in a ditch in north Belfast. It looks like he's the victim of a hit-and-run driver and he's been in the ditch for some time. Sergeant, you're with me.' Spence started moving towards the door.

A reluctant Wilson followed. The thing that hurt him most was the fact that Marie O'Neill had called it from day one.

BOOK 3
Belfast, 2017

69

When Wilson woke he found that he had fallen asleep at the dining table. The Bridget Kelly file was spread out in front of him. On a pad beside his right hand were notes that he had made while examining the file. They had royally fucked-up that investigation. Maybe it was the addition of the coincidence of the file going missing that clinched it. The bastard had slipped them once, but he was determined that there wouldn't be a second screw-up. However, nailing Noel Armstrong was going to be no easy matter. He was no longer a lowly city councillor. He had risen on the political tide of peace. An elected member of the Northern Ireland Assembly, Armstrong had been given a ministry to boot.

The number one task was to find the woman who had been prepared to perjure herself for him fifteen years ago. He had no idea where Margaret Whiticker was, but he was going to find her. Armstrong was Teflon and Wilson wanted to know why. Why was a murderer allowed to go free and why was he aided and abetted by someone, or more likely a lot of someones. Perhaps his IRA colleagues had been employed in the clean-ups at Bridget Kelly's flat and again when Rasa Spalvis's dead body had to be dealt with. There might well be people within that organisation with the requisite skills.

When he had completed his ablutions, Wilson made himself a coffee and a plate of scrambled eggs. While he ate, he opened his laptop and saw that Reid had made five attempts to Skype him. He was going to take some flak from her, but it had been worth it. It was the middle of the night in LA and there was no point in trying to reach her now. Instead, he put the name Margaret Whiticker into Google and came up with nothing. She didn't have an online presence and there were no recent articles with her name, but there wasn't an obituary either. If Whiticker were dead, then so was his investigation. She was the first step in bringing the murderer of Bridget Kelly and Rasa Spalvis to justice.

Outside, daylight was flooding over Belfast and there were large fluffy white clouds in a clear blue sky. The Irish weather god had got the weather wrong again. There was going to be no rain today. Maybe. He picked up the phone and called Spence. 'We need to talk. I'll be in Portaferry in just over an hour.' He put down the phone before Spence had a chance to reply. He quickly remade the file and shoved it and his notes into a briefcase. He was anxious to get on the road.

THE VIEW from Spence's house on a fine day was something to behold. Yachts were already heading into Strangford Lough for a day's sailing or making their way out to the Irish Sea. Donald Spence was seated at a small teak table on the deck in front of his house, nursing a cup of coffee. He stood as Wilson climbed out of his car carrying a briefcase. There was a first time for everything, he thought.

'Where did you get that thing?' Spence said, nodding at the briefcase.

Wilson looked at the black leather bag in his hand as though seeing it for the first time. 'Kate's mother packed it by accident when they threw me out of the apartment. It's one of Kate's old ones. I meant to give it back to her but the occasion never arose.'

'Coffee?' Spence retook his seat and nodded at a coffee pot and cup placed on the table beside him.

'Definitely, and lots.' Wilson pulled the file and his notes from the briefcase while Spence poured a cup for his guest and a refill for himself.

Spence pushed the cup across to Wilson. He could see that his colleague was in a high state of excitement.

Wilson laid the file out on the table. 'Armstrong murdered Bridget Kelly and Whiticker's alibi was bullshit.'

'Okay, take me through it.'

Wilson spent the next half hour going back over the elements of the Kelly case that pointed to Armstrong. He used his notes to expand on the items they had ignored in the initial investigation. 'The people in the Divis Tower were a close-knit lot. Armstrong was their council representative so they were used to him wandering round. Nobody would have thought to mention him when the door-to-door officers were asking about any strangers in the vicinity.'

'What about the clean-up?' Spence asked.

'That's where things get tricky.' Wilson pulled out the autopsy report from the file. 'Campbell estimated the time of death as somewhere between ten and twelve o'clock the previous evening. We have to assume that most of the materials used to clean the flat were already there but that would not apply to the type of bleach used on the body and on the flat itself. Despite his protestations to the contrary, Armstrong had good connections with the IRA. He could have phoned someone and asked for their help.'

Spence sat silently for several moments. He picked up the coffee pot and stood up unsteadily. 'This coffee needs refreshing.'

Wilson watched his former boss move off the deck in the

direction of the kitchen. Something he'd said had shaken Spence. He sat looking out across Strangford Lough and wondered whether this was the way he was going to spend his twilight years. The white sails of the yachts danced across the sparkling blue waters. It was at least ten minutes before Spence returned with the fresh pot of coffee. He sat down heavily on his seat.

Wilson took the coffee pot and poured two cups. 'What's up?'

'Maybe it wasn't someone in the IRA that he called.' Spence spoke slowly and deliberately.

Wilson sat back in his chair. It felt like he had been hit with a bolt of lightning. All the coincidences in the Kelly case coalesced and the conclusion jumped out at him. 'Armstrong was a tout.'

Spence picked up his cup of coffee and there was a slight tremor in his hand. 'A guy like Armstrong wasn't just any old tout. He was one of the men who ran the "Nutting Squad". He sought out the traitors in the IRA, interrogated them and sent them on their way.'

'So, if you wanted to get rid of anyone in particular, he was a good man to have on your side.'

Spence held his cup in both hands and sipped. 'If he was part of the so-called dirty war, the people who ran him will do whatever is necessary to cover up their involvement.'

'Say that he didn't only do Kelly. Suppose that he's still a tout and he did the Spalvis woman. Considering that the body was dismembered and buried in different locations, the almost total lack of evidence – no murder weapon, no initial cause of death, no murder site, no apparent motive – and the fact that someone cleaned up just as meticulously as they did in Divis Tower fifteen years ago, it looks like a match.'

Spence put down his cup, spilling some coffee onto his saucer. 'Jesus Christ, Ian. Gilligan and Jennings had to be part of it. Gilligan is gone, but Jennings is now deputy chief constable. If we're right, these people would have no compunction in removing us from the scene. Can you imagine the importance of someone like Armstrong to the intelligence services? Ex-member of the "Nutting Squad", senior Sinn Féin politician, member of the Northern Ireland Assembly and now a bloody minister. They would move heaven and earth to ensure that Armstrong was safe.'

'I want him, Donald. He's murdered two women that we know of and that's probably the tip of the iceberg. He's a monster.'

Spence took a deep breath. 'Maybe we're running away with ourselves. There's still virtually no direct evidence against Armstrong in either case. We've just been playing a game of "what if". It's all hypothetical.'

'But it fits.'

'That doesn't mean that it's true. Think about it, Ian. Armstrong is a big fish and your chances of landing him are negligible. You go anywhere in the PSNI with this crazy idea and you can be sure that Jennings will hear about it. That means the men in London who covered up these crimes are going to hear about it and the life of a detective superintendent in the PSNI means nothing in the great game of keeping the realm safe.'

'So he walks.'

'He won't be the first and he won't be the last.' Spence looked at the file on the table. 'Take my advice and burn that file. Send it in the same direction as the original has already gone. I curse the day I made the copy.'

'You did it because you smelt something rotten about the Kelly investigation. It niggled at you so much that even when you left the job you took the file with you.'

Spence knew that Wilson was right. He had been the senior investigating officer on several dozen murders. He hadn't solved every case and there were several investigations where he was certain he knew the identity of the culprit but the evidence wasn't there and the final decision of the DPP had been not to prosecute. But he hadn't made a copy of the file of any of those other cases and he hadn't kept it in the box under his bed. Maybe he knew Gilligan and Jennings too well. 'Let it go, Ian.'

Wilson started bundling up his file. 'I can't. The Spalvis investigation is still ongoing.'

'What are you going to do? Put Armstrong at the scene of the crime? You don't have a crime scene to put him at. Check his car for bloodstains? You know that it wasn't him who dismembered the body. Face it, he's going to walk on this one too.'

Wilson started stuffing the file and his notepad back into the briefcase. 'Not if I can help it.'

Spence looked out across the lough. He picked up his coffee cup and drank. His hand was as steady as a rock. 'It's a fine day to be alive.' He looked over at Wilson. 'How are things with Reid?'

'It's close for her mother.'

'Life is such a precious thing. The string that attaches us to it is as thin as a strand of gossamer, but we don't realise it.'

Wilson stood in front of his old boss. 'You've always been a good friend, Donald. And I have dearly tried your patience.'

He held out his hand and Spence took it. 'You've been like a son to me, Ian, and to Miriam. We like having you around and we'd hate it if something happened to you.'

Wilson smiled and let Spence's hand go. For just a second Spence looked old and tired. He picked up his briefcase and started for the driveway.

Miriam Spence came out of the house and stood beside her husband. 'I thought on such a fine day that we'd have lunch outside and that Ian might stay.'

Spence put his arm round his wife as they watched Wilson climb into his car and wave before reversing down the driveway. 'That would have been nice but he has a bit of business to attend to.'

70

Peter Davidson had been a copper for a long time. He put his survival down to his highly developed sense of the relationship between risk and reward and the fact that he had made a lot of friends both inside and outside the force. He was never the first through the door, he left that to the guys who wanted to make sergeant and were willing to put their lives on the line to do so. He had never seen reaching retirement age as having attained the brass ring, but now he felt he'd have to call in some old favours in order to get there. There were many risks associated with the rewards provided by his enjoyable dalliance with Irene Carlisle, but they were dealing with some heavy-duty operators. They? No, he was in this investigation pretty much on his own.

He had been following the trail of the phone that had made the call cancelling Jackie Carlisle's appointment. A company operating in CastleCourt shopping centre had allotted the number to one of its cheapest phones two days before it was used to make only two calls. It had cost Davidson fifty quid to get a copy of the debit card that had been used as identification. A quick check at the station revealed that the card had been stolen. Another dead end, he thought, as he took a seat at a window table in Starbucks on the first floor at CastleCourt.

A man wearing a security guard's uniform put a coffee cup on the table, pulled up a chair and sat down beside him.

'How are they hanging, Pete?'

'Not too bad, Joe, how about yourself?' Joe Hall had been one of those who liked to be first through the door. Unfortunately his bravado came from a bottle and, after a couple of screw-ups in which civilians were injured, Hall was requested to seek alternative employment and accept a reduced pension. He gratefully accepted and launched a new career in mall security.

'So so.' Hall switched off the body cam attached to his uniform. 'We're not supposed to switch this fucking contraption off even if we're in the shitter. Everyone should have a few private moments during the day though. What can I do for you?'

'How long do they keep the CCTV footage in here?'

'Months.' Hall blew on his coffee. 'They're paranoid about personal injury claims being made months later. If some idiot says he slipped on an ice cream and busted his arse, they want to have a record of the event when the insurance company starts to scream.'

'How many months?'

'I've no fucking idea. I work down here on the floor. There's a booth upstairs where a guy monitors the cameras, looking for bag snatchers and shoplifters. You wouldn't believe the kinds of people I've picked up in here. Their purses are full of money and yet they feel the need to steal something worth a couple of quid. Doesn't make sense.'

'So where is all this CCTV footage kept?'

Hall laughed, exposing a mouthful of gapped teeth, and pointed out through the window and up at the sky. 'The cloud. It's all digital these days. None of this searching for a cassette only to find that some idiot recorded a porno movie over the CCTV footage. They can store whatever they want for however long they want it.'

'And say that I needed to see the footage from a certain shopping area on a certain day.'

Hall switched on his body cam. 'The company I work for prides itself on its use of advanced technology. He switched the body cam off again.

Davidson stroked his chin. Hall had been a clown and nothing had changed. 'Give me that in English without the ad.'

'They have a programme. You type in the day, the hour and the camera and, hey presto, you're looking at the recording in seconds.'

'And do you know how to use this programme?'

'Not exactly, but I know a guy who does. Where are we going with this?'

'I need to see some footage, but I don't have a court order and my bosses won't give me one.'

'Doing a little moonlighting, Peter?'

Davidson sighed. 'I wish, at least that might bring in a bit of dosh. We're looking into a possible murder. The hierarchy wants the case closed, but we're looking into it anyway.'

'You still with Wilson?'

'Aye.'

'I'll talk to someone.' Hall stood up. 'Here, same time tomorrow, have a coffee and Danish pastry ready for me.'

Davidson watched Hall waddle down the left corridor of the central mall. This was him in two years' time. Tramping up and down the corridors of some shopping centre or other wearing an ill-fitting uniform and having his arse kicked by some young up-and-coming executive. Having to work for minimum wage to augment the amount of his paltry pension left when his wives had been paid off. Unless, of course, he managed to land the widow Carlisle. And that meant getting her the insurance money from her husband's death. He was putting his head into the lion's mouth, but this time the reward far outweighed the risk.

71

It was almost lunchtime when Wilson returned to the station. On the way back from Portaferry, he had been mulling over Spence's advice. He usually respected his former boss's opinion. Spence had more than twenty years' additional experience and had managed to pilot his way through the political morass that was the PSNI. So why couldn't he take Spence's advice now? Other murderers had walked. The Peace Process had opened the jails and many of the men he had worked hard to put behind bars strolled out to open arms and marching bands. Maybe it was time he grew up. There was a big picture and he occupied only a small corner of it. If he threatened the big picture, he would have to take the consequences. Rory, Harry and Siobhan were working at their desks when he entered the squad room. He asked Siobhan to join him in his office.

As soon as she had closed the door, he said, 'I want you to locate the whereabouts of Margaret Whiticker, that's W-H-I-T-I-C-K-E-R. Fifteen years ago she was a solicitor here in Belfast. I can't give you any other clues, but those magic fingers of yours should be able to find out where she is currently.'

O'Neill wrote in her notebook. 'Okay, Boss, anything else?'

'Yes, and this needs to be kept between the two of us for the moment, I want you to get the plate numbers of all the vehicles that Noel Armstrong MLA has access to.'

O'Neill stopped writing and looked up.

'Is there a problem?' Wilson asked.

'Not really, you just caught me by surprise.'

'Just find out the information and give it to me and me alone.'

She thought that he looked tired. 'Yes, Boss, is that all?'

'No, there is one more thing. It has taken me quite a while, but I've remembered.'

Her eyebrows raised and her eyes widened.

'You were maybe ten or eleven at the most,' Wilson said. 'You sat on the bench downstairs with your sister Marie.'

She smiled. 'Well remembered.'

'I've been re-examining Bridget Kelly's file and it finally clicked with me. Where's your sister now?'

O'Neill's smile faded. 'Dead. She died of an overdose five years ago.'

Wilson hid the shock he felt. 'I liked her. I gave her my psychologist's number and she said she was going to talk to her.'

'Aye, she did. It went really well for a while. When she was in counselling, she gave up the drugs and . . . ' Siobhan's face turned a vivid shade of red as she searched for the words, 'stopped living the way she had been. She even got back with Patrick. But then he discovered that she was doing drugs again and threw her out. Her life spiralled out of control from then on.'

Wilson felt like giving himself a kick in the arse for not following up with Marie. The Bridget Kelly investigation ended up in the bin, as it was supposed to. And he was off tilting at other windmills and meeting Kate McCann. Then Susan was diagnosed with the cancer that would eventually take her life. 'I'm sorry.'

'She liked you,' O'Neill said. 'She used to talk about you all the time when she was seeing the psychologist. I think she had a crush on you.'

Another time, another place, another life, Wilson thought.

'You seemed to be close,' he said. 'You must miss her.'

'Every day.' There was a tear in the corner of her eye that was refusing to flow.

'Okay, get on and bring me Whiticker's address and the plate numbers. And shut the door on your way out.'

Two o'clock in Belfast, six o'clock in the morning in LA and still too early to call. Wilson leaned his chair back and put his legs on his desk. He found himself in the situation that every detective hates the most. Having waded through the crap, he was pretty sure he knew the culprit but was forced to agree with Spence that nailing the bastard was going to be pretty nigh impossible. He assumed that Military Intelligence was ultimately responsible for running such an important asset. The Brits had had dozens of touts in the IRA, but he doubted any others had risen to the exalted heights of Minister Noel Armstrong. Launching an investigation into Armstrong's sexual behaviour was playing with his career. A single word from the minister into the chief constable's ear would be enough to ensure that Wilson drew an early pension. The story of Armstrong's treason to the IRA would never come out while he was still breathing. Once he was laid to rest in Milltown Cemetery, the whispers could begin and the life that had been lived in secret would be exposed. The prototype had already been established with Jimmy Savile, Cyril Smith and others. Spence was certain that Armstrong would never spend a day in the dock. Wilson wasn't so sure.

72

As soon as the small hand hit the four and the big hand hit the twelve, Wilson brought up Skype to call Reid. There were three rings and then her beautiful face filled the screen. 'Where the hell have you been?' there was an edge to her voice.

'Sorry, things have been a little crazy over the past few days. Every time I wanted to get in touch with you the timing was wrong. How are things with your mother?'

'Things have been a bit crazy for me too. You remember the bag that the hospital gave my mother with enough opioids inside to get a small village high? Well, I tried to get the stuff from her but she held on to them for dear life. And she's had a buzz on ever since. She should be having palliative care, but she's running round like a sixteen-year-old.'

'That's good, isn't it?' Wilson said. 'She should be enjoying the last few weeks of her life.'

'What college did you study medicine at?'

'Just trying to be helpful.'

'If you really want to be helpful, get yourself over here pronto.'

'I will. There's just something I need to do first.'

'I'm following McDevitt's reports in the *Chronicle* online. As far as I can see you're up against a brick wall.'

'I think I know who is responsible.'

'Really? Well bang him up as quickly as you can and get yourself to Belfast International.'

'Would that it were so simple. Ever run across a guy called Noel Armstrong?'

'*The* Noel Armstrong? Minister Noel Armstrong?'

'The very same.'

'Yes, I've met him socially and he's a smooth operator. You're in a different league.' Her face froze on the screen and Wilson hit the refresh button. Then he realised that it wasn't a computer glitch.

'Please tell me that you're joking?' she said when her face started moving again. 'I'm not joking.'

'Then please tell me that you have him bang to rights.'

'I haven't any evidence against him yet, but I know that he did the Lithuanian and another woman fifteen years ago.'

'You look tired, Ian. You've been working too hard. You need to get yourself out of there and lie in the sun over here for a while. My mother is going to run out of steam in the next few days and it'll be like removing the last block in a game of Jenga. The whole edifice of her being will collapse. And I'm going to need you here when that happens.'

Wilson swallowed hard. He could see that he was being put on the spot with regard to their relationship. If he failed this test, there would be consequences. Whenever he'd been down this road before, he'd unfortunately been found wanting. 'I'm going to do my best.' He knew that his best might not be good enough.

'There are some other considerations that we need to discuss face to face.'

'That sounds ominous.'

'It's this bloody Skype thing. It's like email. People are not themselves on it. Look, I want you here with me.'

'When I clear the Lithuanian case.'

Reid's mother's head suddenly pushed into the screen. 'Hi, Ian.' She waved. Her face was skeletal. 'Steph and I are going to Malibu for lunch today.'

'I hope you have a great day,' Wilson said.

'We will.'

Reid came back on the screen. 'Stay clear of Armstrong, Ian. He's a heavy hitter with serious connections.'

'He's a murderer who has killed two women that we know about.'

'Jesus, Ian, bin the Boy Scout act. People like Armstrong never see a day in jail, no matter what they've done.'

Wilson didn't respond.

Her face took up the whole of the computer screen. 'Promise me that you're not going to do something stupid.'

'I won't do anything stupid. Enjoy Malibu.' He broke the connection.

He sat at his desk gazing at the PSNI screensaver. In the space of a few hours, two people whose opinions he respected very much had warned him off pursuing Armstrong. He knew their reasons were valid. If Armstrong was a tout for British Military Intelligence, and if they in turn were involved in covering up two murders he had committed, then they would do everything in their power to ensure that their role would never see the light of day. His phone beeped and he looked at the message. Jock McDevitt was offering a farewell drink at the Crown. He was in sore need of that drink.

73

McDevitt was already ensconced in Wilson's preferred snug by the time Wilson arrived at the Crown. 'It may never happen,' he said, looking up from the papers on the table in front of him.

Wilson sat down. 'It's been a tough day following a tough night.'

McDevitt ordered the drinks.

'Guinness and whiskey,' Wilson said. 'Are you spending the film money already?'

'The more I look at it the more I think the film thing is a cod, but they're paying for the trip and I'm a journalist who never turns his nose up at a freebie. No, the whiskey is because I think I'm going to make your day worse than it already is.' He pulled out a sheet of paper and passed it to Wilson. 'That's going to appear in tomorrow's *Chronicle*.'

Wilson read the words slowly – *McCANN, Mrs HELEN is delighted to announce the engagement of her daughter Katherine to Gerald, son of Sir Peter and Lady Geraldine Lattimer of Coleville House, Ballymoney. The happy couple hope to announce their wedding plans shortly.* – Then handed the page back to McDevitt.

The drinks had arrived. Wilson picked up his whiskey and downed it.

'As bad as all that, is it?' McDevitt sipped his Guinness.

'That ship sailed a long time ago.' Despite believing what he said, Wilson couldn't deny experiencing some sense of sadness and perhaps jealousy. There was the feeling of what might have been. But his relationship with Reid was a lot more real than what he'd had with Kate. He had moved on and there was no reason why she shouldn't as well. But still, marriage made it irreversible and final.

'Want to share?' McDevitt asked.

'Possibly,' Wilson smiled, 'if you weren't a journalist.'

'I can stop being a journalist.' McDevitt sensed something deep and disturbing behind Wilson's visible depression and it had nothing to do with Kate McCann.

'Oh yeah, just like a leopard can shake off its spots.'

'You saved my life. I'm a journalist, but I'm also a friend. Right now I think you need the friend more than the journalist. It's the Lithuanian woman's case, isn't it?'

Wilson didn't reply.

'Everyone knows that prostitutes are soft targets and putting the bastards that kill them behind bars isn't easy.'

Wilson sipped his Guinness. 'Please don't say that the police don't follow up because of her profession.' He was remembering Marie O'Neill's prediction.

'It's debatable. Did you read the Byford Report into the investigation of the Yorkshire Ripper case? It was only when Sutcliffe started murdering non-prostitutes that the investigation got serious. Even then he was caught only by chance because he was driving a car with a false licence plate and a young prostitute inside. Judging by the statements released by your crowd, your investigation into this case isn't going anywhere. You have no idea who did it.'

If Wilson had been a twenty-year-old copper full of bravado he would have jumped up and shouted that he knew who had done it but that he just couldn't prove it. Instead, he quietly and carefully stated, 'He's out there somewhere and he's done it before.'

'You've connected two cases?' McDevitt said. 'Now you really have to share.'

'Bridget Kelly, fifteen years ago.' Wilson sipped his drink.

McDevitt's brow furrowed. 'I'd just started on the crime beat for the *Chronicle*. Strangled in Divis Tower, no perpetrator ever found. Is that correct?'

'Not a shred of evidence left at the crime scene,' Wilson said. 'No, I lie. We were able to link two partial prints to men with iron-clad alibis. The flat and the body had been sanitised. It was a very professional job. We thought at the time that a copper might have been involved. The case of the Lithuanian woman, as you call her, has taken it to a whole other level. No crime scene to process, difficulty identifying the victim, no indication whatsoever of who might be involved. You're right, we're looking at a blank wall.'

'Do you think he'll kill again?'

'Now that's the journalist talking. I don't know. He's the only one who can answer that question. The murders weren't premeditated. He likes strangling women while he's having sex with them. Perhaps he likes it a lot or maybe he only needs to satisfy himself occasionally.'

'But you have a theory,' McDevitt said.

'I have a theory.' Wilson waved for a second round of drinks.

'And it involves?'

'I'm finished sharing. What time are you off tomorrow?'

'First thing in the morning.'

'For how long?'

'Up to a week, depends on the other side. We might be booted out on day one.'

The waiter arrived with the second round of drinks and Wilson paid. He took a page and wrote Reid's telephone number on it. 'Contact Stephanie, she's expecting to hear from you.'

McDevitt took the paper and put it in his pocket.

'I envy you,' Wilson said. 'I'd like to be on that plane with you.'

'Remember, life is short and then you die.' McDevitt picked up his whiskey.

74

Wilson woke early and went for his usual run just as light was breaking over the city. Despite the golden sunrise, there was a nip in the air. The meteorologists were predicting a hard winter, but what was new. He pounded the pavement with an unusual intensity. His sleep had been disturbed by another night of mind movies. Every time he closed his eyes, scenes of death floated across his mind, old cases resurfaced and the victims climbed out of their graves to remonstrate with him. His tee-shirt and training top were damp with sweat when he returned to his apartment.

After a shower, he prepared his breakfast and took up his usual position on the couch facing the picture window that exposed the waking city. It was his favourite time of the day. Somewhere out there Noel Armstrong was lying snug in his bed, safe in the knowledge that his crimes had been covered up by the people he had served so well for so many years. It wasn't Wilson's place to judge him or to pursue him for being a traitor to the IRA. He had no truck with terrorists of any variety. But he was sure that Armstrong had murdered two women and that was the reason he would have to have justice. Until that happened, Wilson was going to have a lot more bad nights.

How was he going to get Armstrong? That question ran round in his mind as he watched the city come alive. He was all about shining a light into dark corners, but he was not always happy with what he found there. Armstrong was a product of the dirty war in Northern Ireland. The war that nobody talks about. The war where unseen hands decided who would live and who would die.

WILSON WAS in the station early. He spent a few minutes examining the whiteboard on the Spalvis murder. Nothing had been added in two days. The investigation was moribund. He was tempted to add a picture of Armstrong with the words 'Prime Suspect' written above it. But Rory and Harry would ask sensible questions to which he had no answers. He was sitting in his office when O'Neill arrived. He nodded at her and, after first consulting her computer and collecting some papers, she made her way to his office.

'What have you found?' he asked as soon as she entered.

'Armstrong has one personal car.' She put a photo of a black Mercedes 220 on his desk. 'That's a photo of the actual car so the plate is valid. He also has a car provided by the Assembly that comes with a driver. He has no personal access to that car. His wife drives an Audi A6.' She gave him a copy of the licence plate.

He looked at both papers and put them aside. 'Good, what about Whiticker?'

She consulted her notebook. 'No sign of her in any of our databases. She paid her taxes up to 2006 and then there's nothing. Her membership of the Law Society of Northern Ireland lapsed the same year.'

'So, she's no longer living in the province. That means she probably emigrated.' Damn it, he thought. She could be anywhere in the world. 'Keep trying. See if she has any family members still here who we can contact. She can't have disappeared completely. I suppose you've checked the death records?'

She shook her head. 'Not yet.'

'Find her, Siobhan.'

'I'll do my best, Boss,' she said.

Wilson looked outside and saw that Harry was at his desk. 'Tell Harry I want him.' He watched as she left the office and spoke to Graham.

'Take a seat, Harry,' Wilson said as Graham entered the office. 'I have a little task for you. It's sort of off the books so I don't want it to become common knowledge.'

Graham sat down. He liked working for Wilson, but there were beginning to be too many off-the-books jobs going round. Davidson was on one that could end up getting him killed.

Wilson took the picture of the Mercedes and the paper with the Audi's licence plate on it and handed them to Graham. 'I want to know if either of these two cars were picked up on CCTV in central Belfast on the evening of the thirteenth.'

Graham examined the picture and the licence plate. 'Who are we dealing with here?'

'The Mercedes belongs to Noel Armstrong and the licence plate is for his wife's Audi.'

Graham looked up slowly from the picture of the Mercedes. 'Would that be the Noel Armstrong that I often see pontificating on the late-night news?'

Wilson nodded.

'And we are seriously looking at him for doing the Lithuanian?'

Wilson nodded again.

'I can see why it's off the books. Have you any suggestions how I might ask to view the CCTV from Traffic without informing them as to the ownership of the Mercedes?'

'Not at the moment. But you're an experienced detective and I'm sure you'll come up with something.'

'What do we have on him? I thought we had no suspects. How did he suddenly appear on the radar?'

Wilson told him about the connection to the Kelly case.

'You're pissing against the wind, Boss. And you know what that leads to. If they find out at HQ that you're looking at Armstrong, first they'll have a fit and then they'll transfer you to the back of beyond. Looking at a minister means having a truckload of evidence first.' He looked directly into Wilson's eyes. 'And we both know that that's not the case.'

'Find the car on CCTV and leave dealing with HQ to me.' The number of people telling him to drop the investigation into Armstrong was mounting. Maybe they were right and he was wrong. Harry was right on one point: when it went to HQ he'd better have more than his dick in his hand.

Graham stood up. 'It's your funeral, Boss. I'll do my best on this but without authorisation I wouldn't hold my breath.'

Wilson sat alone in his office. It took five years and thirteen murdered women for the whole West Yorkshire police force to locate Sutcliffe. He didn't have five years or the resources of a complete police force. And even one more dead woman would be a failure on his part.

75

'I don't like you going dark on me,' Yvonne Davis stared at Wilson, who sat like an errant schoolboy in front of her. 'I'm supposed to be briefed daily on progress on the Spalvis case but instead you've been avoiding me.'

Wilson put on his most earnest look. 'Nothing could be further from the truth, ma'am. We've been following lines of enquiry that have led us absolutely nowhere. I'd rather report nothing than have nothing to report.'

'When you prevaricate in this manner, I get very worried. Tell me, Ian, what *exactly* have you been up to?'

Wilson was seated on a comfortable chair, but he shifted uneasily. 'As you are well aware, ma'am, there is precious little evidence in this case. Therefore, we have been forced to develop theories that might possibly fit the crime. One of those theories is that Spalvis may not have been this particular killer's first victim. O'Neill has been looking back through the files to identify similar crimes.'

'And?' Davis prompted.

Wilson had put his foot in the door and he decided that he might as well go the whole way in. 'There was a similar murder in Belfast in 2002. A young prostitute named Bridget

Kelly was found strangled in Divis Tower. By coincidence, I worked on that case myself as a detective sergeant with Donald Spence.'

'And you never found the murderer?'

'No. The similarities didn't end with the occupation of the dead woman or the way she died. There was not a scrap of evidence found at the murder scene except for four latent fingerprints, two of which were traced to males with iron-clad alibis.'

'Why am I getting the feeling that you're not giving me the full story here?'

'I don't know, ma'am. Perhaps it's the fact that when we went to locate the archived file for the Kelly case, it had vanished.'

Davis sat back in her chair. She had a vision of her job in HQ flying out the window with wings attached to each side. 'And what do you think is the significance of that, superintendent?'

Wilson noticed that they were no longer on first name terms. Davis's success had not been the result of her connections, she was one of the minority who had a talent for the job developed over many years of grunt work. He could dance round the issue she wanted to discuss, but sooner or later she was going to drag him back to the point. 'I think that maybe one of our colleagues removed the file with the intention of destroying it.'

'That's a serious allegation. I assume you have evidence to back it up.'

'No, ma'am, but I can't see some guy wandering in to Musgrave Street station, heading down to the basement, managing to divert the attention of the officer in charge and rifling through the files until he found Bridget Kelly's, at which point he stuffed it up his jumper and then left without attracting any attention whatsoever.'

'You have a point.' She had an idea where this was going

and it wasn't good. 'So let's have this hypothesis of yours in full.'

'Perhaps the killer of Bridget Kelly and Rasa Spalvis are one and the same man. There's no evidence in either case. A significant clean-up in both cases left us flapping about like a bunch of idiots. Maybe we should assume that while the killer acted alone in terms of the murder, he may have been assisted in the clean-up by a person or persons unknown.'

She glanced down at her desk drawer. There was a bottle of Rescue Remedy in there for stressful situations and she badly needed it. She doubted it would quell the rising stress in her body, but it was worth a try. 'Let's cut to the chase, do you have any idea who killed these two women?'

Wilson hesitated. Once he dipped his toe in the pool that was facing him there would be no way back. 'I think Noel Armstrong is good for the Bridget Kelly murder and by corollary also for the Rasa Spalvis murder.'

Davis's stomach did a somersault while she tried to compose herself. Wilson had just named one of the most powerful politicians in Northern Ireland as the murderer of two women. 'Continue.'

'According to our intelligence, Armstrong held a high rank in the IRA. Then, like all the rest who had any brains, he morphed into a politician and started climbing the greasy pole. Let's assume for a moment that while in the IRA he became a tout for either Military Intelligence or Special Branch. He would have been a very important asset. Let's say that he had an accident during a sexual encounter with a young prostitute that led to her death. I don't think that he would panic. But he might have made a telephone call to someone. That telephone call would have caused consternation. The loss of such an asset would have been unthinkable for the men who had made their careers running him. So a clean-up squad was sent to Divis Tower and the scene was sanitised. Then the men in charge watched Spence and me wasting our time trying to put a case together. And we almost did. We found the latents that the clean-up had missed. But the investigation was being dogged by a police officer, presumably acting on behalf of whoever Armstrong worked for. The latents were enough to put Armstrong in the frame, but he was warned about them in advance and a cast-iron alibi was constructed. Fast forward fifteen years, another accidental murder and the phone call needed to be made again. Another clean-up, even more thorough this time, so we're faced with an even bigger conundrum. No murder scene, initially no identity of the victim and no forensic evidence. In the meantime the Kelly file was disappeared in case we were able to put two and two together.'

'And all this is hypothetical.'

Davis was now a whiter shade of pale and Wilson didn't blame her. The outline he was putting on the table held enormous risks for both of them. 'Hypothetical, yes, but it fits.'

'And, of course, you know the identity of the police officer who dogged the initial investigation.'

'It was DCC Jennings.'

The silence in the room was the deepest that Wilson could remember. Davis was stunned and speechless. Although her mouth was moving, no words were coming out. Wilson picked up a carafe from the table, poured a glass of water and put it in front of her. 'Drink.'

Her hand moved to the glass and she sipped the water. 'This conversation never took place,' she said as soon as she regained her composure.

Wilson waited until she had finished the glass of water. 'Of course, ma'am.'

'What do you intend doing?'

'My job.' He stood up and started for the door.

76

Peter Davidson was back at a window table in Starbucks in CastleCourt. Joe Hall, security guard and one-time colleague, had called early that morning to confirm that he had fulfilled his request. At the time, Davidson had been enjoying a leisurely breakfast with Irene Carlisle in the conservatory where Jackie Carlisle had died. He was now spending three to four nights a week chez Irene. The accommodation was vastly superior to his small flat and the after-dinner entertainment was of the highest calibre. The widow Carlisle had definitely thrown off her inhibitions and was performing like a wanton houri. Interestingly, the pillow talk continued to centre on how the investigation was proceeding and their life together when the insurance money would roll in. Taken at face value, his life had improved immeasurably and there was the prospect that it could improve even more if Wilson and the team proved that Carlisle had been murdered. People often say 'every cloud has a silver lining', but experience told him that in fact 'every silver lining hides a very dark cloud'. Although Irene professed her undying love for him, he knew there was a good possibility that love might disappear as soon as his usefulness was over. He was a decent lover but an aging one and Irene wouldn't hesitate to trade him in. As he waited for Hall to show up, he ran through some possible strategies he could employ to cement his relationship with Irene. He came to the conclusion that there was really nothing he could do except enjoy the ride.

'Morning, Peter,' Hall dropped onto the seat facing Davidson and in front of a coffee and round Danish pastry. He picked up the coffee and sipped it. 'It's cold.'

'You're late.' Davidson stood up, went to the counter and returned with two more coffees. Meanwhile, Hall switched off his body cam.

'You're looking flash,' Hall said, putting both his hands round the coffee to warm them.

Davidson was wearing a new shirt and jacket that Irene had bought for him. Either by accident or by design she had left the tags on so he knew that both items had been expensive. He felt embarrassed now that Hall had noticed they were far better than his usual threads. 'You said that you'd made progress.'

Hall stopped eating the pastry and fished underneath his heavy jacket. He produced a USB advertising his employer and laid it on the table in front of him. 'It's amazing what they can get onto these things. The bloke who does the programming says that you have the full day's CCTV from the phone shop on that. It's in a zip file, whatever that is.'

Davidson reached across the table towards the USB, but Hall put his hand over it.

'I think you've been telling me little porkies, Peter. There's no way that you're working on something official. If you were, getting a warrant for the phone shop would be a piece of piss. That means that you're moonlighting and sticking a few quid in your pocket. A sound enough bloke like you should push a few quid my way.'

Davidson could see that Hall had made up his mind. He looked at the USB. There was a very good chance that whoever had called to cancel Carlisle's appointment was on it. 'How many quid are we talking about?'

Hall leaned across and felt Davidson's new jacket between his thumb and forefinger. 'What about a hundred?'

Davidson laughed. He had exactly thirty-five pounds in his pocket. Wilson would pay him back but that was in the future. 'This jacket, believe it or not, was a gift from a lady friend. I can give you a score, but it's out of my own pocket.'

'Oh, I believe that all right. You were always very handy with the ladies. Seventy-five.'

'I don't have it, twenty-five and that's the maximum.'

Hall picked up the USB and started to put it back inside his jacket. He looked at Davidson. 'Fifty.'

'Thirty,' Davidson said. 'It's no good to you and it might turn out to be worth nothing to me, but I'm ready to gamble thirty on it.'

'Show me.' Hall started to withdraw his hand from his jacket.

Davidson took out his wallet and counted out thirty pounds on the table. Hall pushed across the USB and pulled the money in his direction. 'You always were a canny wee bastard, Peter.' He stood up. 'Anything else I can help you with?'

Davidson shook his head. 'Not in this lifetime, I hope,' he said when Hall was out of hearing.

77

Royson Jennings dropped two Buscopan tablets into his mouth and washed them down with a glass of water. His stomach had been cramping for the past two days for no apparent reason. He hadn't been sleeping well either and it was beginning to show on his face. Davis's last report on the investigation into the Lithuanian woman's murder had been everything he'd hoped it would be. And yet something wasn't quite right. He kept telling himself that he was in control of events. There was no evidence and no prime suspect. It would take a leap of the imagination for someone to put Icepick in the frame. But then he remembered who the SIO was and the leap of the imagination became a distinct possibility. Why had the silly bastard murdered a woman just as Jennings was about to reclaim his former position? He looked at the mass of paper on his desk. There were reports that he should read and letters that he should sign, but he could not concentrate on them. He had turned his computer screen off because it was oscillating before his eyes.

What the hell was happening to him? He put his hand on his heart and felt to see if there were any palpitations. When he had told his dying father that his ambition was to be the youngest chief constable of the PSNI, his dad had gasped, 'There'll be a price to pay.' Why was he remembering that moment now? He was almost there. If it hadn't been for that idiot Harrison and the ubiquitous Wilson, he would already be sitting in the office down the hall. He had to get a grip on himself. He was safe. The Bridget Kelly file had been destroyed. His role in protecting Icepick would never come to light. His colleagues in Special Branch and Military Intelligence would do everything in their power to ensure that the Icepick affair stayed secret. He tried taking deep breaths. There was still a ninety per cent chance that the whole Spalvis affair would die the same death as the Bridget Kelly murder. He suddenly felt his spine stiffen. And when it did, they were going to have to deal with Mr Icepick. Minister or not, that lecherous bastard was not going to threaten his career again. They would find the incriminating dossier he had left with whoever and they would plant the bastard in six feet of earth.

78

Siobhan O'Neill had spent most of the day staring at a computer screen. Her eyes were red-rimmed. Margaret Whiticker had managed to disappear off the planet. O'Neill had started with Northern Ireland and then checked the rest of the UK. Her first port of call when searching for someone was always HM Revenue & Customs. The motto of the taxman should be 'you can run but you cannot hide'. However, that wasn't the case with Whiticker. Her last filing with HMRC had been in 2006. At that time she did not request a refund, as someone who was leaving the country might have done. She didn't file again and simply vanished off the employment register. The Department for Work and Pensions database showed that she had never claimed any social welfare benefits. A check of the NHS hospital registrations showed that nobody name Margaret Whiticker had entered hospital since 2002. After rechecking several times, O'Neill came to the conclusion that she was no longer resident in the United Kingdom. That was a major problem. Margaret Whiticker was evidently a woman who didn't want to be found. She could be anywhere in the world. If a person wanted to stay hidden and there was no police warrant out for them, then all they had to do was drop out. As long as they had money. She thought about contacting the Missing Persons Bureau at Bramshill Police College in Hampshire, but she knew Wilson didn't want to publicise the search.

O'Neill was frustrated. She desperately wanted to deliver results for Wilson. He had tried to save her sister and it wasn't his fault that Marie had slipped back into drugs and prostitution. She increasingly believed in predestination, and it was Marie's fate to be taken by drugs. Her own fate was to be the one in the family who was ordained to look after their mother. She loved her mother, but she was still young and dealing with someone descending from dementia into Alzheimer's was not for the faint-hearted. The stress had initially affected her metabolism and she had gained weight. Lately she had been seeing the psychologist Wilson had recommended for Marie, and she was beginning to gain control over her life.

She stared at the screen. She needed to start at the beginning. She pulled up the birth record for Margaret Whiticker. The birth certificate showed that Margaret was born on April twenty-seventh 1972 to Rachel and Maurice Whiticker, residents of Finaghy Road, Belfast. That would make her forty-five years old. There was a good chance that at least one of her parents was still living. She looked up Maurice Whiticker and found that he was no longer resident in Belfast. Then she checked the death records and found that he had died, aged sixty-five, in 2007. She returned to the birth records and found that Margaret had a younger brother, Simon, and a younger sister, Alice. She looked up Simon Whiticker and found a Doctor Simon Whiticker attached to Musgrave Park Hospital. It was only minutes from Finaghy Road and worth a shot. She picked up the phone, called the hospital and asked to speak to Dr Whiticker. She was put through to his secretary, who told her that he couldn't be disturbed. O'Neill left the number of the station and asked for the doctor to phone back as soon as he was free, mentioning that it was a police matter.

She tried to piece Wilson's requests together. There hadn't been a briefing in two days, which meant that Wilson wasn't in sharing humour. The boss was holding his cards close to his chest and she was having a bit of difficulty understanding why he wasn't involving the team. First there had been the car numbers. She knew who Noel Armstrong was but had no idea why Wilson was investigating him. It had to be something to do with the Spalvis murder because she'd overheard Harry talking to someone in Traffic, trying to get some CCTV tapes for central Belfast. Then there was this Whiticker woman. Her phone began to ring and she picked up the receiver.

'May I speak to Detective Constable Siobhan O'Neill please.' The voice on the end of the phone was smooth and cultured so there was no way it was one of Siobhan's friends taking the piss. It was the voice of the kind of guy she would like to meet on Tinder.

'Speaking,' she said.

'It's Doctor Simon Whiticker, you left a message for me to call you.'

Now she understood the dulcet tones. 'Thank you for calling back. Are you the brother of Margaret Whiticker?'

'Yes, why do you want to know?'

'We're trying to locate her. Could you please tell me where she lives?'

The phone went dead in her hand. The jerk had hung up on her. At least she had found a relative and his reaction said that he knew where to find his sister. She scribbled his details on a notepad and headed straight for Wilson's office.

79

Wilson grabbed his coat. 'Rory, you're with me.'

Browne put on his jacket and followed Wilson out of the squad room. He was glad of the action. He had been stuck in the office, reviewing the evidence from the Spalvis murder and, despite further interviews with the forensic team and the pathologist, nothing new had come to light. 'What's the deal, Boss?'

Wilson was loath to bring other members of the team into his confidence and that applied particularly to his sergeant. Browne had already admitted that he had been coerced into spying on Wilson by Nicholson. 'This definitely has to go no further,' he said before giving Browne an outline as to why he needed to contact Margaret Whiticker.

They were in the car heading for Musgrave Park Hospital by the time Wilson finished his story.

'You really think that there's a connection between two crimes separated by fifteen years?' Browne asked.

'The crimes are similar in nature, but it's the cover-up that made me look more closely at a connection. Someone went to a great deal of trouble in both cases to ensure that the culprit wasn't found. Whiticker was the vital witness in Armstrong's alibi for the Kelly murder. If that alibi is broken, it's a whole new ball game.'

Musgrave Park Hospital sits on a piece of open parkland between the M1 motorway and the Upper Lisburn Road in south Belfast. Browne entered the hospital grounds and drove directly to the visitors' car park. They walked to the Meadowlands building, where Dr Whiticker had his office and consulting rooms. Wilson showed the receptionist his warrant card and asked to see Dr Whiticker. He refused to give the reason for the visit. They were in the reception area for five minutes before a well-dressed young lady approached them and introduced herself as Dr Whiticker's secretary. The doctor was currently with a patient and would see them as soon as he was finished. If they wished, they could wait in the cafeteria. She estimated that the doctor would be available in fifteen minutes. Wilson and Browne declined and took seats directly facing the interior of the building.

Just over ten minutes later the secretary returned and led them to an office where a brass plaque on the door announced Dr Simon Whiticker MD, DO.

Wilson entered the office first and took his warrant card from his pocket. The man seated behind the desk could not have been more different from his sister. Whereas she was plain, he was handsome with a head of perfectly groomed salt and pepper hair and a well-trimmed red beard . The siblings had no features in common and although fifteen years had passed Wilson vividly remembered Margaret's large nose and lank hair.

'You can put the warrant card away, superintendent,' Whiticker stood. 'I've seen you play many times. In fact, I had hoped that you might have been sent here for rehabilitation after your, shall we say, accident. Please sit. Unfortunately, I'm rather busy today so I can give you only a few minutes.'

Wilson stood aside so that Browne could enter the small office. 'This is Detective Sergeant Browne.' Wilson sat down in a chair facing Whiticker and indicated to his sergeant to take the chair beside him. 'We won't detain you any longer than necessary. I understand our colleague DC O'Neill spoke to you earlier.'

'Please apologise to her for my brusqueness. I'm not usually so bad mannered. It's just when it comes to Margaret my brain appears to malfunction.'

The apology sounded genuine to Wilson. 'As DC O'Neill told you, we wish to interview your sister, but we can't find a local address or telephone number for her. Her registration at the Law Society of Northern Ireland lapsed several years ago. Perhaps you'd be so kind as to tell us where we can contact her.'

Whiticker picked up a pen from his desk and started to depress the button at the top in rapid succession producing a clicking noise. 'My sister had a mental breakdown. She had been suffering from depression and became addicted to opioids. She ended up as a patient in Woodstock Lodge. She has had some sort of recovery, but she is still in a very fragile mental state. It was impossible for her to return to practising law. In fact, I doubt very much whether she will ever be able to work in any capacity again.' He looked at Wilson and saw that he was waiting for an answer to his question. 'I'm sorry, whenever Margaret is the subject of a conversation I tend to ramble on. She was quite brilliant at school and college, first-class honours all the way. Perhaps she pushed herself too hard. And the drugs were the last straw. Why exactly do you want to speak with her?'

'I'd prefer to discuss that with her,' Wilson said.

'As I said, she is in a very fragile state. It would be very easy to send her back to square one. I really would prefer to know what she's facing.'

Wilson was torn between being professional and being human. He could understand Whiticker's concern for his sister, but the reality was that Margaret Whiticker had probably perjured herself and perverted the course of justice and there was no statute of limitations on either of those charges. Thankfully it would not be him who would decide to prosecute. If he explained that situation to her brother, he doubted whether he would learn her present location. 'I understand where you're coming from, but all I can say is that your sister can help us with our enquiries into a crime that was committed fifteen years ago. I can assure you that we will handle our contacts with her with discretion and if there is any follow-up you will be kept informed.'

Whiticker put down his pen and stroked his chin. 'I don't like the sound of this very much. I assume that time is an issue here.'

Wilson nodded.

'I'm going to trust that you're a man of your word and that you'll do everything in your power not to upset her. She lives alone in a cottage on the north coast of Donegal.' He wrote an address on a piece of paper and passed it to Wilson. 'I'll phone ahead and tell her that you'll visit.'

'She won't run?' Wilson asked.

'She has nowhere to run to,' Whiticker said, a tinge of sadness in his voice. 'You'll keep me informed?'

Wilson and Browne stood. 'Of course,' Wilson said.

The two policemen walked back to their car. 'Where to, Boss?' Browne asked.

'Back to the office. I need to pick up a car.'

80

Yvonne Davis studied her face in the mirror of the ladies room at the station. She looked her age. Makeup wasn't the usual stock-in-trade of the policewoman, but Davis thought that she was skilful enough to cover the incipient lines on her face. There would be no concealing the heavy bags that were forming under her eyes, however. She tried to remember the last time that she had had a full night's sleep. She was shocked when she realised that it had been months rather than days or weeks. She supposed it came with the territory. She had already sacrificed her husband and children and now it looked like her health would be the next to go. The past few nights she had woken with her heart pounding. She wouldn't be the first over-achiever to succumb to a heart attack. Perhaps she'd sold her life for a mess of pottage.

Doubtless her recent run of sleepless nights had a lot to do with Wilson and his pursuit of Noel Armstrong. She had been out of her mind not to close down that line of enquiry as soon as Wilson raised it. If Jennings ever found out that they were investigating a minister in the Assembly, she would be for the high jump. She felt a sudden wave of relief at the possibility. They would find a nice little billet for her and allow her to eke out the rest of her days lecturing at some police college. That didn't sound so bad. Back home at a reasonable hour and sleeping soundly at night, but she was in the business long enough to know that it was a mirage. She would die of boredom. She needed to keep everybody sweet until Wilson had played out his cards on Armstrong. She brushed some hair out of her eyes and stood up straight. If she crashed and burned, then so be it.

ACROSS BELFAST, DCC Royson Jennings was chairing a meeting at PSNI HQ. He looked at the faces of the six senior officers seated at the table with him. He knew that one of them had just finished speaking, but his mind hadn't registered the comment. Six faces stared at him, awaiting his response. He wasn't about to admit that he hadn't been listening. 'I think the point is important, but it needs to be fleshed out. Perhaps we could have a paper on it for our next meeting.' The six heads nodded at the sagacity of their leader's comment. 'Now, I'm rather busy so we're finished for today. My secretary will advise you of the date of the next meeting. And I expect to have a discussion paper on my desk by the day after tomorrow.' He stood and walked back to his desk, ignoring the sycophantic mutterings from the men at the table.

As soon as his colleagues had left, he reached into the top drawer of his desk and removed a bottle of white antacid liquid and took a large draught. His ulcer was killing him. The tests performed by his doctor had shown that the ulcer was a figment of his imagination, but he knew better. His stomach was a better barometer of the future than Tarot cards and it was telling him that there was a storm coming. It was a storm that had been brewing for a long time and one that he had stupidly ignored. Davis had been avoiding him and that was a clear sign of trouble. His first instinct was to lash out at her. But he knew that would solve nothing. Wilson was the real problem. He was the kind of detective who would start playing with a little cut, pushing it this way and that, until he opened up a massive wound. What was the bastard working on? According to the latest briefing, the Spalvis case was dying a slow death. There was no evidence to speak of and certainly nothing that would point the finger at Icepick. That was what was happening on the surface, but he knew that something else was going on beneath the surface that he was not being informed about. He couldn't get over the feeling that all was not well. It was time to check out the supposed spy in the camp. He picked up the phone and called Nicholson. 'Find DS Browne and get him here, now.'

81

Peter Davidson had missed out on the computer generation. He watched with amazement whenever his son and his nephews manipulated their control units and made the soccer players on the screen run, pass and score goals. He had attended the requisite PSNI computer courses and he was just about able to do simple searches and compile basic reports. So, when he sat down and plugged in the USB that he'd obtained from Hall, he had no idea what to do when the zip file appeared on the screen. His saviour was, however, sitting just across the room. 'Siobhan,' he called. 'Do you have a few minutes to spare?'

O'Neill stood up and pulled her chair over beside Davidson. 'What can I do for you?'

'I got this USB from a contact. It contains CCTV footage from a mobile phone shop. How do I play it?'

She pushed his chair aside and sat in front of his computer. He caught a whiff of her perfume. It was quite subtle, but feminine and rather appealing. O'Neill had changed over the past few months. She was no longer dowdy. She had slimmed down and blossomed into a very attractive woman. He watched as her fingers skimmed over the keys.

'Okay,' she said finally. 'The footage you have is in RAW. The easiest way to view it is to convert it to .avi or .mpg.' Again, her fingers flew over the keys and he watched the screen as she downloaded a programme and began the conversion. 'This is going to take a few minutes. What are we looking for?'

'The phone that was used to cancel Carlisle's hospice appointment was bought in the phone shop on the day this CCTV footage was recorded. The guy used a false credit card and identification.'

'Any idea what time he was there?'

'Some time in the afternoon.'

She turned back to the screen. 'We're ready to go.' She clicked on a file and the interior of the mobile phone shop in CastleCourt came into view. She expanded the picture and the faces of the service personnel could be clearly seen. 'The resolution is good. If your man looked at the camera we'll get a perfect shot of him.'

'Can you speed it up?'

She clicked on a button at the side of the screen and the people in the picture started to move faster.

Davidson watched the timer. The shop opened at nine o'clock in the morning. When the clock at the bottom of the screen showed that five hours had elapsed, he asked her to return it to normal speed.

They sat close together and watched the screen. 'If you've got something better to do?' Davidson said.

'Not really, I'd like to see this guy.'

Time passed and people came and went from the shop. After about an hour a man wearing a baseball cap entered the shop and went to the desk. Davidson shifted in his chair. It was the first likely suspect that they'd seen. For the length of the transaction the man had his back to the camera. But when he was finished, he turned and the camera caught a very quick look at his face before it disappeared under the peak of his baseball cap. 'Go back,' Davidson said. 'Stop at the shot that shows his face and print the photo.'

The face of the man filled the screen. The printer started to work and Davidson went and took the sheet of paper it disgorged. He held it up. He would go through the rest of the CCTV footage, but he had a feeling that he was already looking at the man who cancelled Carlisle's appointment and who was possibly one of the two men seen outside Carlisle's house on the day of his death.

82

It was late in the evening and Siobhan O'Neill was alone in the squad room. Davidson had long ago departed, taking the photograph of the suspect in the mobile phone shop with him. Browne had popped in before heading home and he had informed her that the boss was on his way to Buncrana in County Donegal and wouldn't be back in the office until morning. Graham had pushed off early. There had been a lot of late nights in the past few weeks and his wife was beginning to complain that the children were forgetting what he looked like. She wandered out to the reception and bought herself a cup of tea from the machine. She walked slowly past the machine that dispensed chocolate treats. A few months ago she would not have been able to resist buying a Twix or a Kit Kat, but she was beginning to see the results of her diet and her days of binging on chocolate were over.

'Burning the midnight oil?' the duty sergeant asked as she pushed open the door to return to the squad room.

She put on a rueful smile and toasted him with her plastic cup. She hadn't really needed the tea, but she wanted to confirm that the station was already in night mode.

Back in the squad room, she deposited the tea at her desk

and went to the whiteboard on the Rasa Spalvis murder. She looked again at the area where Wilson had written the name of Noel Armstrong and put the word 'tout' under it. She'd known Armstrong for most of her life. He'd been to their house on many occasions, supposedly to offer help to her big sister. But she hadn't liked the way he'd looked at Marie. He'd turned up at her funeral, but that had been expected. She and her mother were there to bury Marie, whereas he saw every funeral as an opportunity to press the flesh and garner future votes. When she was older, she'd learned from her uncle that he was a senior figure in the IRA. Her uncle had spoken of him in whispers. Many of the men in West Belfast were afraid of Noel Armstrong. But a 'tout'? Nobody had ever talked about him in that way. And yet Wilson had scribbled the word beneath his name on the whiteboard. It intrigued her. She had been brought up to despise anyone who sold out their people to the British. She returned to her desk and drank some of the tepid tea. She wondered whether she should just head home. Her mother's carer was always anxious to get away but would stay until she got home. She glanced over at Wilson's office. Normally it was locked in the evening but since Wilson hadn't returned with Browne she supposed that it would still be open.

With the cup of tea in her hand she crossed the room and stood before Wilson's office door. She placed her free hand on the handle and pressed. The door opened. She pushed it forward but didn't enter. She took a few moments to make up her mind. If anyone found her alone in her boss's office she'd need to have a damn good explanation. She knew that what she was about to do was wrong, but she walked slowly forward and went to the opposite side of the desk. Wilson had been working on some papers and they were scattered about the desk in front of his chair. He wasn't the neatest boss that she'd worked for, but when he turned that smile on you, things like neatness didn't seem to matter. She set her tea on the desk and sifted through the papers.

Wilson had made notes on an A4 pad and O'Neill began to read them. There were three pages, starting with a review of the case and moving on to Wilson's theory of who had been responsible. It looked like he was preparing a case to present to the chief super and possibly someone higher in HQ. She read the three pages twice. Wilson was sure that Noel Armstrong should be the prime suspect in the murders of both Bridget Kelly and Rasa Spalvis. He outlined the reasons for his theory and his conclusion that both murder scenes had been cleaned in an effort to impede the police enquiry. He made a compelling case.

O'Neill took the notepad into the squad room and photocopied the three pages. Then she replaced the pad where she had found it in Wilson's office. She folded the photocopies and put them in her inside coat pocket. She was more than half an hour late. The carer would be having kittens. She put on her coat and started for the door of the squad room. She had almost reached it when she remembered that she'd left her plastic teacup in Wilson's office. She made a quick U-turn and recovered her cup before closing the office door.

As she left the station, she felt that she was carrying a bomb in her pocket.

83

Rory Browne had just parked outside his cosy two-bed apartment on Stranmillis Road and was looking forward to an evening of pizza, white wine and a binge on season five of *Game of Thrones*. His phone beeped. His first thought was that Wilson had forgotten something, but the caller ID said the message was from ACC Nicholson. His immediate instinct was to bin the message. Instead, he put his phone back into his pocket. Perhaps he had been mistaken to think that once he had put his arrangement with Nicholson into the open, by confessing to Wilson, that he could have the strength to stand up to one of the assistant chief constables of the PSNI. Although still ambivalent about his future as a PSNI officer, the past months working with Wilson had shown him that he had something to contribute to policing in Northern Ireland. He wouldn't be pushed through the door marked exit. When, and if, he left the PSNI it would be because he had made the decision to leave. He sat looking ahead. He could ignore whatever message Nicholson had sent and spend the evening as he had planned. But there would be another message and then there would be consequences if he ignored that too. He took the phone from his pocket and read the text.

. . .

THIRTY MINUTES LATER, Browne knocked on the outer door of the office of the deputy chief constable of the PSNI in the Brooklyn building on Knock Road. He felt a drop of sweat fall onto his neck from the hairline at the back of his head. Jennings' secretary smiled as she ushered him into the DCC's office. She wondered what this pleasant-looking young man had done to earn the disapproval of her boss. As she opened the office door for him, she had the feeling she was sending the poor man to his doom.

Browne entered the office and looked round for Nicholson, but he and Jennings were alone. It was his first time meeting the DCC and he noted the raised platform on which Jennings' chair and desk had been set.

'Take a seat, DS Browne,' Jennings' clipped diction seemed to cut the air in the room like a knife. He was employing his usual intimidatory tactic of appearing engrossed in reading some documents on his desk and didn't raise his head.

Browne sat in a chair in front of the desk and found himself looking at a bald head covered with brown liver spots. He didn't want to leave the PSNI this way. His hands were sweating and he could feel the increased tempo of his heart in his chest. He took a couple of deep breaths, held them and expelled the air slowly. The process calmed him.

Finally Jennings looked up from the papers. He stared into Browne's eyes. He recognised the man from the photographs that Nicholson had delivered to him. Jennings was not a religious zealot like Nicholson. He didn't really care whether someone was Catholic, Protestant, Jew or Muslim. As someone who had no sexual orientation, he didn't care about homosexuality, heterosexuality or bisexuality. They were simply dictionary terms for describing people he'd had to deal with. But every classification of humans gave him an edge that he could use to manipulate them. He neither liked nor disliked Browne.

But he would certainly manipulate the young man to help him survive. He picked up the envelope containing the photographs of Browne and his lover. 'It appears you have been a silly boy,' he said, tossing the photos onto his desk. He knew instinctively that there was no need to rub Browne's nose in it. He had read the man's file. A graduate with a distinguished academic record would have some intelligence. Jennings picked up the photos again, tore them across the middle and dumped them into the wastebasket.

Browne hadn't moved or spoken since he entered the office. His face was set hard. He had expected trouble and had steeled himself to be blackmailed, as Nicholson had done. Jennings, however, considered Nicholson's blackmailing to be crude and naïve. He would prefer to get the desired result without resorting to blackmail. 'There will be no more mention of your sexual orientation. I understand that you enjoy working with Superintendent Wilson?'

'Yes, sir.' Relief flooded through Browne. He knew of Jennings' devious reputation, but so far the man had behaved correctly.

'You are privileged to be working with one of the most highly rated officers on the force. I have the unenviable task of trying to control him. Wilson can act like a free electron, which is sometimes not always in the interest of the PSNI. Whether we like it or not we are a hierarchical organisation. Reporting to our superiors is an essential part of being a good officer. I'm afraid that your boss keeps too much hidden from us here at HQ. That feeling led to ACC Nicholson's rather crude attempt at recruiting you to pass on information on investigations conducted by your superior. As DCC, I am responsible for all investigations being undertaken by the PSNI. As such, I should, by right, be fully informed as to the state of advancement. Unfortunately, that is not always the case, especially where Wilson is concerned. Do you see my point?'

'Absolutely.' Browne could find no flaw in Jennings' logic.

However, he knew that the DCC was a ballbreaker with a hard-on for Wilson. He would need to tread carefully.

'How is the Spalvis investigation going?' Jennings asked.

Browne had no idea what Jennings already knew. 'Slowly, there's a distinct lack of forensic evidence.'

'But surely Wilson has developed a hypothesis.'

'If he has, he hasn't shared it with me. We've been re-examining what evidence we do have over the past few days. To be honest we're getting pretty frustrated.'

Jennings suppressed a smile. 'And where is your boss at the moment?'

Browne thought for a minute and could see no harm in telling the truth. 'Off on some wild goose chase to Donegal. He's gone to interview some woman called Whiticker.'

Jennings' heart almost stopped beating. Margaret Whiticker had disappeared into the sands of time. He'd heard that she'd had some sort of mental breakdown. How the hell had Wilson stumbled onto the one person who could bring him down? 'What has this Whiticker woman to do with the Spalvis investigation?'

'I have no idea.' Browne noticed that Jennings had lost it for a moment when he'd heard the woman's name. He hoped he hadn't just put his size-nine foot into his mouth.

'Your boss hasn't confided in you?'

'No.'

Jennings leaned forward and stared into Browne's eyes. 'Are you sure?'

Browne stared back. 'Yes.'

'Thank you DS Browne, you may go.'

Browne stood up. 'Good evening, sir.' He started for the door, noting that Jennings didn't reply

84

It was a glorious autumn evening when Wilson left Belfast heading north-west on the M2. An hour later the sky was darkening and he could see the thunderclouds building over Derry in the distance. The rain had started in earnest by the time he was skirting Derry and it was coming down in sheets as he crossed the border into the Irish Republic and headed north towards Buncrana. Dark clouds hung directly over Lough Swilly, turning the water an ominous grey colour. He almost missed the small left turn after Buncrana that led to Ned's Point Fort and the shores of the lough.

Margaret Whiticker's cottage was set back from the road and partially covered by a stand of mountain ash. Wilson parked his Skoda at the foot of the short path that led to the small whitewashed house. Whiticker's abode was about as far away from the rush and bustle of Belfast as you could get. As he sat watching the rain beating against the windscreen, he wondered how an ambitious young city solicitor came to bury herself in such a remote location. He switched off the engine and steeled himself to cover the twenty metres between the driver's side of the car and the front door of the cottage. If Whiticker was not at home he was in for a drenching for nothing. He opened the car door and, already in a bent position, sprinted for the cottage. He made the cover of the small thatched overhang above the door without getting completely soaked. He pulled in a deep breath of ozone-laden air before knocking on the door.

He had a memory of Margaret Whiticker in his mind, but the woman who opened the door and beckoned him in bore no relation to the person he had interviewed during the Bridget Kelly investigation. Whiticker could be no more than forty-five years old, but this lady looked to be over sixty. Her hair was completely white and ran wild round her small pinched face. Her blue eyes were lifeless. She was dressed in a loose-fitting Aran sweater and jeans. Despite the fit of the sweater, he could see that she had lost an enormous amount of weight since he had last seen her. 'Margaret Whiticker?' Wilson said as he entered.

A slight smile played on her thin lips. 'Sergeant Wilson, you haven't changed much. Come inside to the fire. It's a wild evening out there.'

Wilson entered the living room and looked round. Every space on the walls was covered by paintings of the scene directly facing the cottage. One painting featured an evening sunset with the waters of the lough reflecting gold and red. Another showed black clouds engulfing the lake. Wilson would never have made a living as an art critic, that had been his former partner's bailiwick, but he reckoned Margaret Whiticker had a talent. 'It's Detective Superintendent Wilson these days.'

'I'm honoured.' She indicated a sofa. 'Sit down and I'll make us a nice cup of tea.' She walked to the rear of the cottage and disappeared through the back door of the living area.

The room he was in was well lit and bright but devoid of any object relating to its occupant's previous life. There were no photos, no certificates on the wall, no knick-knacks. He noted that none of the paintings contained a human figure.

Wilson could hear a conversation going on in the kitchen and wondered who else was present in the house.

Whiticker returned carrying a tray with a teapot, two cups and saucers, a milk jug and a sugar bowl. She placed the tray on the coffee table that dominated the centre of the small room.

'Aren't you going to ask your friend to join us?' Wilson asked.

Whiticker looked puzzled. 'Superintendent, I assure you that we are alone.' She poured tea into one of the cups, put it on a saucer and handed it to him. 'You can add milk and sugar yourself.'

Wilson took the cup and poured a dash of milk into it. 'Your brother called and told you that I would be visiting?'

'Yes, I think so.' She poured herself some tea and added sugar and milk. 'Time has a different feeling here. I sometimes forget what time of day it is, and the only way that I can tell the seasons is by looking outside.'

'I understand that you've been ill?' Wilson sipped his tea.

'I had a mental breakdown. Simon says that I shouldn't just say that I was ill because it was quite a severe mental breakdown. He sent me to a private psychiatric hospital and they made me better.' It sounded like a series of sentences that she had learned by rote.

'Do you remember meeting me before?'

'Of course, I thought you were very handsome.'

'Do you remember why we met?'

'I was very busy in those days. Maybe that was why I had the mental breakdown. They told me it happened in 2004. I was taking quite a lot of tablets at the time. My recollections are not really so good.'

'We met two years earlier. I was interviewing you about an alibi that you gave Noel Armstrong in a case I was investigating at the time.'

She was drinking her tea and the cup stopped halfway to her mouth. 'Yes.'

'Do you remember?'

'Yes.' She seemed to be concentrating on Wilson's face. 'I remember that I thought you were handsome and I wasn't happy that I was lying to you.'

'So your alibi was false?' Wilson placed his cup on the table. He wasn't enjoying the interview. He could see why her brother had been so concerned about his visit. She was a very vulnerable lady and he didn't like adding to whatever pressures had pushed her over the edge. The psychiatrists may have made her 'better', but they certainly hadn't brought her back to her former self.

She tossed back her head and laughed. 'Of course it was.' There was a matter-of-fact tone to her voice, as though it was something that should have been obvious to everyone. 'You more than anyone should know that.'

'Why should I know it?'

She looked confused. 'Because it was organised by the PSNI.'

Wilson wondered whether he had stumbled into some alternative reality when he had entered the cottage. 'Tell me about how the PSNI organised the alibi.'

'I was doing lots of drugs with my friends back then and I was caught making a buy. One of your people said that he'd wipe the slate clean if I gave an alibi to one of his friends. I didn't have a choice. If I'd been charged, it would have been the end of my career. I didn't know that my career was about to end anyway.' She looked at his face and smiled. 'How droll, you obviously weren't in the loop.'

'Who exactly made this deal with you?'

'A horrid little man. Inspector Jennings I think his name was.'

It all came together in a flash in Wilson's mind. Jennings had been monitoring their investigation, Jennings knew about the fingerprints, Jennings prepped Armstrong for the interview and Jennings arranged the alibi. The dots had been there, but Whiticker had provided the piece of information that allowed him to connect them. He looked at the pale face of the woman sitting across from him. She had been conned into perverting the course of justice but that wouldn't make any difference to a judge and jury. A decent brief would destroy her on the stand. He had no doubt that she was telling the truth, but much as he would like to see Jennings in the dock for suborning perjury and perverting the course of justice, it wasn't going to happen. As soon as the DPP met Margaret Whiticker, the jig would be up. Wilson slumped in his chair. Armstrong had probably murdered two women, but he was going to skate. Somewhere behind Jennings there was someone else who was pulling the strings. That someone was never going to allow the murderer of Kelly and Spalvis be brought to book. Marie O'Neill had been right. Nobody really cared about the death of two prostitutes. Armstrong and Jennings would go on their merry way, protected by forces that the ordinary man in the street had no comprehension of. 'Thank you for the tea.' Wilson stood. 'I'm sorry but I have to get back to Belfast.'

She stood with him. 'You seem sad. I hope that I haven't depressed you. That's how it started with me. I can't remember why, but one day I found myself in a very dark hole and I had no idea how to climb out.' She walked across and took the painting of the sun casting its glow across the waters of Lough Swilly. 'I want you to have this. Whenever you look at it, you'll remember your visit here.' She handed him the painting.

'Thank you.' He took the painting from her. It would be a constant reminder of his failure to put Armstrong where he belonged.

She opened the door and looked outside. The rain was pouring down. 'Be careful driving back to the city. And thank you for coming to tea. I don't get many visitors.'

Wilson ran down the short drive with the painting under

his arm. He jumped into the car and tossed the canvas onto the back seat. His last sight was of a woman whose life had been ruined by her brush with evil. She was waving as though he was a long-lost friend. He felt an incredible sadness as he turned the key in the ignition.

85

'Where's the fire?' Malin tossed his raincoat on a chair in the corner of the Nissen hut at the rear of Thiepval Barracks. He'd been at dinner when he'd received a frantic text from Jennings demanding an immediate meeting. There was a scent of panic hanging over Jennings and the only way their project could unravel was if one of the participants lost the plot. He looked at the two men sitting at the table. Rodgers appeared to be holding it together, but Jennings looked like he hadn't slept in days. He didn't like weak links and he would never have believed that Jennings would have been the first to crack. He took his seat at the top of the table.

'Wilson has found Whiticker,' Jennings said. 'He's probably meeting with her as we speak. She'll give me up for arranging Armstrong's alibi for the Bridget Kelly murder.'

'She probably has already,' Malin replied calmly. 'But so what? The Icepick project is so important that it has been under constant surveillance. We've been watching Whiticker for the past fifteen years. She's currently a basket case living in a cottage in Donegal. I wouldn't be surprised if she thinks that there's an alien living in a cupboard in her kitchen. So, who do you think is going to believe that the current deputy chief constable of the PSNI committed perjury? Wilson is an intelligent man. He's met Whiticker now, so he knows the truth of what I'm saying. Whiticker is a flake. She'll never take the stand against anyone. She's part of the collateral damage of this project.'

'You don't know Wilson,' Jennings said. 'Give him an inch and he'll take at least a foot. I'm the man in his sights and I don't like the feeling.'

'We have worked through every possible eventuality. This project is watertight. The only fear is that one of us three will start to lose that belief. The word from London is unequivocal. Icepick is to be protected at all costs.' Malin looked at Jennings. 'That means that we have no intention of leaving anyone in the lurch. It's time for all good men to hold their water. The only enemy is panic.'

Jennings could feel himself breathing easier. Perhaps he would survive after all. He and his colleagues were protected by the powerful. But the downside was that Wilson now knew about his role in obtaining an alibi for Armstrong. Whiticker might be a flake today, but if she recovered her faculties, then where would he be.

Malin looked from Rodgers to Jennings. Rodgers' eyes were hooded, whatever was going on behind them would remain hidden. He was a listener not a talker. His role in the project was minimal and he didn't feel the same fear as Jennings. The DCC was beginning to look more at ease. His body had responded positively to Malin's mollifying words.

'One additional piece of news that should reduce tension,' the MI5 man said. 'We have located the source of Icepick's insurance and we have prepared a plan to obtain it should the need arise. Now, gentlemen, I think that concludes our business. I can safely say that the Icepick project is once again safe.

And may I say that we three have done our duty to ensure that our asset remains safely in place. Our service will, I am sure, not go unnoticed.' He stood up from the table, picked up his raincoat and put it on. 'Filthy night.'

86

Siobhan O'Neill stepped out of the black taxi and ran up the short path of the small two-up-two-down house in Trostan Way in Anderstonstown. The door was opened before she could knock and she was bundled inside.

'Filthy night,' Rose Muldoon helped O'Neill out of her coat and the two women hugged. They had been friends since attending primary school together. 'How's your ma?' Muldoon asked.

O'Neill frowned. 'There's less of her there every day. It's beginning to be a twenty-four-hour job looking after her.'

'What about a home?'

Siobhan didn't want to say that the idea was actively under consideration. Well, maybe a little more than that. 'Not just yet.'

'You've done enough, Siobhan. If your mother needs full-time care, you should think about a home.' Muldoon smiled. 'You've lost weight. You're looking tired but good.'

O'Neill smiled back 'Unintended consequence. Is he here?'

'In the living room.'

O'Neill walked along the corridor and pushed open the door to the living room. The man she had come to meet was sitting in an armchair watching a football game. As soon as she entered, he pushed a button on the remote control and the sound was muted. Ronan Muldoon had been one of the most handsome boys at school. He had the dark Celtic good looks that had made Colin Farrell famous. Now in his thirties, and with a divorce behind him, he was wearing his age well. His head of dark floppy curls and boyish good looks belied the man behind them. Ronan Muldoon was the commandant of the Belfast Brigade of the IRA.

He rose from his chair. 'Siobhan, darling, and how is our woman in the PSNI doing?'

O'Neill put out her two arms to keep him at bay. 'This is purely business, Ro.'

He stopped, a shocked look on his face. 'I remember the days when the other kind of business was all you had on your mind.'

'Get over yourself and sit back down.' She knew that she wasn't the only girl in West Belfast who'd lost her cherry to Muldoon.

Rose's head came round the door. 'I'll put the kettle on and make us a nice cup of tea.'

If anyone at the station asked, O'Neill would simply have visited an old school-friend and enjoyed a cup of tea. And she wouldn't be lying.

'What's so damn important?' Muldoon retook his seat. 'I thought that you people were busy with that Latvian prostitute.'

'She was Lithuanian, you eejit!' She looked again at Muldoon. He hadn't been the sharpest knife in the box at school. She had been. But somehow his charm and vicious streak had been ideal to rise in the ranks of the IRA. She was going to have to start at the beginning and it was possibly going to be a long night.

An hour later Ronan Muldoon sat examining the three sheets of paper that she had copied at the station. You had to give it to Siobhan O'Neill. She wasn't as good looking as her sister Marie, but she had stacks of the grey matter inside that pretty head. She could have been anything. Number one in school and he'd heard that she was number one at college.

'Noel Armstrong! Do you believe this crap?'

'Ian Wilson is the best detective in the PSNI. If those are his conclusions, I believe it.' O'Neill had some reluctance in handing over Wilson's conclusions to Muldoon. She was certain that she was signing Noel Armstrong's death warrant, which was totally inconsistent with her role as a police officer. But the RUC officers who had handed over information on members of the IRA to the Protestant death squads hadn't worried about such inconsistencies. The only things that really mattered to her were that Bridget Kelly was avenged and that Armstrong would be stopped from killing anyone else.

'Armstrong is the arsehole who was responsible for having my cousin shot,' Muldoon said. 'If I bring this to the Northern Command, it's going to look like revenge on my part.'

'If you don't, a British spy who has been at the centre of the organisation you represent is going to keep on handing your secrets over to the Brits.'

Muldoon reread the pages. 'Armstrong has weight. He's going to laugh these charges off.'

'I thought you people knew how to interrogate traitors.'

'Why do you want this guy so badly?' Muldoon asked.

'Not because he betrayed you and your pals. This son-of-a-bitch killed Bridget Kelly and walked away scot-free. Bridget was like a sister to me. I want him for that and I also want him for the Lithuanian prostitute. You can have him for your cousin. I don't care. I just don't want him to walk away again.'

'I don't know. This is heavy duty.'

'I always thought that you'd be a limp-dick when it came to it. It's all right flashing it at a group of schoolgirls, but it's a different matter when the odds are raised.'

'I know Armstrong. If he wriggles free from this, he'll have me killed.'

'Then don't let him wriggle free. And make sure that he admits to killing Bridget.' She needed to know that she had done the right thing.

'You know that phrase about "shooting the women first"?'

She nodded.

'Now I know where it comes from.'

87

Why does it always seem that the return journey is so much longer? The rain that had been falling in sheets in Buncrana followed Wilson all the way back to Belfast. The darkness hanging over the land mirrored his mood. He would keep going with the investigation. There was no alternative. Somewhere out there was the scrap of real evidence that he could use to build a case against Armstrong. Some cases were resolved in days, some in weeks and others took years. It had been fifteen years since Noel Armstrong had put his hands round the neck of Bridget Kelly and choked the life out of her. It might take another fifteen years to put him behind bars, but the case was going to stay live as long as Wilson could draw breath. Everyone knew that there were several thousand unsolved murders in Northern Ireland. He would try to remove the killings of Bridget Kelly and Rasa Spalvis from that list. There was no certainty that he would succeed. As he approached the outskirts of Belfast, he toyed with returning to the station or visiting the Crown. The station would be empty and that would only increase his despondency. The Crown would be lively and show him the emptiness in his own life. In the end, he headed home to Queen's Quay. It was approaching nine o'clock, which meant that Reid would be available on Skype.

'IT'S NOT YOUR FAULT, IAN,' Reid said once he'd brought her up to date on his investigation.

He sipped his whiskey and stared at her beautiful face. Maybe she was right. Perhaps he wasn't to blame, but it was his job and that of his team to bring the bad guys to justice. 'I can't see a way forward.'

'You're not done yet. Something will come up.' She could see the marks of tiredness on his face. It had been three weeks since she'd left Belfast. She remembered how tired and worn out she had been when she landed in Los Angeles. Now she had been revived by the sun and the rebuilding of her relationship with her mother. Okay, that relationship was terminal and she would always be sorry about the time they had lost, but she was also thankful for what she had gained. She wished she could be more help to Ian, but she had a problem closer to home. She looked round before speaking. 'My mother is going into the hospice tomorrow. The doctors have given her a week perhaps two at the most. I need you here.'

Wilson felt like he had been kicked in the stomach. He was a self-centred arsehole. Reid's mother was dying and their call up to that moment had concentrated on him and his problems nailing Armstrong. 'I'm sorry, Steph. As soon as I clear up things here I'll be on a plane.'

'I need you now, Ian. Armstrong is protected by government agencies with a vested interest in making sure that you can't put him away. My mother has days to live.'

He could see tears forming in her eyes. He looked down at his coffee table at the photographs of Bridget Kelly and Rasa Spalvis he had placed there. They deserved justice, but he was losing hope that such an outcome was possible. 'I'll do my best, I promise.'

The line went dead. He looked at his computer and there was still plenty of charge. Reid had shut him down. He picked up the bottle of Jameson and poured himself another double. His free hand hovered over the redial icon as he lifted the glass to his lips. There was no point. It had ended badly, but if he pressed that icon there was a chance that it might get worse. He had avoided telling Reid that Kate McCann's marriage announcement had appeared in the *Chronicle*. He wondered why he hadn't mentioned it. Every relationship he had seemed to crash on the rocks of his damn job.

88

Wilson's mouth felt like the bottom of a parrot's cage when he woke after another night of fitful sleep. He had no idea how much he had drunk or when he fell asleep. He looked at the bottle of Jameson. It was still close to the top. He felt crap about the way Reid and he had finished their call. He knew it was all about his insensitivity and egocentricity. He stood up unsteadily from the couch. He went to the toilet, and then to the kitchen, where he made himself a strong coffee. He had made a prime mistake at work as well. An investigating officer should never become emotionally involved in a case. Maybe it had something to do with his and Spence's failure to solve the Kelly case fifteen years previously. Or maybe it had something to do with his failure to save Marie O'Neill. He thought about going for a run but opted instead for a hot shower. It was going to be a difficult day.

AS SOON AS Wilson entered the station, the desk sergeant put on his most mournful look and pointed upstairs. 'The chief super, and pronto!' Clearly, the boss was not happy and he was the source of her unhappiness. Wilson marched up the stairs like the accused mounting the steps from the cells to the dock. He knocked on Davis's door and entered as soon as he heard a sound from inside.

Davis was dressed in full uniform, which was immediately a bad sign. 'Don't bother taking off your coat. We're wanted at HQ and by the sound of the DCC's phone message, we're already late.'

'Top of the morning, ma'am,' Wilson said, holding open the office door.

'You're in good humour, Ian. I hope it's not misplaced.'

'I assure you not, ma'am.'

On the way to HQ, Wilson filled her in on the latest lines of enquiry, including his trip to Donegal and the result of his interview with Margaret Whiticker.

'So, do I now know everything? There's no way the little bastard can blindside me?' she said when he was finished.

'I can confirm that you now know everything, but I can give no guarantees as far as the little bastard blindsiding you. Jennings is knee-deep in the cover-up of two murders, but he has the security services at his back. There's only one strategy for us and that is to allow him to run and see what we can learn. We have to assume that he knows everything we know, so there's no point in trying to hold anything back. He may try to raise our hackles, but we have to resist.'

'They told me that dealing with you was going to be a rollercoaster ride.'

'Some people like rollercoasters, ma'am.'

JENNINGS HAD ASSEMBLED his usual Greek chorus of Nicholson and Grigg. He didn't bother to greet either Davis or Wilson but simply nodded at Nicholson, who then ushered them to their appointed seats at the table in the corner of the DCC's office.

Wilson recognised that all the elements of a ritual slaughter were in place. Except that today he wasn't in the mood to play the part of the sacrificial lamb.

Jennings walked slowly across the room to take his place in a chair whose legs were longer than the other seven chairs. He allowed a file he was carrying to fall on the table with a loud bang.

Wilson had to suppress a smile. He hated being part of a bad piece of theatre.

'Do you recall the instructions I issued with regard to being kept abreast in the case of Rasa Spalvis?' Jennings looked directly at Davis when he asked the question.

'I do,' she said.

'Then why haven't you complied with my instructions?'

'You asked to be briefed every day on the direction of the enquiry and that is exactly what I have done.' She could see the red streaks rising in Jennings' neck.

'That is an outright lie.' His voice had risen almost an octave. 'When were you aware that Minister Noel Armstrong was a suspect in the murder?'

Davis continued with the theatrical motif by looking quizzically at Wilson.

'Don't look at him for help,' Jennings shouted. 'Answer my question.'

Davis returned her gaze to Jennings. 'It's just that I wasn't aware that Minister Armstrong was a suspect in the Spalvis murder. And I doubt if Detective Superintendent Wilson was either.'

'It has come to my attention that Detective Superintendent Wilson is himself looking at Noel Armstrong as a suspect in the Spalvis murder.'

There was silence in the room.

'Are you going to divulge the source of this information?' Davis said eventually.

Jennings surveyed the table. Davis and Wilson were totally

relaxed. Nicholson and Grigg were the ones on edge. He looked at Wilson. 'Where were you yesterday?'

'I noticed some similarities between the murder of Bridget Kelly fifteen years ago and the recent murder of Rasa Spalvis. I was looking into whether the murders might have been committed by the same person. It was a simple line of enquiry. It certainly had no connection to Minister Armstrong. But now that you bring up the issue . . .'.

'I did not bring up the issue.' Jennings looked quickly at Nicholson. 'And I want that noted.' The interview wasn't going at all the way he intended.

'The lack of evidence is a major problem in the Spalvis case,' Wilson continued. 'The lines of enquiry are limited and as of yet we have not developed a list of suspects. Is it your message that we should look at Armstrong as a possible suspect?'

The red streaks that had started on Jennings' neck had engulfed his head. He looked like he might explode at any minute. 'That is certainly not my message. Quite the opposite, in fact. Let me be clear. I do not want the minister mentioned unless there is concrete evidence against him. And since there appears to be no physical evidence in this case that is a very unlikely outcome.' He looked directly at Davis. 'I think that we have wasted enough resources on an investigation that is going nowhere. I'm sure that the superintendent and his team have plenty on their plates without the distraction of this moribund case.' He tapped the file on his desk. 'The murder of the man found in the boot of the BMW in Helen's Bay, for example.'

'We can't just close the case,' Wilson said. 'There are still lines of enquiry that need to be followed. We have to keep it open until we find a culprit.'

Jennings looked at his acolytes but there was no help there. 'Of course the case remains open but at a lower level of resources.' He looked at his watch. 'I have another meeting scheduled. I think that I have made my feelings clear.'

Nicholson and Grigg nodded their heads, dutifully playing out their role in the meeting.

Davis and Wilson stood together. 'It's comforting to know that the hierarchy is taking such an active interest in our work,' Davis said.

Neither Wilson nor Davis spoke until they were in the rear of Davis's car. Then they looked at each other and laughed. But the laughter didn't last long.

'What do you intend to do?' Davis asked.

'I intend to nail the bastard. I know that he's a murderer and I know there's evidence out there that'll prove it. Right now he and his dark friends are laughing up their arses at us. Two young women's lives have been taken and we can't put the murderer away because he's an asset to the British Secret Service. I've had enough of this bullshit.'

'By the book, Ian.'

'Yes, ma'am, by the book, I promise.'

89

Wilson had called a briefing to bring the team up to date on the Spalvis case. They stood at the whiteboard, looking like a group of errant schoolchildren. 'What's up?' he asked.

'Nothing,' they chorused.

Wilson stared into their faces. 'Are you sure?'

'Problem with the CCTV,' Harry Graham said. 'My mate over in Traffic says there was a bit of a screw-up that night. Most of the footage from central Belfast was corrupted. The bottom line is that we have no possibility of checking whether the two cars of interest to us were in circulation.'

'That's one hell of a coincidence. But why am I not surprised?' Wilson said. 'Everywhere we look it seems like the evidence is miraculously non-existent.' He briefed the team on his visit to Buncrana but left out the fact that Jennings had suborned Whiticker's perjury. It wasn't the first time that they knew who the murderer was but weren't in a position to prove it. He moved on to the meeting with Jennings.

'So where does that leave us?' Rory Browne asked.

'Up shit creek without a paddle,' Wilson replied. 'Despite that, we're going to keep at it. We're going to go back over every piece of information we have and find something that leads to Noel Armstrong. If he strangled two women, then it's possible he almost strangled others who have survived. We have to find these women, if they exist. But we do not give up. Now get to work.'

He went back to his office and fell into his chair, which creaked loudly in protest. He wondered whether his counterparts in Liverpool, Birmingham and other cities had to put up with the crap that he had to. He knew that the answer was probably yes. They more than likely didn't have MI5 to deal with, but they would have local MPs and councillors sticking their dirty paws into investigations. It was probably the same the whole world over. That was the reason for the high level of divorce, alcoholism and suicide among police officers. It was seldom about justice. It was always about expediency. His thoughts were beginning to descend into a dark place when he saw Browne approaching his door. His sergeant looked like someone had just killed his favourite dog. He motioned him in. 'Tell me,' he said as soon as Browne was inside and had closed the door.

'Jennings called me to his office yesterday evening,' Browne began. 'I think I screwed up.'

'You told him that I was on my way to Buncrana to see Margaret Whiticker.'

Browne was staring at the floor. 'He threatened to fire me from the PSNI.'

'He can't do that. Anyway, you did no harm. I'm not trying to hide the lines of this enquiry. Everything is in my day-book and I'll be adding a note on the meeting to the file.' A heavily redacted note.

'You look tired, Boss.'

He smiled. 'We all look tired, Rory. It goes with the territory. The criminals dress well, are bejewelled and take lots of holidays in top-of-the-range hotels and villas in sunny climes. The world is ill-divided. Don't worry about Jennings and his ilk. As far as we're concerned they're simply an occupational hazard.'

'I'm sorry, Boss.'

'Think nothing of it.' He watched Browne leave the office with his head held a little higher than when he entered. It wasn't easy to motivate the troops when his own motivation was so low. Rory was right. He was tired. He'd been on the treadmill for too many months now and it was beginning to tell. The insomnia and the drinking were evidence enough. He thought about Reid. He wasn't being fair to her. If he had any gumption, he would be on his way to Los Angeles now to be with her. Instead, he was wasting his time fighting the powers that be. He noticed Peter Davidson was now heading in his direction. He would soon have to dub his office 'the confessional'. He motioned him in.

Davidson sat on the chair in front of Wilson and placed a sheet of paper face down on the desk. He briefed Wilson on his progress with the mobile telephone that had made the call cancelling Carlisle's hospice appointment.

Wilson had to decouple his mind from the Spalvis case to Davidson's one-man investigation.

'I managed to get the CCTV footage from the shop for the day that the mobile was bought, Davidson said. 'I'll be putting in a chit for the cost. This is the result.' He turned over the sheet of paper and pushed it across to Wilson. 'This is the guy who bought that phone. It's the only clear shot that we have of him.'

Wilson picked up the sheet of paper and looked at the face of the man in the hoodie. It was a face that he knew well. 'I know this man. His name is Sergeant Simon Jackson and he's a member of PSNI Special Branch.'

'Holy God, no way, Boss.'

'I'm afraid so.'

'What the hell have we got ourselves into? I know Special

Branch is composed of a bunch of cowboys, but I didn't expect their involvement in Carlisle's murder.'

'We always knew that investigating Jackie Carlisle's death was going to lead us to places we might not want to go.' Wilson tapped the picture on his desk. 'This man is very dangerous. If he gets wind that we're investigating him, he and his pals will not sit idly by.'

'Where do we go from here?'

'We start looking at this guy, but we do it in the most circumspect way possible. We walk round him. We see who his contacts are. But at all costs we don't alert him to our interest in him.'

'That's a big ask. And I'm not sure that I'm the right man for the job, Boss.'

'I don't know anyone more capable. You've already accomplished a great deal, but don't raise your head above the parapet.'

'Easier said than done.'

'Just keep plodding but gently.'

Davidson stood up and displayed a singular lack of enthusiasm. 'I'll do my best.'

'That's all I expect.'

When Davidson left the office, Wilson half-expected Siobhan O'Neill to be the next penitent to enter, but the door remained closed. He looked into the squad room and saw that she was beavering away on her computer. There had been something awkward about her at the briefing, but obviously she wasn't ready to share it with him yet. He was happy to be alone. He had both the Kelly and the Spalvis files on his desk, but he had no desire to go through either again. The breakthrough would have to come from patiently, and very carefully, raking the ground around Armstrong.

90

Wilson looked out over the narrows of Strangford Lough and could make out the tower of Strangford Castle in the distance. He was sitting on the deck of Donald Spence's house in a brand-new Adirondak chair that had been crafted by a local carpenter. The two men cradled cups of coffee to warm their hands as they watched a single yacht make its way steadily towards Portaferry Sailing Club. Wilson had brought Spence up to date on the course of the investigation. Spence hadn't interrupted or asked questions.

'The bastard did it,' Wilson concluded, looking into his empty cup. 'He did it fifteen years ago and he skated because he was more important to some people than giving Bridget Kelly justice. It looks like he's going to skate again because that's what the same people who protected him then still want. Rasa Spalvis was just a foreign skank who had a lousy life and an equally lousy death. On the chessboard of Northern Ireland she wasn't important enough to be even considered a pawn.'

Spence nodded in agreement. He knew the pain that Wilson was feeling. He had been there many times himself. It's always about results, whether it was school, college, any institution or the police. The progress through life hard-wires humans to follow the task through to the end. 'I would love to have been at that meeting with Jennings.'

'A spot of light in an otherwise dark picture, but I took no joy in it.'

'Those two cases are your scourge now. If that's what you want to make them. I've beaten myself up with the Kelly case for the past fifteen years and the only thing that I've learned is that it's the road to no town. You did your best, but the odds against you were too much.'

'Life shits.'

'You need to believe in a greater power. I content myself with the thought that while I'm enjoying the singing of angels in Heaven, hundreds of little devils will be sticking hot pokers into Armstrong's genitals in Hell.'

Wilson felt a blast of cold air and pulled his jacket tighter round him. He hoped that Spence was right and that there would be some kind of reckoning further down the line. 'Maybe he'll slip up.'

'And maybe he won't. In any case, if you're right about him being a tout for MI5 there'll always be someone to clear up his mess.' Spence shivered. 'I love sitting out here watching nature, even when the weather's cold. I won't allow the shit to bury me. You should have the same outlook. Go to the States and be with that woman of yours. She's a lot more important than bringing the likes of Armstrong to book.'

Miriam Spence shouted out the front door, 'Come inside the pair of you before you get your death of cold.'

Spence stood up. 'Looks like we got out orders.'

They stood up and went inside. Miriam was busy in the kitchen and Wilson caught a glimpse of a still picture of Asrmstrong on the television. 'What's that about Armstrong on the news?' he asked.

'Oh the DUP are up in arms because Armstrong failed to turn up at some big meeting to resolve the political crisis.

Apparently, they're more than a little upset at him. He's not the type to go AWOL when there's such delicate negotiations underway.'

Spence turned to Wilson, who shook his head.

'We left our cups outside,' Spence said. 'We'll just go and get them.'

Miriam turned and smiled. 'Is this the new Donald Spence I've been promised for the past forty years?'

They went outside again. The yacht had almost reached the sailing club's moorings.

'Hell of a coincidence,' Spence said.

Wilson knew there was no such thing as a coincidence. ' Could be anything. Or it could be that someone wasn't willing to wait on the greater power to sort things out.'

'As long as it wasn't you. Any ideas?'

'Could be his friends cleaning house?'

'Or maybe his old friends got wind of his treachery?'

Wilson put out his hand. 'I need to get back to town.'

'Mind what I said.' Spence ignored the hand and hugged Wilson. 'Your relationship is the most important thing right now. When Stephanie gets back, Miriam insists that you both come to supper.'

Wilson nodded. 'Tell Miiam goodbye.'

91

Detective Chief Inspector Jack Duane of the Garda Síochána Special Detective Unit sucked the cold dregs from his cup of coffee and tossed the empty cardboard cup into the rear of his car, where it fell among a mass of sandwich wrappers, burger cartons and plastic bottles. He had already wolfed down a breakfast roll bought at a service station just outside the north Dublin suburb of Swords. He was approaching the town of Dundalk and he knew that he shouldn't be driving. The previous evening he had been celebrating Galway winning the All-Ireland Hurling Final with some friends at a city-centre nightclub and had crawled into bed at three o'clock in the morning the worse for wear. Next thing he was receiving a six o'clock wake-up call from a frantic garda at Dundalk station. There's a standing order for all police stations on the southern side of the border to call DCI Duane first when a body is discovered. The second order is to cordon off the site and then do nothing until Duane arrives.

Approaching Dundalk, Duane stayed on the M1 and skirted the town on his right before making his way onto the familiar R177. He knew this area and the many small roads that cross the invisible border between the south and north of Ireland like the back of his hand. He took a right turn and continued north until he reached a string of crime scene tape. He parked his BMW 312 and approached the policeman on duty holding his warrant card aloft. He ducked under the tape and started walking up the quiet stretch of road towards a group of police officers ahead. He could see that they were standing round a body. Shit, he said to himself as he approached the group.

'Duane?' A garda wearing sergeant's stripes asked.

'Yeah.' Duane didn't bother with introductions but moved the group aside so that he could get a good look at the body. 'Double shit.' He said when he examined the face. Noel Armstrong had been officially missing for eighteen hours and he knew his face well enough. He bent and examined the body. Armstrong had been shot once in the heart and twice in the head. He hands were still tied behind his back with a set of cable ties. An A4 sheet of paper pinned to his chest read '*I am a tout and a murderer.*' His face was puffed and a series of bloody marks suggested that he had been beaten during an interrogation. The body had all the hallmarks of an IRA punishment shooting, which meant that nobody would be found responsible. Everyone would have alibis up the wazoo.

Duane stood up and looked round. A bloody minister in the Northern Ireland Executive found on his side of the border. He contemplated having the body bundled up and driven a mile or two down the road. Then it would be the business of the PSNI to look into how it happened. It wouldn't be kosher, but it would make his life significantly easier. He looked at the faces of the three officers watching him. They had fine Irish faces and they would be spilling their guts to their mates about the find before the day was out. So the trip down the road was a non-starter and the headache he had set out on the trip north with was pounding away.

'Okay,' Duane said, beckoning the officers over. 'Get something to cover the body and let's have the pathologist here as soon as possible.' He took out his phone and called the forensic service in Dublin. He doubted that they would find anything useful. The murder had probably taken place up north and he was standing on the dump-site only. The journalists would be on them like flies on honey soon and he couldn't face that. He took out his mobile phone and photographed the body from different angles. 'Stay here and keep the locals at bay,' he instructed the uniforms. 'I'll be in the Dundalk station and I'll need the pathologist to contact me.' What an almighty fuck-up, he was thinking as he walked back towards his car.

92

Wilson had passed by the station early in the morning, deposited a request for two weeks leave and exited immediately. By nine thirty he was standing outside the Belfast City Crematorium at Roselawn Cemetery in the hills to the south-east of Belfast. The crematorium's first client of the day was being unloaded from an undertaker's vehicle by two men dressed in black suits. An onlooker might have assumed that the small basket contained the body of a young child, although the absence of mourners might have belied that. As the wicker basket was carried inside, Wilson was the only person who followed. He watched as the last remains of Rasa Spalvis were loaded into the furnace. The rest of her body would probably never be found. He waited until the curtain was pulled across and then left.

Outside the building he checked his mobile and saw that a message had arrived from Jack Duane. The message read *'Found on our side of the border this morning. You lucky beggar.'* There were a series of photos attached. The first showed the dead face of Noel Armstrong. The most interesting for Wilson was the one showing the paper pinned to his chest bearing the legend '*I am a tout and a murderer.*' Wilson walked across to where a taxi was waiting. He opened the rear door and sat in. He let out a deep sigh. 'I hope you burn in hell,' he said.

'What's that, pal?' the taxi driver asked.

'Belfast International.'

AUTHOR'S NOTE

Author's note

I hope that you enjoyed this book. As an indie author, I very much depend on your feedback to see where my writing is going. I would be very grateful if you would take the time to pen a short review on Amazon. This will not only help me but will also indicate to others your feelings, positive or negative, on the work. Writing is a lonely profession, and this is especially true for indie authors who don't have the backup of traditional publishers.

Please check out my other books on Amazon, and if you have time visit my web site (derekfee.com) and sign up to receive additional materials, competitions for signed books and announcements of new book launches.

ABOUT THE AUTHOR

Derek Fee is the author of the DCI Wilson series. He has also authored several standalone books and two Moira McElvaney novels.

He is a former senior diplomat and oil company executive. He live in Connemara with his wife of 47 years, Aine.

Printed in Great Britain
by Amazon